*The Cowgirl Ropes a Billionaire*

By Cora Seton

*To my husband, my partner on this journey.*

**The Cowgirl Ropes a Billionaire** is Volume 4 in the **Cowboys of Chance Creek** series, set in the fictional town of Chance Creek, Montana.

**Sign up for my newsletter HERE.**

www.coraseton.com/sign-up-for-my-newsletter

# Chapter One

"NO—I CAN'T TAKE any more kittens!" Bella Chatham pointed to the closed sign posted prominently in the door of the Chance Creek Pet Clinic and Shelter. It was past seven o'clock in the evening and she'd already done a full day of appointments and surgeries. Now that she'd finished her errands, she looked forward to polishing off the fast food she'd picked up before she switched her attention to the animals waiting for their fair share of love and attention in the shelter out back. After a few hours of caring for her *long-term* guests, she'd make her way to the small airstream trailer she lived in at the far back of the property, take a shower and collapse into bed.

Dick Schneider stood on the other side of the door, however, holding a box emitting the all-too-familiar sound of kittens meowing. Their plaintive cries barely carried through the glass separating her from the cool October evening air. Dick owned a large spread about ten miles outside of town, and when the feral cat population became out of control out there, he caught all the kittens he could and delivered them to her.

"You'll have to come back tomorrow," she tried again.

She couldn't take in any more kittens. Her shelter cages were filled with kittens. Despite her best efforts at promoting a spay and release program for feral cats, Chance Creek, Montana was still full of them. And their offspring all ended up here at her combination clinic and pound. Feeding them ate all her income and more. Last month she'd had to pay part of her receptionist's earnings with the change from the big jug of coins she'd been adding to since she was a teenager.

She wasn't sure how she'd pay Hannah this month.

Dick shrugged. "I'll just take care of them myself," he called through the door and turned around.

For one brief second, Bella thought he meant he'd keep the kittens after all, but she quickly realized his true intentions. She yanked the door open. "Don't you dare kill those cats!"

Dick spun around on his heel and she caught his smile before he suppressed it. Darn it—this was her problem in a nutshell; everyone in Chance Creek knew she wouldn't turn away strays. She might deal with disease and death on a daily basis in her clinic, and she administered lethal doses to animals who needed their way smoothed as they died, but she could not bear to euthanize animals just because they'd had the misfortune to be born.

So she didn't.

And since most people hated the idea just as much as

she did, they brought their unwanted kittens and puppies to Bella, knowing that even though they'd turned an animal in to the pound it would survive and their consciences could remain clean.

Bella propped the door open with her hip and accepted the box. "I don't suppose you'd consider a contribution to the clinic to help offset their care?"

Dick sighed heavily and pulled out his wallet. He carefully selected a ten dollar bill and handed it over.

"Ten dollars?" Bella bit back a curse at the piddly amount; she couldn't afford to alienate Dick, even if she knew darn well he could afford ten times what he'd given her. "Thank you!"

"You're welcome." He climbed back in his truck and pulled away.

Bella retreated into the clinic, placed the box on the floor, and sat down beside it. Now that she was stuck with them, she might as well see what she had. Pushing the cares of the day out of her head for just a moment, she opened the lid with the same sense of anticipation she'd opened her gifts on Christmas morning as a child. She loved all animals. *Well, all except horses*, she thought, with the habitual frown she reserved for the four-legged monsters that were all too common in ranch country. Horses were dangerous, careless, overwrought beasts that had no business living among humans. She might sport cowboy boots and a hat just like all her neighbors, but she was terrified of them.

Five calico kittens stared back up at her. At least they were old enough to be weaned and she wouldn't be up all night with an eyedropper like she sometimes was. They mewed piteously and she picked them up one by one, rubbing their tiny faces with her cheek. Kitten cuddles were one of the best perks of this ridiculous job.

A ridiculous job she wouldn't hold onto much longer, at this rate.

"ANOTHER MONTH AND this will all be mine," Nate said as he barged into Evan Mortimer's ultramodern office and plunked a framed five-by-seven photograph of himself, his wife, Brenda, and his four-year-old daughter, Katy, on the gunmetal-gray desk.

Evan eyed the photograph with narrowed lids. "A month is plenty of time for me to get married, so don't start moving in your things just yet."

"Come on, if you were going to marry you'd have done it by now. You're incapable of dating a woman for longer than twenty-four hours, let alone getting engaged. Time to admit defeat and hand Mortimer Innovations over to me."

Evan would rot in hell before he did that, or he'd marry the 72-year-old cleaning lady, for that matter. "What's got you so excited? You found some more farmland you want to destroy?"

"It's called fracking, and it's the next big thing," Nate said. "We're already late to the party. We should have invested years ago. Why aren't we in North Dakota right now, buying up those farms, blasting that bedrock and getting rich on oil?"

"Because we're already rich, and we're in San Jose,

trying to promote technologies that will free us from our oil habit once and for all," Evan said. They'd been over this a million times.

"Hand your shares over, buddy, and let me get this company into the twenty-first century," Nate said.

Evan stood up, and was frustrated to find himself eye-to-eye with his younger brother. It had been so much easier when he stood a foot above Nate. "Sorry, man, but I'm not going anywhere. If I don't find a fiancée the old-fashioned way soon, I've got a backup plan."

Nate snorted. "What kind of backup plan? Are you going to marry a mannequin? I don't think that counts, buddy." Giving his family photograph a final pat, he left the office as abruptly as he came.

Evan couldn't believe he needed to marry at all. But the strictures around who got to run Mortimer Innovations were ironclad. He needed a wife.

Nate was right; time for plan B.

He reached for his phone and tapped the link for his secretary. "Amanda, get me on that show."

WHEN BELLA CHARGED through the door the following morning, late and disheveled, still twisting her unruly blonde hair into a ponytail, her cowboy hat—a tan affair she'd had since she was twelve—tucked under her arm instead of on her head, she noticed Morgan Matheson stood behind the reception counter with her sole employee, Hannah Ashton. Morgan's husband, Rob, sat on one of the waiting room chairs, his hands laced behind his head.

The two women looked guilty, like Bella had caught them dipping into the petty cash, and she felt the usual pang she did when she saw them together. Hannah was twenty-five and she had worked for Bella for four years. Bella counted her as her closest friend.

However, when Rob Matheson brought his fiancée in to pick out some kittens last month, Hannah and Morgan instantly took to each other. As soon as Morgan returned from her honeymoon, she began to stop by the shelter several times a week. She spent a lot of time with the animals, and even more time with Hannah—often inviting her out to lunch when she came by. It wasn't that the other two women excluded her exactly—Bella always worked through lunch, as Hannah knew all too well—but she still felt left out. Bella knew she'd neglected her friendship with Hannah; while they saw each other at work every day, they didn't hang out after hours, or go out to eat, or shop, or anything else women did together for fun. She simply didn't have time. She worked all day at the clinic, all night at the shelter, fell into bed as soon as she got home, and woke up and did it all over again.

Not to mention it was getting harder and harder to look Hannah in the eye when they both knew Bella would have to let her go soon. The one time she brought it up Hannah told her not to talk crazy, but the woman needed the money as badly as she did. She couldn't work for free.

She had to fix things, but she didn't know how. Her

only option was to institute the same euthanization program all the other shelters had for their unwanted pets. She wasn't ready to do that.

"Bella! Great, you're here. I've figured it out!" Hannah said, breaking into her thoughts.

"Hi, Morgan, Rob." She nodded to the Mathesons and turned to Hannah. "What did you figure out?" She gratefully accepted the cup of coffee her receptionist offered her. Hannah lived a few miles out of town and passed the Bagel Bookshop—Chance Creek's best source of java—on her way in to the clinic. As much as it shamed her that her receptionist was buying her coffee these days, she hadn't been able to make Hannah stop, and she did love her coffee.

"How to get all the money we need!" Beside her Morgan nodded like she knew all about it, her thick, dark hair swinging. Bella suppressed another pang at the thought the two had discussed her situation behind her back. Judging by the grin on Rob's face, he was in on it, too. A tall, blond cowboy with wide shoulders, and an easy-going personality that had gotten more serious in the time he knew Morgan, he was one of four brothers who'd grown up on a ranch not far from town. Now Morgan and Rob were busy starting a winery and lived with two other couples on the Cruz ranch, next door to the spread where Rob lived as a child.

Bella grew up on a ranch, too. Her parents still lived there, although they'd had to sell about half of the land, but she hardly ever went home to visit, even if it was only ten minutes away. Her family wasn't close anymore;

they hadn't been in a long time. She envied Morgan and Rob's tight-knit group of friends who all worked together to support each other. In these difficult times, a person needed friends like that. She knew the Cruzes, the Mathesons, and the Lassiters, but she wasn't among their inner circle.

Looked like Hannah was getting there, though.

Suppressing that catty thought, she grabbed the daily patient list off of the high counter that separated Hannah's reception station from the clinic waiting room. She was pretty sure she had some paying customers coming in today. That would offset the ongoing cost of spaying and neutering all the abandoned and feral animals she had in the kennels out back. Bella bit back a sigh. Maybe if she didn't spend all her time taking care of animals, she wouldn't have declined so many invitations and she'd be part of that inner circle, too.

"Bella?" Hannah said, breaking into her thoughts.

"What?"

"Don't you want to know how?"

"How?" she said as she scanned the front end of the clinic to make sure all was ready for the day. Shelves of pet food, common medicines and accessories stocked? Check. Floor swept and front windows clean of streaks? Check. "Oh, you mean how I'll get all that money? Sure—how can I strike it rich overnight?" She tried not to sound as impatient as she suddenly felt. She was going to lose everything she loved—her clinic, the shelter, the animals who depended on her...

"You'll be the winning contestant on *Can You Beat a*

*Billionaire?"*

Bella had reached to tug the venetian blinds on the front window a little higher, but stopped mid-pull. "I'll be what?"

"You know that show—the one where they pit a poor person against a billionaire? If the poor person wins they get five million dollars. If the billionaire wins, he or she gets to pick some humiliating punishment for the loser. Last time the billionaire made the poor guy clean his house for three months. And it was a mansion! As in—huge!"

"You're kidding, right? You know those shows are all fake. I bet no one actually wins anything." She shook her head. Hannah was so gullible. Why didn't Morgan say anything? Morgan was in her thirties; old enough to know better.

She glanced at Rob, whose smile grew even wider. "Some of them win," he said.

"Actually, they do," Morgan said. "I'm sure some scripting goes on and the producers stick people in situations guaranteed to show their rough spots, but the contests are real and several people have walked away with the five million dollars."

"Remember that guy last year who used the money to refurbish a whole block in his inner city neighborhood?" Hannah chimed in. "I read a follow-up article about him. He turned around the lives of a bunch of people. They have testimonials from the families on the website."

Bella did vaguely remember that. She never watched

the show—she didn't have time—but Hannah watched it religiously and filled her in on the latest gossip every week. Her receptionist cried with relief each time the poor contestant won and got the money, as had happened once already this season, if memory served her. And if the rich contestant won, she'd stomp around angry for a week.

"Okay, so maybe it's not all fake. So what? I'm just a country vet who's going broke. I bet they get thousands of interesting applicants—what makes you think they'd pick me?" Satisfied with the height of the blinds she turned around in time to catch the look Hannah and Morgan exchanged. Hannah began to blush, and since she was blonder than Bella—her hair a corn-silk tassel compared to Bella's honey locks—the red stain was all too obvious on her pale cheeks. Rob leaned forward, as if eager to see how this next bit played out.

*Uh oh.* Warning bells went off in Bella's head. "What did you do?" she demanded.

"Submitted your application," Hannah said in a small voice. "Three months ago."

Bella's mouth dropped open. "Take it back! Make them delete it—I don't want to be on some stupid reality TV show!"

"It's too late." Hannah cringed as if she thought Bella would jump the divider and tackle her. "They already picked you."

Morgan hurried to add her two cents. "When Hannah first told me what she'd done I reacted like you did, but after I thought about it, I decided it's a great idea!"

"Yeah, ought to be fun," Rob said.

"No way." Bella shook her head, instinctively taking a step back. "You started this and you can put an end to it. Call them up and tell them I'm not interested. I'm sure they'll understand."

"I can't." If Hannah slumped any further in her chair she'd be under her desk, Bella thought. "They're on their way over right now for your first interview. Besides, you need the money. You know you do!"

Bella's cheeks heated at the words Hannah didn't say—they both needed the money. Otherwise, they'd both be out of a job, something Hannah couldn't afford, even if Bella was determined to go down with her sinking ship.

"I've got appointments all day," she said, grasping at straws. "I can't do interviews. I don't want to do interviews!"

"Actually I rescheduled all of today's appointments," Hannah said. She stood up and came around the partition to take the clipboard out of Bella's hand. "Come on, I knew you'd be upset so I left a little time for us to talk. Let's go out back—I want to show you something."

"I don't want to talk!" But Hannah took one arm and Morgan the other, and with Rob taking up the rear, Bella had no other choice but to allow them to lead her through the clinic to the shelter in the back. The facility had both indoor and outdoor spaces for the pets awaiting placement in adoptive homes. Additionally, Bella had built ad hoc sheds around the wide yard to house the pets that probably wouldn't ever be adopted. A whole band of volunteer schoolchildren took turns coming in the afternoons to feed and play and walk and socialize with the animals, so Bella knew they received adequate love and attention. She also knew that every pet deserved a forever home with a loving person they could call their own, and her heart ached for the ones that didn't get one. "What am I looking at?" she said brusquely. She couldn't believe Hannah had added another responsibility to her already crushing schedule. That she thought such a hare-brained scheme could possibly work.

And that she'd told Morgan all about it and never mentioned it to her.

"All of these animals depend on you, and more come in every day. These beauties weren't here when I left yesterday." Hannah pointed to the calico kittens, safe now in their own small cage. "Think about what five million dollars could do for these animals. Think of the food it would buy. Think of how much you could expand the spay and neutering program. We could get a truck and do a mobile clinic so people wouldn't have to try to lug feral cats into town. Maybe we could actually solve the feral cat problem!"

Bella took a deep breath as she considered Hannah's words. Five million dollars would go a long, long way. If she didn't have to worry about money every minute of the day, she could do so much good for the animals of Chance Creek.

"Right? It's a good idea, isn't it?" Hannah prompted her.

"Maybe," Bella conceded. "But filming a whole television show? That must take weeks. I have to come to the clinic every day."

"It only takes one week," Hannah said and held up a hand to forestall her protests. "Yes, you can take a week off. When was the last time you took any vacation at all? If you keep working like this, you're going to have a heart attack, and then where will the animals be? Look, I've already moved all your appointments for the next two weeks back and I've put a notice in the paper that we'll be closed until you're done. The volunteers and I will take care of the rest of these beasts while you're gone, and your brother's agreed to take any emergency cases that come up."

Bella grimaced. She hadn't talked to Craig in months. He probably thought she should just close down her clinic for good. Her older brother was the *real* veterinarian in town—at least, that's what she'd heard more than one rancher say—the veterinarian who wasn't deathly afraid of horses. You called Craig when your cattle had hoof rot. You called Craig when your mare was foaling for the first time. You called Craig for any and all problems concerning livestock—the bread and butter of the ranches that ringed Chance Creek. She was just the *pet doctor*—the one who gave Spot and Mittens their shots, rid them of their fleas, and made their last days a little easier. She knew no one took what she did seriously, but she also knew someone had to care for Chance Creek's pets—they couldn't all be hotshot livestock vets like her brother.

"We'll all help out while you're gone," Morgan said.

Rob nodded and put an arm around his wife's waist. "Don't you worry about a thing. We've got your back, Bella."

"The show's coordinator is coming in twenty minutes," Hannah said. "She'll ask you a lot of questions, go over the paperwork and you'll have to sign a bunch of forms. Your flight to Canada leaves tonight at seven."

"Tonight?" Bella squeaked. This was all happening way too fast. "I haven't even agreed I'll do the show! And why Canada?"

Hannah bent forward and gripped her face in her hands. "Five million dollars, Bella. Focus on the five million dollars. All you have to do is win a couple of contests. It's in Canada because it's located in Jasper National Park—you know they use a new exotic location for each show. Just be grateful you don't have to fly to Australia."

"Although Australia would be pretty cool," Morgan put in. "But Jasper's great, too. I've been there a bunch of times."

Fine, she was grateful. *Not.* She couldn't believe Hannah and Morgan were ganging up on her, and just because Morgan—a Canadian by birth—vacationed in Jasper, didn't mean it would be any fun at all to film a reality television show there. In fact, it sounded downright cold. "What if I lose?"

"Uh... you'll have to..." Hannah held the clipboard in front of her face and mumbled something unintelligible.

"I'll have to what?" Bella demanded.

Hannah's face grew red again. "I already agreed to that part—there's no way to change it now," she said, lowering the clipboard slowly. "If you lose, you have to marry the billionaire for a year."

EVAN MORTIMER PICKED up his cell phone on the first ring. "Speak to me." He sat at an oversized mahogany desk in the plush headquarters of Mortimer Innovations and he'd been waiting for this call from his longtime personal assistant, Amanda Hollister. Amanda was the one person he could count on—he knew this because he paid her ten times her worth, footed the bill for all six of her grandchildren to attend private universities and matched her contributions every year to her rather hefty pension plan. Every expense was worth it. He had to have an ally he could trust implicitly in this cutthroat industry. He'd learned the hard way that people like Amanda were few and far between.

"I still can't believe you're doing this crazy show," she said.

"We've been over all of that. What's the dirt on this Bella woman?"

"She's a cowgirl," Amanda said flatly. "Wait until you see her photograph—hat and everything."

A cowgirl? Evan stifled a chuckle. "What else?"

"She's thirty-one, lives in Chance Creek, Montana, and seems like a nice girl," Amanda said, making the adjective sound like a dirty word. "Smart—graduated top of her class in Chance Creek Senior High. Did well in veterinary school, too. Attended Montana State University for undergrad, Colorado State University for the vet program. Came back home to Chance Creek to start her own clinic. Specializes in house pets."

"House pets? You said she lives in Montana—shouldn't she be handling livestock? I bet she'd make more money."

"You'd bet right," Amanda said. "Here's where it gets interesting. Bella has an older brother, Craig. Five years older. Looks like big brother sewed up the livestock veterinary business and left Bella to take care of the cats and dogs."

"You'd think Montana might require more than one livestock vet." Evan ran a hand through his thick, dark hair and gazed out the window at downtown San Jose. If he lived on the east coast, he'd be high over some city in a penthouse office, but no one built skyscrapers in earthquake country. Still, this was home—always had been. San Jose suited him. Some of the best minds in the world toiled away just minutes from his office, and he was positioned to capitalize off the fruit of their mental labor. Mortimer Innovations bought up patents from aspiring scientists and inventors and held on to them until the market suited his exact needs—only then did he resell the patents; right at the point he could make the most money off of the companies dying to get their hands on them. The millions he made each year went to funding his own innovative projects. Evan had a dream that one day instead of factories that ate up resources and produced waste and products that ended up in landfills, he would build closed systems that produced useful objects whose components could be reused again and again.

He remembered the day he'd stumbled on the concept of a factory cleaning the water it used; returning it to the surrounding watershed in better condition than when it entered the plant. He'd been in college, his growing awareness of the damage his family's holdings were doing to the environment piling up on him like so much trash in a dump, and the idea that it could be different—that industry could help the environment instead of hurt it—fueled him to study engineering and put his family's money to good use.

Nate thought he was crazy, but while there might be money in oil and natural gas, Evan was sure there was money in green technology, too, and it was the kind of innovation that could put Americans back to work. He saw himself as part of a new breed—both environmentalist and capitalist. He intended to make his money work—for himself, his family, his company, and the rest of the good ol' U.S. of A.

This Bella person was a fool if she'd let her brother push her out of the most lucrative segment of her business. But most people were fools when it came to money. He'd realized as a teenager that his grandfather and father didn't have any special characteristics that set them above the crowd; they were just willing to think about money morning, noon and night. "What you focus on is what you get," Grandpa always said. By the time he was fifteen he'd decided to focus on his dual loves of cash and nature. A shy child, and an awkward teenager, he was never happier than when he was either alone in the wilderness, or supervising experiments.

"I don't know about that. What I do know is Bella isn't a businesswoman. I managed to get a hold of her tax returns for the last five years—she's losing money fast."

"Losing money?" He wrinkled his nose. "A vet should turn a profit, even if her specialty is pets—what's the problem?"

"A tender heart," Amanda said sarcastically. "People bring her strays, but she won't euthanize them."

"Can you blame her? Putting down kittens doesn't sound like a fun time."

"Maybe not, but it's part of the job," Amanda countered.

Evan shrugged. She was right. "So she keeps every stray she sees, feeds them all, provides medical care...."

"And the money going out tops the money coming in. Her bank account's nearly empty. She's got a couple more months and it's good-bye clinic, good-bye trailer, see you later, cowgirl," Amanda finished for him.

"Trailer?" Evan rolled his eyes. He owned a five-bedroom, five bathroom luxury home in the San Jose hills, complete with a pool. Who the hell lived in a trailer?

"Trailer—at the back of the same lot her clinic is on. We're talking white trash here, Evan."

"Doesn't matter. In fact it's for the best."

"Seriously? You're going to marry this Betty Bumpkin?"

"I'll do what I've got to do to keep control of the company, you know that."

Evan's great-grandfather, Abe Mortimer, was a Bible-thumping, stiff-necked, pain in the ass by all accounts, but he started Mortimer Innovations and set up the corporation so that the family's shares could only be held by one family member at a time—the oldest male, who was required to be married or forfeit control to the next in line. If the oldest male family member was under twenty-five, the stock would be held in trust for him until he reached his twenty-fifth birthday, at which time he had a year to find a wife. If he was older than twenty-five, but unmarried, he had six months from the moment he inherited to get hitched. Evan's grandfather had already been married when he took the helm, as had his father. Now that his dad had passed away five months ago, Evan was running out of time to find a wife.

Trouble was, he didn't want one.

After a whole lot of looking, he'd found a loophole within all the legal gobbledygook that was going to save him from that fate—the marriage requirement only lasted a year. Evidently women in Abe's time often expired early due to complications of childbirth, and Abe had taken that into account. He wasn't required to stay married, therefore. No—all Evan had to do was find a woman whose time he could purchase for one year, or better yet, win for free. Betty Bumpkin might not know it at the moment, but she was doomed to be Mrs. Evan Mortimer for at least twelve months, right after he beat the pants off her on this stupid reality TV show.

"Yes, Amanda—I'm going to marry her."

"Thank God for prenups."

He'd made sure Hammer Communications, the parent company of the network that ran *Can You Beat a Billionaire*, knew there was no way he would expose half of Mortimer Innovations assets to some TV contestant. They'd fallen over themselves to agree—thrilled they'd managed to catch one of the West Coast's richest bachelors.

"Amen to that," Evan said, leaning back in his chair.

"Why don't you just buy some prostitute? They're a dime a dozen."

Evan rolled his eyes. They'd been over this before, too. "And let the newspapers have a field day when they figure it out? Nope—not into it."

The TV show gave him a bizarre, yet legitimate, excuse to get a wife no one had ever heard of before—someone his competition couldn't possibly have tainted beforehand—and dump her a year later. The network assured him no one would care what actually happened to the couple once the show was off the air.

"What if she refuses to divorce you?"

"First of all, no court will make a couple stay married these days if one person wants out. Second, look at her résumé—the one time she left Montana it was for school, after which she made a beeline back home. She'll hate it out here in California. The minute I let her go, she'll be gone!"

"If you say so—not many women will walk away

from a lifestyle like yours."

"I'll give her a nice donation to start her clinic back up again. I'll give her some business tips, too."

"Like—you can't save all the kittens in the world?" Amanda said dryly.

"Something like that. What's she look like, anyway?"

"I told you about the hat, right?" Amanda laughed. "I'm sending over her photo right now." She hung up on him and he turned to his computer and clicked the refresh button on his email. He clicked again on the image Amanda attached to her message and stared at Bella Chatham.

*Hello.*

A golden-haired beauty stared back at him. Well, maybe beauty was too strong a word. She was fresh, wholesome, wore little makeup that he could see. She stood in a yard filled with large enclosures, surrounded by dogs, cats, rabbits and other animals. She held a puppy in her arms that was obviously squirming and she was laughing—all bright eyes, thick, wavy hair, legs that went on for a mile, and a cowboy hat perched atop her head. She could be the poster child for middle-America—a healthy, happy, well-adjusted country girl.

His total opposite.

He'd never dated anyone like her, not that he'd dated much. When your family was worth billions a certain amount of suspicion crept into your personality. His mother, especially, thought they were surrounded by vultures ready to rip them apart at the slightest sign of weakness. She'd practically hand-picked Nate's wife from the children of her small circle of friends. While Nate and Brenda seemed happy enough, Evan had no interest in marriage to a woman like that.

His own attempts at dating had been disastrous. A few girls back in college who made it clear they expected a steady stream of expensive gifts, and called him cheap when they weren't forthcoming. Several more women in his twenties who didn't mention money at all, but talked frequently of their friends' impending weddings, all the while shooting him furtive looks from gleaming eyes that he swore held the reflection of dollar signs.

He never got past a few weeks of dinners, dancing and trips to museums or concerts before he broke it off. A constricting feeling would build in his chest until the idea of seeing them again made him physically ill. He was ashamed to admit he broke up with most of those women over the phone, several by texting, but that feeling of being caught—of being trussed up with no way to escape... He couldn't bear it, and couldn't take the risk that if he met with them in person, he'd end up running away.

That had happened once—only once—but he'd never forget it, and he'd never put himself in that position again.

He shook his head and dragged his thoughts back to the present. His money was a blessing. No way Evan would feel sorry for himself because it hampered normal relationships.

Bella was nothing like the sophisticated, calculating women who'd given him so much trouble in the past.

He'd have no problem keeping her at arm's length and controlling the outcome of the show.

She'd do fine for his wife.

Just fine.

## Chapter Two

"HERE SHE IS," Hannah blurted when Bella came through the front door of the clinic for the second time that day. She had raced home to the trailer to shower, pluck her eyebrows, throw on a little lipgloss and smooth her wild hair back into a barrette, but she was still shaking with anger that Hannah had done this to her—set her up on a show whose outcome was fixed, for all they knew. Sure, she might win the five million dollars and solve all her problems, but she might just as well end up some city slicker's wife. The sick pit of fear in her stomach grew a little deeper. What if she lost? What if she had to give up her clinic and shelter—and had to leave Chance Creek and everyone she knew to marry a stranger and live in California for a year?

What would the man expect of her?

There was no way she'd go through with this if it wasn't for the sad smile Hannah had flashed at her as she left the clinic to go get changed. Desperate times called for desperate measures. If she won, she'd save Hannah, too—the woman who'd worked for her for years at slave wages because she loved the animals as much as Bella did.

She'd do it; she'd go on this crazy show and she'd give it her best shot. At least then if she lost she'd know she'd done everything she could to save her business and her home. She now wore a sundress she'd found in the back of her closet and a pair of sandals, which were slightly dressier than her cowboy boots. Behind the reception counter, Morgan gave her a thumb's up. Bella's heart sank when she noticed three more cowboys had popped up in the waiting room. Rob's best friends Ethan Cruz, Jamie Lassiter and Cab Johnson sat near him on the stark, plastic seats. Hmm, maybe she was closer to that inner circle than she'd thought.

"Hi," she said to them.

"Don't mind us, we're just providing *local color*," Ethan said.

"Doesn't get much more colorful than a county sheriff," Cab added, pretending to polish his badge.

Bella turned to Hannah for an explanation.

"Bella, this is Madelyn Framingham, the director of *Can You Beat a Billionaire*, and her assistant Ellis Bristol. They arrived a few minutes ago," Hannah said, waving to a woman who was just emerging from the corridor that led back to the shelter.

"Ten minutes ago." Madelyn stepped forward and offered her hand, although everything about her radiated displeasure. The woman was intimidating. Tall, bony, with ebony hair pulled back into a sleek chignon, she wore scarlet lipstick, a dark power suit with a skirt that stopped just above her knees and three-inch-high stiletto heels. No one dressed like that in Chance Creek. The cowboys in the waiting room watched her as curiously as if she were a leopard in a zoo.

"Sorry to keep you waiting," Bella said and shook her hand.

"So this is your…clinic."

"It is. We're very proud of our facility," Bella said. She didn't like Madelyn's attitude one bit. The director was now making her way around the room checking out the furniture, shelves—even the paintings on the walls, done by the local artist Ingrid Deck.

"If you're interested in the artwork," Bella began. "I can…"

"I'm not." Madelyn turned to her. "Tell me why you became a vet."

"Uh…I…" Bella struggled to recite her usual pat answer to this question. It didn't help that she had an audience of cowboys as well as Madelyn and her assistant waiting to hear what she had to say. "A family pet died when I was ten after being hit by a car. As you might expect, I was quite saddened by the experience. I guess I decided then and there to learn to care for hurt animals."

She didn't add that Caramel's death had been her fault. Or that the incident had also nearly bankrupted her family. She'd been playing with the dog back behind the house near the stables and corrals where her father and his hired hands worked. She'd been told a hundred times to skedaddle when the men were handling the horses, but she hadn't listened that day. Truth was, she rarely did. As the baby of the family and the only little girl on a ranch full of men, she was spoiled, which drove her older brother Craig wild with resentment. That day Craig was helping the men, though, and he'd lorded it over her that he was big enough to join in while she had to keep away.

Cyclone was a new horse; a thoroughbred stallion her father mortgaged the ranch to purchase with the hope that he could charge exorbitant stud fees and breed new generations of thoroughbreds to sell. Her father was thrilled that he'd landed his first customer, and his voice rang out as he called directions to the rest of the men helping to load the horse.

She'd been far too young to realize how precarious the family's finances were. The ranch had been owned by Chathams for generations. Chance Creek was her whole world. As she ran and played with Caramel she felt just as safe and loved and carefree as she'd ever felt growing up there.

So she hadn't stayed in the front yard as she'd been told to do. Instead she brought Caramel out back to play catch. She'd been crouched down beside the dog to congratulate her for returning the ball she'd thrown, rubbing her fur, too absorbed in her fun to hear the commotion behind her. She hadn't noticed the men trying to load Cyclone into the trailer. She hadn't seen him break free of his handlers and gallop away.

She didn't see Cyclone at all until he was almost on top of her, rearing high into the air at Caramel's sudden barks of warning. She looked up to see his hooves above her, the entire weight of the stallion about to crash down on her head.

That moment drew out impossibly long in her memory. People shouting, Caramel barking, the horse wheeling around, and the sickening crack as its leg shattered when it tumbled down to earth. Her father's bellow. Another sound—sharp as a slap.

Caramel's bark of pain.

The dog struck out like lightning across the hard-packed earth of the yard, past the house, past the driveway, and toward the country highway.

Bella leapt to her feet and raced after her. She heard the squeal of brakes and Caramel's anguished yelp of surprise. By the time she reached the road Caramel was shuddering with pain. With the driver's angry words in her ears, and tears streaming down her face, she held her dog in her arms as Caramel breathed her last.

Even today she remembered that gut-wrenching helplessness—holding Caramel, feeling the life drain out of her, unable to stop it, knowing it was all her fault…

And then the gunshot.

"We're on a very tight schedule," Madelyn snapped. Bella blinked, dragged back to the present too abruptly. "This morning we'll do an interview and your paperwork. The camera crew will be in to get footage for our opening sequence—the contestants in their milieu."

"Their what?" Still struggling to catch up, Bella caught Hannah's eye behind Madelyn's back and frowned. Hannah shrugged, but Morgan waved her hands at the office as if to say, *the place where you live and work, dummy.* Well, Morgan probably wouldn't call her a dummy. Out loud.

"Their home environment," Ellis explained, gesturing at the cowboys in the waiting room. "Hi, Bella—great to meet you. You're probably feeling a little overwhelmed right now." Ellis looked young—twenty-five or twenty-six, Bella guessed, dressed in black jeans and a black turtleneck that must have been hot on this sunny fall day. He gripped a pile of file folders and kept fiddling with his cell phone.

"Of course she's overwhelmed," Madelyn said. "What does Bella know about being on television? Nothing. So we'll teach you." She put an arm around Bella's shoulders in what she assumed was supposed to be a friendly hug but felt more like a vise grip, and led her to an empty chair in the waiting area. "Have a seat and I'll quickly explain the layout of the show."

As Bella sat down she saw Hannah pull out a small notebook and pen. Thank God—she doubted she would remember any of this. Morgan leaned on the counter soaking up every word, too. The cowboys relaxed in their chairs.

"The whole show is shot over seven days, with two days for travel and five days of filming. Once you step on our private jet you will have no contact with anyone except the show's personnel. At the show's conclusion we will either deliver you back here or to the home of Evan Mortimer. If you win, we will shoot additional coverage of us presenting you with your winnings, plus a follow-up show in three months' time to check in on how the money has changed your life. If Mr. Mortimer wins, we will shoot your wedding, of course, plus a follow-up show in three months' time to see how your marriage is going."

"Wait a minute," Bella said. "There's a question I've got to ask. Why would a billionaire want to marry me?"

Madelyn frowned. "Billionaires are not like you or me, Bella. Who knows why they do what they do? But the terms of our contract state that if you lose the contest you will marry him. Do you understand? There's no surprise here—we discussed this at length in our emails."

Bella glanced at Hannah again, who chewed on her pen, a sure sign of nervousness. Madelyn must be referring to emails she'd exchanged with Hannah. A momentary urge to throttle her receptionist swept over her, but Bella remained in control. Barely. "Right. I just think it's strange, that's all."

"Moving on," Madelyn said.

"Can I see him?" Bella interrupted.

"See who?" Judging by the way she tapped her foot on the clinic floor, the director was getting irritated.

"Mr. Mortimer. Can I see what he looks like?"

Ellis juggled through the file folders and pulled out a photograph. "Here he is. Meet Evan Mortimer—billionaire. Must be nice, huh?"

"I guess." Bella chewed on the end of her hair thoughtfully as she looked over the photograph. It showed a man in his early thirties with dark hair and cool, assessing eyes. He had a strong face that spoke of a sharp mind and decisive personality. He looked to be an impressive adversary.

Suddenly this all felt like a very, very bad idea.

"That ain't a man, that's a weasel," Jamie pronounced, looking over her shoulder. "Look at that getup he's wearing. No way he can do an honest day's work in that. You ought to marry a cowboy, Bella. Don't we know anyone?" He looked meaningfully at Cab, the only single one of the bunch.

"Leave Cab alone," Ethan drawled. "He'll get married sooner or later."

"Emphasis on later," Rob said. "The man's slower than molasses."

"Who you calling slow?" Cab said.

"Time, people," Madelyn snapped. "We have a lot of ground to cover."

Bella tried to ignore the cowboys and listen to the woman's description of the shooting schedule, the types of contests she might face and a list of rules that seemed endless, but her attention kept returning to Evan's photograph. Despite Jamie's assessment of his suit, he was very handsome.

What if she lost? Could she really marry this man and spend a year with him? Would he expect her to sleep with him during that time? She felt her cheeks begin to heat—it had been a long time since she'd slept with anyone; she wasn't sure she knew what to do anymore. He seemed so self-assured, he probably knew exactly what to do, and he'd quickly become bored with her limited repertoire of sexual moves.

*Whoa. Earth to Bella; you're not going to sleep with him, no matter what.*

She gave herself a little shake. She definitely wouldn't sleep with someone she married after losing a contest. That was ridiculous.

And besides, if she lost it meant she'd have to close the clinic for good. She'd only been able to open it in the first place because she'd received a small inheritance. That was long gone, so once she shut down—even temporarily—it would be just about impossible to start it up again.

Her stomach sank at the thought. She'd lived through her parents' money troubles and knew how awful that was. She'd have to go to work for someone else—like her brother, Craig. She'd be an employee rather than her own boss, and if he mandated a time limit that abandoned animals could stay in the pound, she'd have to euthanize the ones that overstayed their welcome. She couldn't bear that.

And she couldn't bear being around horses, either— not close up like Craig was on a daily basis. Horses reared and tried to smash you to bits. They bit and kicked and threw their riders. She hadn't been able to go near a horse since the day Caramel died.

The gunshot rang again through her mind. The bullet that had ended Cyclone's life. That was her fault, too. If only she had listened to her father, both Caramel and Cyclone would have lived. Her father would have made a mint on Cyclone's stud fees.

They wouldn't have had to sell half the ranch that

had been owned by Chathams since the 1800s.

"Do you understand what I've said?" Madelyn asked, breaking into her reverie, and Bella had the awful feeling it wasn't the first time she'd repeated the question.

"Yes—of course!"

Madelyn gave her a long look. "Take a minute to read over the contract. One minute—we're already very behind. Ellis, call the camera crew—see when they're arriving."

When Bella glanced over at the receptionist's desk, Hannah waved her notebook—now full of notes—and Bella breathed a sigh of relief. She had to pay attention from here on in. What happened during the next seven days could determine the course of her life. One thing she knew for sure—she couldn't become Mrs. Evan Mortimer. Because if she did, most of the animals she loved would die.

"JASPER NATIONAL PARK? In Canada?" Evan said into his cell phone as he pulled together notes for his next meeting.

"Yep. Canada. It's supposed to be gorgeous," Amanda said.

"Hell, what's wrong with Yosemite? I could be there in a few hours."

"Yeah, and you know it like the back of your hand—unfair advantage."

Exactly his point. He'd take all the unfair advantages he could get if it meant he could marry Betty Bumpkin the cowgirl and get the board of directors off his back.

"So—wilderness challenges, that kind of thing?"

"Most likely. I've generated a list of the challenges they've thrown at contestants in previous years. There's nothing here you can't handle."

He felt pretty confident about that. He was an expert cyclist, a strong sailor, he'd been skiing since he was ten years old and he was even a fair hand at rock climbing. He hadn't tackled Half Dome yet, mind you, but he was getting there.

"All right. When are they picking us up?"

"Five o'clock. I'll have your bags and passport ready."

"Fine—you've made sure my phone has coverage in Canada?"

There was a pause on the other end of the line. "Evan, didn't you pay attention when I read you the rules? Once you get on their plane, you can't have any contact with the outside world, remember? That includes me."

Something in her voice told him she was looking forward to the break, and the thought stung him. He talked to Amanda on the phone far more than he saw her in person, but she was part of his day-to-day life—an invisible genie smoothing the road before him in a million different ways. He guessed he couldn't blame her for wanting some time off—she was really too old to work as hard as she did, although if anyone said so she'd be the first to eviscerate them. Evan swallowed the feeling of abandonment that swelled his throat for some unaccountable reason.

"All right; I'm heading into my last meeting right now. I'll be ready to go at five."

"Go get her, killer. You can take that cowgirl."

"Damn straight. Get ready to meet the wifey, Amanda."

"I hate her already. Good luck."

And she was gone. Evan clicked off the phone and stared out at the view. He'd never been to Canada before—something of an oversight, now that he thought of it. He called up a browser on his computer and checked out the Jasper National Park website. Looked pretty cool. Maybe he'd get some climbing in.

Seven days away from work, without even a cell phone to keep him tied to his desk. Evan straightened with new determination. This would be fun.

Yeah, right.

# Chapter Three

BELLA CLIMBED OUT of the SUV and stared at the rustic lodge in front of her. She felt off-balance from the hours of travel behind her. First the plane ride to Calgary and a night spent in a passable hotel by the airport. Next, she'd been hustled into the SUV and driven 298 miles to Jasper, via Banff. The scenery along the Icefields Parkway between the two towns in the Canadian Rockies was jaw-dropping, and she'd wanted to beg the driver to stop at least once at one of the many viewpoint turnouts, but other than a brief layover for lunch at the Num-Ti-Jah Lodge they drove straight through.

The rules of the *Can You Beat a Billionaire* television show forbade her from bringing a cell phone or camera, and it killed her to watch glacier-fed lakes, spectacular mountains and wildlife of every description slip past without snapping a shot. *I'll come here again*, she promised herself, and nearly snorted out loud. She was broke— about to lose her business and her home. If she wanted to go sightseeing again in this lifetime, she'd better win the show.

She'd better win if she wanted to stay single.

Her thoughts drifted back to the conversation she had with Madelyn at the airport the night before, and her lips thinned with distaste. Madelyn Framingham wasn't even human. The way she played with people's lives and apparently relished pitting them against each other—there was something grisly about that. The director had taken her aside as they waited to board the network's corporate jet.

"You've probably considered throwing the show," she announced.

"Why would I throw it?" Bella had no idea what she meant.

"Marrying a billionaire? Probably sounds like a dream come true to a girl from the sticks."

"Uh…not really," Bella said. "I'm not looking for a husband, I'm looking for money." Aside from saving her business, she would finally be able to pay her father back for the land he'd lost. Only then would she feel like she'd made up for the damage she'd caused him all those years ago.

Maybe he'd forgive her.

"Right. I don't believe you," Madelyn said. "So let me make it clear. If Evan wins, you will sign an ironclad prenuptial agreement so when he divorces you after a year you will walk away just as poor as you are today." She leaned closer, her scarlet lips inches from Bella's face. "He's looking for a prop, not a partner. In order to remain in control of his family's business he must be married for a year. So don't get excited…and don't think you can profit from throwing the show."

"You've got to be kidding," Bella said, rounding on her. "You think I'd give up five million dollars to be Mrs. Evan…Whatever his name is? That's insane!" Even if the man was as handsome as a rugged movie star.

"What's five million compared with five billion?" Madelyn arched an eyebrow. "Surely you're smart enough to do the math."

"I wouldn't want five trillion if it came with a man attached to it." Bella shook her head at the woman's stupidity. And she was the one in charge of this show?

Madelyn considered her, a calculating look in her eyes. "You're really that dead set against marriage? Even to a guy like Evan?"

"Hello—if I lose, it's bye-bye Chance Creek Pet Clinic! What do you think happens to all the animals living there? You think magically they'll all get adopted? Even the ones missing a limb or an eye or maimed by the neglect of their previous owners? No—they won't. They'll be killed. Murdered! And people like you won't even bat an eyelash. Just another dead kitten—no big deal! Who cares about that puppy—I want more wedding cake!"

Bella knew she was losing it. A number of people in the corporate waiting room had turned to stare at her as her voice raised, but she couldn't help it. She'd never been away from the clinic for a single night since she'd accepted her first batch of unwanted puppies, and now she'd been gone for eighteen hours. What if something happened and her brother was too busy to come and help?

A wave of panic crashed over her, and suddenly she knew for certain disaster had struck back at home. Hannah couldn't handle emergencies like she could, and her brother would never prioritize a pet over a *useful animal*, as he termed horses and cows.

"Give me your phone." She snatched at Madelyn's state-of-the-art device. "Give it to me—I need to call the clinic!"

Madelyn looked over her shoulder and made a strange, rolling gesture with her right hand. Bella turned to follow her gaze and was horrified to see that the camera crew had crept up behind her to film this interchange. She looked up and ducked in alarm at the microphone boom one portly crew member dangled over her head.

"What the hell? What are you doing?" Crimson with rage and humiliation, Bella ducked and covered her head with her arms. Damn it, she must look and sound like an utter fool, and they were planning to broadcast that? Now she understood all too well what she'd let herself in for. She would have to be in perfect control for the next seven days and never betray her true thoughts to the show's producers or its audience. She couldn't let them turn her into a laughing stock or ruin in her life.

If they hadn't already.

"Cut!" Madelyn said with a sigh. "We're filming back story. Our viewers want to know what makes you tick and I think we just found out. You care more about those animals than you care about your own sex life. Kinda sad, but makes for great television. There's our plane. Come on, everyone—get your gear together. We'll board in ten minutes."

Now, viewing their first night's rustic accommodations, Bella wondered for the thousandth time how she'd survive this week. If she won, she'd have smooth sailing for the rest of her life and the means to save thousands of animals. If she lost, she'd lose everything—including herself, body and soul, for a year to a man who cared for nothing except making money. What a lonely, awful year it would be as the puppet wife for a callous, jaded businessman. And then what would she do? She'd have to go home to her parents, her tail tucked between her legs until some other veterinary clinic took pity on her and hired her on.

Maybe she could move to a larger town where the pound was separate from the veterinary clinics and she wouldn't have to see the animals who were doomed to die.

She'd know they were out there, though. And she couldn't bear the thought of leaving Chance Creek.

She had to win. That was all there was to it. No matter what, she had to win.

SEVERAL HOURS LATER, Evan stepped out of a second SUV and surveyed the log-framed lodge before him. As he took a long breath of the fresh mountain air, he acknowledged that this break from work was probably good for him. He'd return sharper, clearheaded.

He'd return with a wife.

She was in there somewhere, he thought as he ran his gaze over the rustic exterior of the lodge. A crew member informed him she'd arrived earlier and was already ensconced in her room. They'd meet over dinner tonight and hear a last round of rules and directions from Madelyn Framingham, and the taping would begin tomorrow morning at eight.

Would she be as lovely as her photograph?

What would their wedding night be like?

He knew he needed to keep his mind on the contest to come, but the idea of a wedding night had preyed on his mind during the long ride to Jasper. His situation had made him a loner and he missed female companionship more than he'd admitted to himself. Generally he was too busy to give his choice to remain single a second thought, but he wasn't a monk, and Bella was beautiful.

If they were man and wife they'd have to spend time together, right?

He hadn't actually planned on that. He'd figured he'd set her up in one of his extra bedrooms, and spend more time than usual in his laboratories and on his trips. They'd barely need to see each other, except for the occasional public appearance to make it all seem on the up-and-up.

Now, however, he was rethinking that strategy. With the question of marriage and money already solved, maybe he and Bella could enjoy each other's company. Get to know each other.

Have some fun.

Something stirred to life within him; a part of himself he'd done his best to ignore for quite a long time. Would Bella be different from the women he'd known? Could the two of them get beyond his money to the things that really mattered?

No. No woman had ever gotten past his money. Bella would be the same as the rest of them; why else would she go on a show like *Can You Beat a Billionaire?*

"Evan Mortimer. Welcome to Jasper!" Madelyn's jarring voice brought him back to the present.

"Madelyn. Good to see you again." He put the image of Bella out of his mind. This was just another business transaction.

"Come right in. Your room is ready for you. Dinner will be in one hour and we'll let you get some rest."

BELLA SMOOTHED HER hands over the long denim skirt she wore, paired with a mint green shirt and leather sandals. She'd been instructed to bring clothes suited for intense outdoor activities, plus one casual but dressy outfit for this first dinner. She hoped she'd gotten it right. She wore simple, small hoop earrings and a silver bangle bracelet as her only jewelry, and she'd kept her makeup light. All in all she looked neat and fresh, she thought as she fluffed her hair. She wore it down around her shoulders in soft waves for this occasion. She planned to return to her usual pony-tail for the rest of the contest.

Taking a deep breath, she grabbed her purse, turned out the lights and let herself into the hall just in time to hear the clack of Madelyn's unmistakable high heels. Would she wear them when they got to the outside portions of the show?

"You're dressed, good. Let's get you to makeup." Madelyn waved her along the corridor.

"I've already done my makeup." But Bella, caught up in the director's wake, followed her helplessly to another room.

"Television requires different makeup. Bolder. Otherwise you'll look like a cup of milk onscreen." Madelyn opened the door and pushed her into a room where the beds had been removed and additional portable tables set up. Bella sat down uncertainly in the chair she indicated and a small, cheerful, middle-aged woman with curly auburn hair in a jumble on top of her head pounced on her, makeup brush in hand.

"I'm Natalie," she said, swiping the brush over Bella's face. "You'll be seeing a lot of me, so get used to it!"

She set to work with a vengeance, covering Bella's face, neck, upper body, and even her hands in foundation. She pencil-darkened her eyebrows, lined her eyes and applied shadow and mascara. She swiped various shades of blush and powder all over her cheeks, nose and forehead, lined her lips with a pencil and filled them in with lipstick. Bella felt like she was wearing a mask by the time all was said and done—a stiff, itchy, uncomfortable mask.

"Voila!" Natalie exclaimed, turning her toward the mirror.

Bella gazed at her reflection with horror. She looked

as made up as a rodeo prostitute. "I'm sorry—I'm sure you're very good at your job," she said to Natalie, "but I look…" she waved a hand.

"The cameras will love it," Natalie assured her. "You don't wear makeup very much, do you? I made you up to look natural. If we were going for a glamour shot, I'd have applied twice as much." She laughed at Bella's expression. "Get going—you'll be late for dinner."

Madelyn snagged her as she left the room and dragged her back toward the main entrance of the lodge. Bella's forehead itched, but she was afraid to scratch it. She was afraid to touch anything. She was uncomfortable and suddenly felt ridiculous in her denim skirt with Madelyn still dressed for the city.

"Maybe I should change," she began as the woman tugged her toward the main dining room.

"Too late now," Madelyn said. "Come on."

DENIM? FOR DINNER? Evan bit back a smile as Madelyn ushered his opponent into the lodge's dining room, hearing his mother's critical voice in his head. He didn't care what women wore, but she sure had, and she'd judged every eligible girl in sight on their poise and taste whenever they left the house. He stood up while Bella took her seat, then sat down again and took his time appraising her. She'd obviously also undergone the tortures of Natalie's ministrations, but she seemed far more uncomfortable with the results than he was. Hell, he'd been on camera dozens of times as spokesman of Mortimer Innovations. Still, he was a guy—he should be the one holding himself stiffly, afraid to even fold his hands in his lap or take a sip from his water glass. A woman ought to wear enough makeup to be familiar with the process.

He suspected Bella thought a dab of eye shadow and a rub of lip gloss were adequate for any occasion. Would Amanda be able to give her a few hints when the time came for Bella to accompany him to charity balls and other events as his wife, or would the cowgirl step up her game on her own without help? He had no idea how he'd even bring up the matter. Maybe there were classes for that kind of thing. He made a mental note to have Amanda look into it. While she was at it, she could enroll Bella in business classes as well. Anyone who lost money as a veterinarian obviously needed to revisit the basics.

He allowed himself to smile at the pretty, miserable woman across the table, who became even more miserable when the television crew snapped on a series of bright lights and aimed their cameras at them. "Hi—I'm Evan Mortimer." He reached out his hand.

Bella glanced at Madelyn, and extended her own to take his. "Bella Chatham. Nice to meet you."

"Fine, fine, niceties dispensed with," Madelyn said acerbically. "Here comes Jake. Let's get this party started."

Jake Cramer was *Can You Beat a Billionaire's* legendary British host. With his upper-crust accent, he made a trip through a jungle or a wild ride down a river on a raft sound as elite as dinner at Buckingham Palace. The show's writers gave him plenty of face time and snappy one-liners, Evan had learned when Amanda sent him a highlight video to watch for preparation. While the contestants tended to look like drowned rats by the end of the first episode, Jake remained spotless, well-tanned, and as poised as a debutante about to make her entrance.

"Welcome Bella, Evan," Jake boomed as he entered the dining room. He shook hands with each of them, and took the third seat at the table. The cameras caught all of this, and Evan swore at least two of them were getting close-ups of Jake's face at any moment. "Let's get down to business, shall we?" He gave each of them a radiant smile and Evan wondered how much the man spent on his teeth. Not that he hadn't spent a pretty penny, himself. "As you know, our contestants call this meal the last supper—because it's the last time you'll be well fed and indoors for the next five days. We've rounded up all kinds of adventures for you kids, so I hope you're ready for the trip of a lifetime!"

He turned to face a camera. "This season, our contest pits billionaire Evan Mortimer against veterinarian Bella Chatham. As always, if Bella wins, she'll walk away with five million dollars!" He patted Bella's arm. "And if Evan wins," he gave a big, toothy grin, "he'll gain a wife for one year. That's a different twist, isn't it, folks?"

Evan tuned out his blather as he focused on Bella again. He had to admit her casual clothes fit her far better than the overdone television makeup did. She was worried—he could tell by her tight frown. Well, she ought to be—when it came to outdoor solo sports he bet he had a hell of a lot more experience than she did.

She glanced in his direction and her eyes widened when she saw him looking back at her. A slow blush crept up her neck and cheeks, but she didn't look away. Even in all that makeup, her eyes were beautiful, hazel green with sweeping lashes that didn't require any mascara.

"Evan, tell us," Jake said, leaning forward. "If you had to pay the prize would you miss the five million dollars?"

Evan blinked. "Not at all, Jake," he said, shifting his attention away from his adversary reluctantly. "First of all, I can find five million dollars between my couch cushions. Happened last week—true story!" He grinned for the audience. "Second of all, I'm not going to lose. I may have to slog through five days of your evil challenges, but I plan to walk out of here with my beautiful, new wife."

The crew members grinned at each other, apparently happy with the way things were going so far. "Bella." Jake turned his attention to her. "What about you? How will five million dollars change your life?"

"It won't change my life very much," Bella said. "But it will change the lives of Chance Creek, Montana's animals a whole bunch. I'm a veterinarian who specializes in house pets—cats and dogs, things like that." She hesitated and Jake nodded, urging her on. "Caring for the pets who have a home is no problem, but like most towns Chance Creek is filled with unwanted, stray and feral cats and dogs who would be rounded up and put down if it wasn't for the voluntary services my clinic provides. We currently house and feed over a hundred animals and that number keeps growing. With five million dollars I could launch a spay and neutering program that would limit the number of feral cats and provide housing and health care for any animals who don't find a forever home with a member of the public."

"And if you lose?" Jake winked broadly at the camera. "What will it be like to be Evan Mortimer's wife—the wife of a billionaire?"

Bella turned pale, and looked like she might be sick. "If I lose, I'll lose my home and my clinic...and more than one hundred animals will lose their lives," she stated baldly. "I don't think I'll care who my husband is if all that blood is on my hands."

"Cut...cut!" Madelyn yelled. "For crying out loud, our audience doesn't want to think about slaughtered animals. Try it again—you can't say blood."

Bella looked stunned and it was plain to Evan she hadn't been acting, nor had she been trying to be melodramatic. She obviously believed that the animals she cared for would die if she lost. Her distress gave him a momentary pang of guilt, but he tamped it down. He'd take care of that little problem himself if he won by farming the animals out to a shelter and writing a check. Nothing to it.

Jake composed himself back into his high-eyebrowed pose. "And if you lose? What will it be like to be Evan Mortimer's wife—the wife of a billionaire?" he repeated.

"Ummm....boring, I guess." Bella shrugged. "I wouldn't have anything to do."

Boring? Evan felt like he'd been slapped. Being his wife would be boring? He was a billionaire, for crying out loud. Women would kill to marry him!

"Cut! Boring? Are you kidding me?" Madelyn stalked over to Bella. "This is television. Play to the audience. You can't say boring. The audience doesn't want to be bored. Never, ever say boring. Roll cameras!"

Jake leaned forward a third time as Evan tried to force a smile back to his own lips. Wouldn't do to look like she'd surprised him. He planned to remain calm, unfluttered and completely in control at all times.

"And if you lose?" Jake boomed again. "What will it be like to be Evan Mortimer's wife — the wife of a billionaire?"

Bella blew out a breath and looked straight at Evan.

"It'll suck."

BELLA NEARLY LAUGHED loud at the look on Evan's face. The hotshot must think every woman in the world was standing in line to marry him. What a pretentious, egotistical snob. Madelyn was bad enough for insinuating she'd blow her chance at five million dollars for the privilege of bedding down with Mr. Money for a year. Fat chance of that. If Fate truly hated her guts and she lost, she'd make the lawyers write it right into his precious pre-nuptial: No sex.

Evan was staring at her again, his dark eyes cold and hard. Oh, she'd ticked him off good, hadn't she? Poor little rich boy was used to getting anything and everything he wanted at the snap of his fingers. Well, count her out of that game.

After a couple of chirpy comments about her answer, Jake launched into a description of their first day of competition.

"We will meet at the starting point tomorrow morning at eight. Good luck to both of you, get a good night's sleep…and enjoy your final supper!"

On cue, two perky waitresses began to set platters heaped with delicious food upon the table, until the space between them was full of dishes, each one more appetizing than the last. Unfortunately, her appetite was gone, so while she scooped some salmon, new potatoes and salad onto her plate, she only picked at it. The cameras still rolled, which made her ultra-self-conscious about chewing, and she kept dabbing at her face with her cloth napkin for fear of drips.

"What made you become a veterinarian?" Evan asked, startling her so that she dropped her fork to her plate with a clatter.

"What do you mean?" she said, picking it up again. She didn't feel like rehashing this question.

"Was there a particular incident with a pet that made you choose your line of work? A cat who met a bad end?"

"A dog, actually," she forced herself to say, the muscles of her face tightening. "Caramel. A family pet."

"What happened to her?"

"She was struck by a car."

"So you decided to save all the other dogs."

She glanced up to see if he was making fun of her,

but his voice had softened, and genuine sympathy shone in his eyes. Locked with Evan's intelligent, questioning gaze, she sensed he was someone she could open up to.

Oh, hell no.

"I decided to do my best," she said, hoping her clipped tone would signal an end to that line of questioning.

Evan studied her intently but changed tactics. "Have you done a lot of camping?"

Camping? "I was a girl scout for years," she said cautiously.

"So...not for the last decade?" He helped himself to a steak.

Bella thought back. The last time she spent a night in a tent she'd been ten years old. "Something like that."

"The gear has changed a lot."

"Really?" She pretended to be bored—*screw Madelyn*—but secretly began to worry. What if she couldn't pitch her tent at night? And what would it be like sleeping alone in a tent in this...wilderness? She didn't scare easily, but this was bear country and as much as she hated horses...she hated bears more. She slid a glance at Madelyn who conversed in whispers with Ellis in the corner of the room. What would the director do if she found out about her fears?

Exploit them to the fullest, no doubt.

Her unease grew as she considered what she'd do if one of the challenges involved riding a horse. Could she get over her old fears and do it? Or would her campaign to win the show come to a screeching halt?

Would she lose and have to marry Evan?

"Yep. It's no biggie for me, though," Evan continued, oblivious to her rising panic. "I camp all the time. I like to rock climb, so I get out into the wilderness every chance I get."

"You also brag every chance you get, don't you?"

Damn, had she said that out loud? Her mother would send her to her room for days if she heard her speak like that to a dinner companion. If there was one thing Sylvie prized, it was good manners. Her family excelled at good manners.

Evan sat back. "At least I don't blame my greed on helpless animals."

This time she deliberately dropped her fork. "I beg your pardon?"

"If I don't win, hundreds of animals will be slaughtered," he mimicked in a high-pitch whine. "Please—spare me. You think anyone's actually going to buy that sanctimonious act?"

"There's nothing to buy. Everything I say is for real. Not like you—you probably hired someone to write you a script for the show. I'm not worried about what's going to happen out there tomorrow, because I bet whenever you "go camping"—she finger-quoted the words—"you take along at least five other people to cook, clean, set out your clothes, put up your tent and carry you down the path to your destination. Now if you'll excuse me, I'm tired and frankly," she turned toward the camera crew with a defiant look, "I'm bored. I'm going to bed." As soon as she'd crossed the room and pushed through the door to the corridor, out of sight of the cameras, she raced down the hall to her own room.

Once inside, she rushed to the bathroom, locked the door, and began to scrape the makeup off of her face. Why had she let Hannah persuade her to go on this stupid show, anyhow? She hated Madelyn and Jake…and she despised Evan Mortimer.

# Chapter Four

EVAN STOOD AT a trailhead at eight the following morning dressed in khaki convertible hiking pants, boots, a black t-shirt and sun hat. He sipped the coffee Ellis handed him as soon as he got out of the SUV that conveyed him here from the lodge, and watched the crew scurry around to set up the morning's first shot. Bella stood across the clearing clutching her own cup in two hands, as if she was trying to draw heat from it, although the fall morning was already getting unseasonably warm.

Madelyn barked orders to all and sundry like an army lieutenant. The sun blazed in a clear sky, throwing all the mountains surrounding them into relief. They'd seen two bears and several elk grazing by the side of the highway as they made their way here, but although he'd kept a sharp lookout, he had yet to spot any of the mountain goats the park was known for.

Another SUV pulled up and Jake Cramer stepped out, followed by Natalie the makeup artist, a hairstylist and a third assistant whose job seemed to be to get yelled at.

"Great—Jake's here. Let's get started!" Madelyn said. "Evan, Bella—stand here." She pointed to a spot on the ground. "Jake—you're here." She indicated another spot, facing them. Ellis took the coffee out of Evan's hands and led him to his place. A moment later Bella stood by his side.

"Ready to get your ass kicked?" Evan said to her, figuring he might as well liven things up.

"Ready to die a slow, painful death?" she returned, her glare positively venomous. Evan was momentarily taken aback—he'd just been engaging in some friendly banter—but then he grinned. When was the last time anyone had spoken so freely to him? Apart from Nick and Amanda, that was. Most people treated him with kid gloves, as if billionaires were an entirely different breed who might explode at the slightest provocation. Bella just treated him like...dirt. It was kind of refreshing.

"I'm ready if you are," he said.

"Roll 'em!" Madelyn shouted.

"Evan, Bella, it's great to see your shiny, happy faces this morning—the first morning of a grueling five-day contest of strength and stamina and cunning designed to push both of you to the limits of your endurance. I suspect you won't look quite so shiny or happy at the end of the day." Jake grinned as if the prospect pleased him no end. "Each day you will travel a number of miles. Each morning and afternoon, you will also encounter a challenge—an activity you must complete that offers the chance to pick up five points. Once you've reached the finishing point for the day, you will find supplies to set up camp for the night. Do you understand?"

Evan nodded. So did Bella.

"Cut!" Madelyn pushed forward. "Nodding does not make for good television. If Jake asks you a question you answer out loud. If he doesn't ask you a question, keep your mouth shut. Got it? Let's take it from 'Do you understand?'"

Jake leaned forward, his expression serious, and repeated his line. "Do you understand?"

Enthusiasm, huh? "Yes," Evan shouted.

"Cut!" Madelyn put her hands on her hips. "Seriously? Save the drama for later, this is only day one. Take it again," she waved to Jake.

Jake seemed put out, too. Evan frowned. He wasn't used to getting yelled at or taking directions. A glance at Bella told him she was enjoying this all too much.

"Do you understand?" Jake intoned a third time.

"Yes," Evan said, hoping he sounded confident and calm.

"Yes," Bella echoed in firm, but measured tones.

"Good. Here are your maps." Jake moved forward to hand each of them a colorful, laminated tri-folded map. "These show your starting point, the ending point and the location of the two challenges. Grab your daypacks and set out as soon as you're ready. Let the fun begin!"

"Cut! Okay you two—that's your cue to cheer, shake hands and run for your packs! Roll 'em!" Madelyn interrupted to say.

Evan exchanged a look with Bella. "Uh...right on,"

he said unconvincingly.

"Yay?" she said.

"I don't hear you!" Madelyn hollered.

"All right!" Evan said, hoping he didn't sound like a complete idiot.

Bella let out a whoop that made his ears ring, grabbed for his hand and shook it awkwardly, and sprinted for her daypack. Evan hesitated for only a moment before he raced after her, unwilling to let her get a head start. She already had her pack on and was consulting her laminated map when he caught up. As she strode off quickly toward the trail, Madelyn bellowed, "Hold on—where are you going?"

"Um…I'm following the trail," Bella said, halting in her tracks.

"Not so fast, chickie. You need your crew. Paul, Nita, you're with Bella. Chris, Andrew—you'll take Evan." She tugged Bella back into the clearing as the crew members hustled over. A cameraman and assistant assigned to each of them, Evan noted. The assistant held a microphone and both packed extra equipment on their backs.

"Here's how it works," Madelyn went on. "One—your camera crew will be on your tails every minute of every day except for powder breaks, of course. If you're not answering nature's call, they have the right to monitor and record every move you make and every sentence you utter. No matter how tired, frustrated, annoyed or just downright ornery you might be, you may NOT take it out on the crew, do you hear me?" She waited for them to answer.

"Got it," Evan said.

"Sure," Bella said.

"Good. Two—your camera crew does not exist. I repeat—they do not exist. No matter what, you do not look at them, speak to them, ask them for help, ask them for a drink of water, ask them if you are headed in the right direction. At challenges you'll find additional camera crew in position. At night there will be crew members camped nearby, but out of sight. You may not interact with them. They will not answer you. They will not help you." She looked from Evan to Bella to make sure her point was driven home. "Ignore all crew members at all times, unless they give you a direct order. These guys are trained professionals. No matter how many times you break this rule, they will definitely ignore you.

"Three—you are competitors, but you may not sabotage each other. No holes in each other's water pouches, no tripping or pushing, and so on. Sabotage equals automatic disqualification. You may, however, trash talk and generally annoy the hell out of each other. In fact, we're counting on it. Is all of this clear?"

"Yes," Evan said. He snuck a glance at Bella, who once more seemed a little pale.

"Yes," She nodded, and her pony-tail swung.

"All right—go get 'em!" She clapped her hands together. "Get out of here!"

Bella broke out into a run and Evan only hesitated a moment before running after her. In several strides he caught up, pushed past her and raced onward with a rush of speed designed to leave her far behind. When he looked back thirty seconds later, all he could see past his camera crew were the trees crowding the trail. This was child's play.

BELLA STOOD IN a crook of the trail and studied her laminated map. If she'd heard everything right, this contest wasn't about speed—it was about accuracy. She would gain the points she needed to win at the challenges, not by exhausting herself racing from point to point. She looked at the map legend and back to the trail marked out by a dashed line. In total, she would cover eight miles today. That didn't seem so bad. Of course, if the trail was hilly—and it looked to be hilly—it could be quite strenuous. She found the midpoint and noted that the two halves of the trail were bisected by the challenge points. So, she had maybe two to three miles to go before the first challenge, a longer four mile hike to the second challenge, and two more miles to the day's campsite. She could do this.

She wasn't exactly a fitness buff, but her work required her to move all day long, lifting animals, feeding them, exercising them. She had plenty of stamina. The trail looked very well marked, too, so she wouldn't have to worry about getting lost, at least at first. Setting out at a steady pace, she tried to ignore the crew members following after her. How did her butt look in these shorts? She hoped it looked good, because with Paul's camera pointed right at it, the viewers were definitely going to notice.

Before long, the path began to climb. They were traveling through a mixed forest in which cedar, hemlock and pine predominated. The air smelled different from home. Although the day was warming up fast, there was a sharp hint of snow in the air—probably from the wind sweeping over the mountains. On the drive the previous day they'd passed more than one glacier, so she assumed some nearby peaks never lost their snow cover, no matter the time of year.

As they continued, the going got rougher and she began to breathe heavily. Paul and Nita huffed and puffed behind her, and when she risked a look over her shoulder, she saw Nita push back her heavy, dark bangs, already damp with sweat. Good—she wasn't the only one struggling.

She wondered how far ahead Evan was. He'd looked all too handsome this morning, completely at home in his hiking gear—even that funny, brimmed hat he wore. She felt kind of dorky in the brand new water-wicking shorts the show had provided for her, and the t-shirt they'd given her hugged every curve, making her adequate breasts look absolutely huge. Madelyn had allowed her to keep her cowboy hat—thank God. Although she avoided horses, it was as much a part of her daily uniform as her own skin. It would be too strange to part with it now.

By the time she'd traversed the first couple miles she was covered with a slick of sweat. She hadn't stopped for a break yet, but if she didn't find the first challenge soon, she'd need to stop and rest. The trail rose consistently and became quite steep in places. Add in the weight of her water pouch and daypack and she was tiring fast.

Just when she was about to give up and stop by the side of the trail, it leveled out and she entered a moderately sized meadow. Two targets were set up about fifty yards from where she stood. Evan stood in front of one, a recurve bow upraised in his hands. As she watched, he pulled the string back to his ear and let an arrow loose. It flew at the target and hit it with a thwap. His two crew members clapped. Another man she didn't recognize wrote something on his notepad. "That's four."

Four? As in, four arrows in the target? If each arrow equaled a point, Evan had nailed four out of five points in the first challenge. She'd never picked up a bow in her life—there was no way she could beat that.

Evan took another arrow from a quiver at his feet, set it on the string and lifted the arrow again. She watched him carefully, trying to note his stance, the way he set the arrow to the string and how he positioned the bow. Obviously, he'd done this before.

Was Madelyn aware of that? Was this contest rigged against her? She realized she had no way of knowing. Maybe this whole thing was going to be an exercise in humiliation, with the loss of her clinic and animal shelter the final blow.

She had to do something. What had Madelyn said? They weren't allowed to hurt each other, but trash talk was encouraged?

She waited until Evan pulled the arrow back to his

ear and steadied it there. Right when she judged he would let it loose, she yelled, "Bear!"

Evan jerked and the arrow swung off course, missing the target altogether. Everyone in the clearing tensed and scanned the area.

"Sorry," Bella called and stepped forward. "My mistake—it was just a tree. I'm a little jumpy."

Evan turned on her. "You did that on purpose."

She shrugged. "I haven't spent a lot of time in the woods. My specialty is pets, not grizzlies. Like I said, I'm a little jumpy."

"You're going to be a whole lot jumpier before the day's done. You realize you've only spoiled one shot of mine. I'll be here to spoil all five of yours." He held her gaze as he came to stand close enough to her she could smell the sweat from his morning's exertions. It should have disgusted her, but instead it seemed to waken something deep inside. He was clean shaven this morning, still neat and tidy despite the hike, but as handsome as he was now, she had the feeling that the wilder this trip got, the hotter he'd look. Rugged outdoorsy activity suited the guy far better than his suits did. She doubted it had the same effect on her appearance, though.

He handed her the bow and Bella swallowed, all too aware of the way his hands wrapped around the polished wood. Strong hands with blunt fingers. Hands that could caress and squeeze and stroke…

"You'll lose your head start," Bella said, suddenly eager to send him on his way. Her hands weren't shaking out of nervousness about handling a bow for the first time, nor because he obviously intended to taunt her while she shot. The thought of Evan touching her made her feel warm. Delicate. Womanly.

Interested.

Crud. Of all the men to react to like that. Why couldn't she fall for one of the businessmen of Chance Creek, or even one of the cowboys working the ranches around town, like Rob's brother Jake? Or the county sheriff, Cab? She got along great with Cab, but there'd never been a spark between them—not like this.

Cab didn't have Evan's hands.

Surely she was losing it. Who cared about hands? It was a man's heart, his brain, his capacity for love that was really important, if you cared about things like that. She didn't care about men one way or another.

But her thoughts returned to the way Evan's hands could make her feel alive. They could tease and torment her until she writhed with desire.

Seriously. She needed to get laid.

Did Evan feel it, too, or was she the only one being shanghaied by hormones? He stepped closer and for a second she thought she saw her own interest echoed in his eyes. He frowned and bent nearer. "I'll always beat you in a race, Betty Bumpkin. I've already beat you at this challenge. I've got this contest in the palm of my hand. Pretty soon I'll have you in the palm of my hand, too. At least for a year."

Betty Bumpkin? Heat rushed into her cheeks. He called her Betty Bumpkin on national television? What an asshole! And what did that last crack mean—having her in the palm of his hand? She could think of any number of dirty interpretations for that sentence.

Now she saw him as he truly was—a cocky, arrogant, self-absorbed jackass who'd inherited a bunch of money and thought it made him superior to everyone who worked for a living.

"We've got a long way to go, so step aside, Money-buns. Let's get on with it." His snort of disgust at the crude nickname made her smile, but her anxiety rose as she approached a white line spray painted on the ground. One of the extra crew members took the bow Evan had handed her and directed her to a rack full of them.

"This one's much too big for you," the young woman said. "Try a few of them out and see which ones you can pull back all the way. You want the biggest one you can handle, though. The bigger the bow, the faster the arrow flies—making it more likely to stick in the target." Bella chose a bow and Evan smirked at her as the woman helped Bella put on a wrist guard and gloves, led her back to the line, and pointed to the quiver of arrows. "Fire at will."

Everyone stepped back behind the line. She knew the cameras were rolling—several of them. Evan stood nearby, his powerful arms crossed over his chest.

Hell. This was going to be embarrassing.

She selected an arrow and nocked it just above a small metal bead attached to the string. She raised the bow out in front of her, held her left arm straight, took hold of the arrow and string between the second and third fingers on her right hand and drew back as far as she could. It wasn't as easy as Evan made it look. Her right arm trembled, more and more as she waited for Evan to begin heckling her. He didn't say a word. Finally, unable to wait any longer, she loosed the arrow and cringed when it flew barely half the distance to the target before hitting the ground.

Bella wiped her sweat-slick palm along her shorts. This sucked. Still, it was just one contest. Surely there'd be others she excelled at. She glanced at Evan, who saluted her cockily. "Great shot."

"Shut up." She bit her lip, angry at herself for being baited. That wasn't the stinging comment she'd like to have made. She selected another arrow, nocked it and raised the bow again. This time she angled it higher, figuring that if the arrow went higher in the air, it would travel farther. She took a breath, pulled the arrow back and released it as quickly as she could, before Evan even had the chance to say anything.

This time the arrow made it three-fourths of the way to the target, but veered off to the left.

"You're pushing the arrow. Keep your fingers at your chin and just release."

Bella spun around to glare at Evan. He was giving her archery tips?

He met her gaze coolly. "You're not going to hit the target anyway. Might as well learn something."

Hmmm—Mr. Moneybuns liked to show off his knowledge and couldn't stand to see someone doing something wrong. She filed that information away for later use. She pulled a third arrow from the quiver and raised the bow again. This time she pretended she was in her operating room at home, focused solely on the task at hand, allowing all distractions to slide away. She was alone with the target, the bow as much a part of her arm as her scalpel usually was. She raised it another inch, nocked the arrow and pulled it back until her fingers rested just below her ear, and let go, just like Evan said.

The arrow sailed straight through the air and hit the target.

"That's one," the man keeping score said.

Bella let out a whoop and nearly danced with excitement. She did it—she got one!

"I'm still beating you," Evan said.

"Better hold on tight, Moneybuns," she said. "I'm catching up!"

Confident now, she selected a fourth arrow and let it loose before Evan could say a word. It hit the target, too.

As she picked a fifth arrow, however, Evan evidently decided not to take any chances.

"Archery is one of those sports women think they can excel at, but they never really match up to the strength and accuracy of men," he said, coming closer. "Women suck at depth perception, and archery, really, is all about depth perception."

She shook her head. He'd have to do better than that if he wanted to throw her off. She liked nothing better than proving arrogant men wrong. After all, her brother told her for years women made lousy vets and she'd shown him. She outscored him in every class and every test on her way to becoming a vet. Of course, he still lorded it over her that he cared for livestock while she stuck with pets, but that had nothing to do with strength, accuracy…or depth perception, come to think of it. She raised her bow and got ready to release the arrow.

"The only thing women don't suck at," Evan said, drawing nearer and dropping his voice. "Is sucking…"

Bella jerked just as the arrow left her fingers and she knew instantly it would miss. She closed her eyes and lowered her bow in frustration, but when she heard a distinct *thwap*, she opened them again.

"Three," the scorekeeper said and she blinked in amazement. Her arrow dangled from the very bottom of the target, but its head was definitely stuck in the ticking. She'd hit it after all.

With another whoop, Bella did dance this time. "Three—I got three!" she crowed at Evan.

"I got four," he said. "Give it up, Bumpkin."

"Not on your life, Moneybuns! I'm just getting started." She grabbed her daypack and her map and darted off to a well-marked gap in the trees on the other side of the meadow.

"Hey, wait up!" Paul the cameraman yelled after her, but she didn't miss a stride. Sure, she was losing. Sure, they had nine more contests to go. She didn't care. She'd won three points when by all accounts she should have scored zero.

She was still in the running.

EVAN PICKED UP his daypack and map and followed more slowly behind Bella, his crew trailing behind him.

How had he let her get three points? Hell, she wouldn't have scored at all if he hadn't yelled out those instructions. Was he insane? Or had she hypnotized him with her long legs and incredibly curvy curves. That t-shirt had been distracting enough back at the starting line. Now she'd exerted herself for a few hours, it clung to her damply, and he struggled to keep the reaction in his groin from embarrassing him on national television. It wasn't just her curves, either. Her insults revved him up even more. He loved competition, but he'd always pursued solitary sports, and when he did compete he went up against other men. Her taunts turned him on, and so did the way she breathed heavily when she got angry. The rise and fall of her breasts was mesmerizing.

Her abundant, curvy, wonderful breasts.

Yep, that part of himself he'd tried to bury was alive and well, thank you very much.

If he wanted to win this contest, however, he needed to keep a clear head. He could pursue her after he'd married her, he thought with a grin. Everything would be settled—he wouldn't need to worry about losing control of Mortimer Innovations, and he wouldn't need to worry about being rejected on national television. He'd been publicly humiliated before. He didn't care to repeat the experience.

Focus. First he needed to win this contest.

He decided to hang back and let Bella keep her lead for now. He bet she'd get nervous after a while, and sure enough he caught her looking back from time to time, probably wondering why he didn't speed up and pass her by again.

*Not this time, honey*, he thought. *This time I'm watching you. That's right—you should be worried. What am I plotting?*

Not much—unless you counted all the positions he was trying out with her in his mind. He really needed to stop thinking about that. His groin twinged. Definitely needed to stop thinking about that. He hadn't spent as much time in the sack as a guy his age should have, but he'd spent enough to know what he liked.

And he liked Bella.

The trail climbed even more and toward noon the trees thinned out. Evan was starving by the time Bella stopped for lunch. She put down her pack and glanced back at him, tensing as he approached.

"There's a whole mountain—can't you eat somewhere else?"

"Don't you want company?"

"No."

"Well, I do." Company that would actually speak to him, not just trail after him like his camera crew did. Besides, this was the perfect occasion for him to get to know his future wife. He sat down on a rock and opened his pack, hoping the show provided decent food. He pulled out several sandwiches, some trail mix, an apple and an orange. Enough food to get by, but not very generous. He supposed it was Madelyn's aim to keep them tired and hungry, so they'd bicker more and make mistakes.

Bella remained on her feet. So did Paul and Nita, although he thought the two of them might rebel if she didn't sit down and eat her lunch. They must want to grab their own meal.

"Aren't you going to eat?"

"Yes. I just…" She glanced around, color rising in her cheeks as she found all four crew members watching her along with him.

Aah—she heard the call of nature. "There's toilet paper in your pack. Just find a handy tree."

She frowned, but opened her pack and took out a plastic pouch filled with toilet paper. "Okay." She headed reluctantly into the bushes. When she reappeared a minute or two later she wouldn't meet his eye. Paul, Nita, Chris and Andrew had all settled down to eat but he was positive the cameras and microphones were still on.

"Seriously, Bumpkin. People piss every day; it's no big deal," he said.

She ignored him and looked in her pack again. She didn't appear any more enthusiastic than he felt when she pulled out her lunch.

"That's it?"

"Think of it as a bonus diet," Evan said. "You may lose the show but at least you'll get rid of those pesky last five pounds."

"I don't need to lose five pounds," she said. She selected a sandwich, the apple, and the trail mix, and tucked the rest back in her bag.

Evan had to give her points for that response. Most women were so touchy about their weight they might deny needing to diet, but they would have felt very self-conscious afterwards. Bella didn't seem bothered a bit. She ate in silence and Evan bit into his sandwich, too.

"Do you hike a lot?" he asked after a minute.

"Sometimes."

"Do a lot of camping?"

"You already asked that."

He laughed. "Right. Girl scouts. Tell me about it."

"No."

He could almost hear the collective groan of the camera crew—this wasn't interesting television. How could he rile her up some and forestall a lecture from Madelyn the next time they saw her? God—what if Madelyn made them re-do the day? He could just imagine her yelling, "Cut—get back to the starting line and let's hear more trash talk this time!" He wasn't interested in that scenario.

"Do you have a boyfriend?"

This time she did turn around. "No, I don't."

"Aren't you going to ask me if I have a girlfriend?"

"I don't care."

"I don't. Not a steady one, anyhow," he amended since he didn't want to come off like a total dork.

"You mean you have one night stands."

Hmm, her disapproval about that idea was palpable. "Sure. Or two-night stands. Sometimes seven-night stands, even. I'm versatile." Let her chew on that. He hadn't even had a one-hour stand in a long, long time, though. Way too long, now that he was sitting close to Bella.

"You're a slut." She shot him a look. "I bet you have

to pay for it, too."

Anger surged within him. That was taking trash talk too far. And the fact that he'd entertained the idea once or twice out of pure desperation made it all the worse. "Betty, I never have to pay for sex."

She just raised her eyebrows. "But let me guess—you do pay for dinner, entertainment, hotels, plane tickets, gifts..." She ticked the items off on her fingers. "You may not hand them hundred dollar bills at the end of the night, but you most definitely pay for sex, Moneybuns."

Evan opened his mouth, thought a second and closed it again. She'd hit a bull's-eye, but she'd also missed the target altogether. He didn't date because it felt like paying for sex. The women were so sure a billionaire would lavish them with gifts that he felt compelled to do so, or ruin their good impression of him. He could never simply be with them; never know for sure if they even liked him.

He didn't trust women.

He didn't trust anyone, come to think of it.

## Chapter Five

BELLA WATCHED THE COLOR SURGE into Evan's handsome face. Score one point for her. Was he thinking over past dates and wondering whether they'd have gone so well if he hadn't spent so much cash? She bet guys like him never found out. They were probably so addicted to the high life they rarely ever got their credit cards back into their wallets before it was time to flash them again.

Poor little rich boy, she thought, and bit into her sandwich. She hoped the show planned to provide them a big dinner tonight, because while the food in her pack might get her through the rest of the afternoon, it wasn't going to satisfy her at the end of this hike. She was ravenous.

She finished as quickly as she could and allowed a crew member to top up her water supply. Apparently they might starve her, but they weren't going to allow her to get dehydrated. She recalled Evan's diet comment. Most women might fuss about their weight, but she wasn't one of them. She was comfortable with her body and she saw no reason to change it. Who cared about frivolous things like that when there was so much suffering in the world?

Speaking of suffering—how was Hannah doing with the animals? Had she remembered all their special diets? Had she played enough with the dogs in the back kennels? What about emergencies?

"If you need a nap, you can curl up by me," Evan said suddenly, startling her out of her thoughts. "I'll keep a watch on…things," he let his gaze dip to her breasts and raised it again, "while you sleep."

"Shut up," she said and bit her lip, catching his mischievous grin. Darn it—he always made her sound like an adolescent when he caught her off guard. He obviously enjoyed the opportunity the show gave him to act like a teenager. Somehow she knew he didn't normally behave this way. Her body hummed with interest over his insinuation, though. As much as she wanted to dislike Evan, she was attracted to him at some basic level. The thought of him looking at her? Yum.

No, yuck. She gathered her trash and stowed it away, shouldered her pack and began to walk again, determined to focus on the contest, not her adversary. That proved to be harder than she expected, though.

It was bad enough worrying about the cameraman focusing on her bottom. Now Evan dogged her every step and whenever she glanced back she could swear he was staring at it, too. She tried to curb the sway of her hips, but that made her walk stiffly and soon became uncomfortable. *Okay, America*, she thought as she gave up trying to repress her natural stride. *Take a good long look at my butt. Hope you like it.*

Knowing Evan was unabashedly staring at her hindquarters kept her all too aware of him throughout their hike. Worse were the images of her and Evan in a more intimate setting. She pictured them peeling the clothes off of each other. Taking their time. Touching...

She was thoroughly unnerved by the time they reached the colored flags that signaled their second challenge of the day. Her boots had begun to rub and she pulled the small first-aid kit out of her pack and held her breath as she opened it. Thank goodness there was a Band Aid big enough to cover the blister building on her heel. She shucked off her boot and sock, applied the bandage and pulled them back on. Only then did she allow herself to survey the challenge.

Wait a minute. Where was the challenge?

She caught sight of a rope dangling from a nearby tree and followed it up—and up—and up—until she spotted several people standing on a platform high overhead.

Back on the ground, a crew member approached carrying something that looked like a cross between a vest and a harness. Her stomach sunk. A zip line course? She was not a huge fan of heights. She had managed to help fix the gutters on her clinic last year, but she'd never tried anything like this before. Was the challenge simply to live through it?

As one crew member helped her into the vest, another explained the rules.

"Once you climb to the platform, you'll be at the first of five zip lines we've installed. You'll be handed a beanbag at each platform and you need to pitch it into a basket positioned somewhere along each zip line. The challenge is to spot the baskets and make each shot for a possible total of five points."

"We have to throw things while we're zipping?" she said, and cringed at the squeak in her voice. "Aren't we supposed to hold onto something?"

"It only takes one hand to control your speed," Evan said as a crew member finished fastening him into another harness. "It's no big deal to throw something, too."

Control your speed? She hadn't even thought about that. And why did Evan seem so confident about this task, too? Was he as much an expert at this as he was at archery? This whole thing was rigged, wasn't it? The show's producers must have it out for her.

Miserably, she allowed herself to be fastened into her harness and led over to the tree containing the first platform. Evan, already halfway up, waved down to her. "Come on up!"

"I'll wait," she said.

His laughter rang out above her. "What's wrong, Bumpkin—afraid of heights?"

"No." *Yes. Kind of.* She wasn't afraid of balconies, or even ladders up to a point. This particular ladder, attached to this particular tree, however, seemed to go up and up and up—much higher than she'd ever climbed before.

When Evan disappeared from view she took a deep breath and began her ascent. Paul and Nita climbed beneath her, Paul still filming. Terrific. This must be a very flattering angle. Her arm muscles began to ache about halfway up, but she knew better than to hesitate even for a second. She also knew better than to look down. The ladder seemed sturdy, so as long as she focused only on the next rung, everything was okay.

"Just a few more rungs," a voice said above her. She glanced up and saw the underside of the platform looming overhead. A trapdoor was open and a man she didn't recognize looked down through it. "I'm Jim, your instructor," he said as she climbed through the door. He steadied her as she awkwardly flopped onto the platform's floor. "Come on, I'll show you the ropes."

Evan was there, leaning casually against a railing as Jim began his safety spiel. She tried to pay strict attention to everything Jim said, but her gaze kept trailing back to Evan's strong shoulders and wide-legged stance. Even in a harness he was hotter than hot. Would marriage to him for a year be so bad? What would it be like to be cared for by someone else for a while? To let him worry about bills and costs and... She snapped herself out of her reverie. Evan wasn't interested in saving animals' lives. Marriage to him meant an end to the clinic and possibly to her career.

She turned her attention back to Jim as he finished outlining their task.

"Who wants to go first?" he asked.

Evan looked to her.

"He can go first," she said. "He's been watching my ass all morning. Turnabout is fair play."

His eyebrows shot up. "We don't have to take turns, Betty. You can watch my ass anytime you like."

He made a big show of keeping his posterior pointed her way through the entire process of connecting his harness to the zip lines. Jim handed him a beanbag. "Good luck, man."

"Thanks." Evan turned to Bella and winked. "I'll be watching for you."

"Whatever."

He took off, zipping down the line and out of sight. A second later, they heard a slap of something hitting wood.

"I think he got a basket," Jim said, obviously impressed. "Your turn."

Her stomach writhed at the thought of leaving the platform and skimming through the trees with the ground so far below her. "I don't think I can do this."

"Sure you can. It's easy."

"No, really—I don't think I can!"

Jim clipped the end of a tether to her harness and to the zip line, and helped secure a second connection. "See? You're attached in two ways to the line; no way you'll fall down, no matter what. Keep your left hand on the brake," he showed her how, "and use your right hand to throw. Easy, peasy!" He put the beanbag into her right hand and pushed her to the edge of the platform. "Jump!"

"But I don't…"

Jim shoved her, and she fell forward, jerking sharply when the connection between harness and line brought her up short. She dropped the beanbag immediately and clutched the brake with both hands, screaming so loudly she hurt her own ears. The forest zipped past her in a blur, so she closed her eyes. That was worse. She opened them again and fought to keep from throwing up with fear. Something caught her eye and she blinked, surprised by the incongruity of a florescent orange post in the middle of this pristine forest. It stuck straight up and culminated in what looked like an old-fashioned bushel basket.

The basket!

Bella let go of the brake with her right hand, threw, and realized she no longer held the beanbag. Damn— she'd lost another point, and Evan had scored this one— she'd heard the thunk. Well, now that she knew what she was shooting at, she wouldn't miss next time.

By the time she saw the platform approaching in the distance, she had her emotions under control. As she approached, she reflexively drew up her knees and pressed the brake harder. This zip line business wasn't that difficult after all; and not that scary once you got past jumping off the platform. The brake did put her speed under her control.

And the burn of competition helped a lot.

Having never considered herself all that competitive, the feeling surprised her, but it also gratified her. Somehow, the unquenchable desire to kick Evan's ass made her feel powerful, and she hadn't felt that way in a long time. She slowed to a stop and landed on the second platform. As she allowed another helper to unclip her from the first line and escort her around the tree to the second line, she was only dimly aware of the cameraman also landing and making his way around the tree. She gripped the beanbag tightly and positioned her left hand over the brake with confidence.

"Need a push?" the young man asked.

"Nope—I've got it."

She pushed off and relished the feeling of freedom zipping down the line gave her. She kept her eyes peeled for the target and slowed down when she spotted it—there! Winding back for the throw, she remembered her years in little league. She could place a ball accurately.

Thunk. She hit the basket, but on the outside. Bella watched the beanbag fall to the ground in disbelief. Double-damn! Two points down.

The next target went better. She scored, and scored again on the fourth basket. When she arrived at the fifth platform, Evan was just taking off.

"Help me—hurry up," she called and this time a young woman helped move her tether from line to line. Evan was already almost out of sight, but she yelled after him anyway. "Hey, Evan—your butt crack's showing!"

He twisted and swore and the young woman helping her laughed out loud. "That's the way to get him."

Bella took her time getting ready for the next leg— her last chance for a point today. Taking a deep breath, she perched on the edge of the platform and gripped the beanbag. This was it—she had to score. She took off, keeping her speed well in line this time, and slowed down considerably when she spotted the basket. She aimed, held her arm steady, and threw as hard as she could.

Yes!

She let go of the brake and allowed herself to pick up speed as she kicked her legs in a happy dance. Three points! Even if Evan got five she hadn't fallen too far behind. The next challenge had to be better, right?

"Bella!"

She would show him tomorrow—she would run his butt into the ground and find a way to get him off his game so she could...

"Bella—you're going too fast!"

She opened her eyes, unaware she'd even closed them in her celebration, to see the platform hurtling toward her. Evan and a stranger—another zip line attendant—stared back at her in shock. She grabbed for the brake, missed it and grabbed again, but it was too late. Evan threw himself in the space on the platform between her and the tree trunk and she slammed into him at speed, knocking the wind from her lungs.

When she came to, she was tangled in a pile of arms and legs, the attendant yelling and swearing at both of them. Evan's breath tickled her neck and she breathed in his smell, masculine and woodsy. She hadn't been in such an intimate embrace in...well, years, frankly, and it stirred something within her that had been sleeping for a long time.

"Let me up," she said shakily.

"What the hell were you thinking?" Evan said as he climbed awkwardly to his feet and dragged her up with him. "You could have been hurt. You could have killed yourself!"

"I would have stopped her," the attendant said pettishly, and Evan turned his glare on him. The attendant slunk off to the other side of the platform. The cameraman landed, still filming.

Bella ignored him. "I'm fine. Thank you for saving me." She meant it, but somehow the words came out sarcastically and Evan scowled.

"I did save you. They'd be hauling you off in an ambulance right now if I hadn't been there." Bella tried to shrug off his hands, but he gripped her harder. "Look at me."

She did so reluctantly, but instead of anger she saw concern in his eyes.

"What do you care if I get hurt?" she demanded. "You'd win, right?"

He frowned. "Sure—maybe, but that's not how I want to win. I want to beat you fair and square."

He was so close she could see the shades of brown in his irises, warm tones that intrigued her and hinted at possibilities she hadn't considered with Evan. His jaw was strong and his features handsome. A kissable mouth. He pulled her a fraction closer.

"Bella." His voice was rough.

For a second she thought he was going to kiss her. She held her breath, anticipating his move, and her body tingled in awareness of him.

Then the moment ended. He shook himself, glanced over her shoulder, and she realized the camera was still rolling. She stepped away automatically and suddenly the attendant was back to help unhook her from the zip line and get her prepared for the descent to the ground. There was a difficult moment when she moved from the platform onto the ladder that led down the tree, but once she'd navigated it, she found it easy to move down the rungs. Back on solid ground, however, she found she was shaking and she was grateful for the bustle of removing the harness and retrieving her hat, pack and map to bring her back to herself.

When she shot a quick look at Evan, however, she found him looking back at her. His expression was inscrutable, and she had no idea now if he'd ever really meant to kiss her on the platform or if that was all in her head.

It didn't matter, she told herself. She wasn't here to find a husband. She was here to beat a billionaire.

HELL, HE'D NEARLY kissed her. On national television, no less. After making a fool of himself diving between her and the tree, Evan trudged down the trail after Bella in the late afternoon sunshine, berating himself for his lack of focus, his stupidity in placing himself in danger, and his even bigger idiocy for letting his groin dictate his actions.

What was wrong with him? One day in Canada and he was acting like a college kid on spring break. Hmm, maybe that was it, he thought as he rounded a corner and sighed as the trail headed upward again. Maybe he was reacting to his first real bit of time off in years. He took vacations all the time, but he always had his cell phone with him and even when he rock climbed he checked in two or three times a day minimum to issue orders and make sure business was progressing smoothly in his absence. He went alone for the most part, although sometimes when he climbed he joined up with some other guys. Still, once the climb was over, he generally chose to head off on his own.

"You put the lonely in loner," Amanda said to him once in the early days just after she'd come to work for him. "Who ever heard of a personal assistant who never sees her boss?"

She was right—he knew he took his privacy to the extreme, but having people too close to him made him claustrophobic. Amanda's office was separate from his. He took his meetings over the phone, handled all correspondence through email and texts. He liked to keep moving—that way people couldn't corner him and box him in.

A memory surfaced briefly—he'd been twelve years old when his mother caught him in the foyer as he tried to slip out the door, his uniform on. "No more baseball games; I've removed you from the team. Mommy needs you here. Daddy's out of town again."

He shuddered. It didn't take a shrink to figure out why he hated attachments now. His mother's neediness had overwhelmed him and ultimately pushed him away. Thoughts of those years when her need for constant attention kept him from joining activities, making friends—even going to school, often—left him desperate for movement. He picked up his pace.

Soon he caught up with Bella, who was decidedly limping. She sighed as he passed her, and stopped to bend down and fiddle with her shoe. He stopped, too. "Something wrong?"

"My ankle. Stupid boot is rubbing. Go ahead, I'm going to put another Band-Aid on it."

Evan hesitated. He should go on, but really there was no rush. He wouldn't earn extra points for making it to the campsite first and he didn't like to leave her behind.

Even if their camera crews made a small crowd on the path.

"I can wait."

"Fine." She took out her first aid kit, shucked off her boot and sock and picked the Band-Aid off.

"Better put some ointment on that." He didn't like the red, raw look to her ankle.

She dabbed some on and applied a fresh Band-Aid. Once her boot was securely back on, she stood up and re-shouldered her pack.

"Probably another mile to go, huh?"

"Yeah."

They plodded on in silence. Bella moved slowly, obviously in pain, and Evan kept having to stop and wait for her. Thankfully, the trail evened out, moving parallel to the ridge above them. Normally he would have covered the last mile in a matter of minutes, but he estimated it would be another half-hour at the rate Bella was traveling. Finally, he fell back and took her arm.

"I can do it," she said.

"I know you can." But he kept his arm in place.

Soon she gave up protesting and leaned on him heavily. He waited to feel the usual claustrophobic tightness he felt when someone got too close to him, but it didn't come. They continued on for twenty minutes, until the path curved and a vista opened up beneath them of the Maligne River Valley. Bella gasped and they stumbled to a stop.

"It's beautiful," she said.

He enjoyed the way she leaned against him. He could feel the rise and fall of her shoulders as she caught her breath, and her curls tickled his nose as he turned his head. He could still smell traces of her shampoo, despite the exertions of the day, and it was a clean, feminine scent that stirred animal lust within him.

He spotted a blue and white ribbon just a little farther down the trail. "Look—I think we made it."

BELLA PLUNGED DOWN the trail alongside Evan, thankful to reach the campsite at last, so when they rounded another curve at the blue and white marker and found themselves in a small clearing, empty of everything except for a pile of gear, she was brought up short.

"This is it?" she said aloud. Aware of the camera crew behind her, she tried to keep her voice from wobbling. She was hungry, tired and hurt. And the TV crew didn't even bother to set up camp? She felt anger radiating from Evan beside her, but he only said, "I guess it's up to us to make ourselves at home."

He approached the pile of gear and began to sort through it. Moments later, however, he stopped, stood up and paced away, his hands in fists at his sides.

"What?" Bella forced herself to ask. She didn't like being around angry men and Evan looked furious.

"There's only one of everything."

"What do you mean?" He wasn't making sense.

"They've left us one tent, one sleeping bag, one pillow."

"Are you kidding me?" She rounded on the camera crew, despite all of Madelyn's warnings against doing such a thing. "What the hell is this? Where's our gear?"

Paul, who hadn't said a word to her all day, waved her away.

"No! I want to know what the hell is going on!"

"Bella, forget it—it's part of the show." Evan appeared behind her and led her away from the cameraman.

"That's baloney! What are we supposed to do, flip a coin for it?" She rounded on Paul again, but Evan caught her arm.

"Yes, that's exactly what they want us to do—fight over it." He held her there until his words sunk in.

Of course. She let her shoulders slump as she pictured Madelyn's smug grin. A grown man and woman fighting over limited gear made for great television. "So, what do we do?"

"We could share it." He sounded as enthusiastic about the prospect as she felt. But what other choice did they have? The day was still warm now, but no matter where you were, nighttime in the mountains meant cool temperatures, and the change from hot day to cool night would most likely bring a heavy dew and soak anyone sleeping outdoors.

"Fine. What did they give us?"

It didn't take them long to pitch the tent, unroll the single, thin sleeping mat and place it inside. They agreed not to unroll the sleeping bag until it was time for bed.

"We'll just unzip it and use it as a cover," Bella pronounced.

"Sure," Evan agreed.

Next they unpacked their dinner. Bella had finished all her food except her banana earlier in the afternoon and she was pretty sure Evan was low on grub, too, so she was pleased to see their portions were slightly more generous this evening.

"Oooh—smoked salmon," she said, lifting up the package. "And cream cheese and crackers."

"That must be the appetizer," Evan said. "We've got some stew here, too."

"We'll need a fire for that."

"They actually provided us some wood and matches."

"Really?" Bella's anger over the single tent began to slide away. A hot meal would do her a world of good. Evan worked on getting the fire started while she undid the packages and poured the stew into a small, cast-iron pot she found in the pile of gear. They shared the salmon while the stew heated, then dug into the main course.

Sitting on the ground, leaning against an outcropping of rock, she ate her fill while watching the fire flicker and dance. She could have used a hot bath right about now, but overall she felt good.

Except for her ankle. She'd better change the Band-Aid again.

Before she could move toward her pack, however, there was a commotion down the trail and Jake appeared, leading a small band of crew members.

"Bella, Evan, congratulations on surviving your first day." A crew member scuttled forward and set up a tripod next to him. It held a placard inscribed with both their names. Dots of Velcro were placed next to them. Evan stood up and slowly she did the same. Soon crew members ringed them to film the day's wrap-up.

Jake spoke in his plummy announcer voice. "Your first day consisted of an eight mile hike and two challenges. You both did very well, but Evan—you did better overall. You had a strong start with the archery competition, scoring four out of five possible points. Well done." He bowed his head to Evan and Evan answered with a nod. "Bella, you seem like a newcomer to archery. Am I right?"

"Yes." *Thanks for pointing that out*, she thought.

"But with a few tips from your adversary," he nodded to Evan again, "you did all right. Three points out of five." He stuck a card to each set of Velcro dots—one emblazoned with a four next to Evan's name and a three next to hers. "Your next challenge was even harder. You needed to overcome your fear of heights and use skill and accuracy to win the zip line beanbag challenge. Both of you found this somewhat difficult. Evan, again, you went after this contest with a fair bit of skill and scored your first four baskets. Bella here, however, helped you miss your fifth. That makes eight points in all for you today, Evan." He turned to Bella. "I believe you're scared of heights?"

"Sort of," she said. "But not too much."

"You got off to a shaky start," he agreed, "but you did seem to get the hang of it. You made three shots, as well. That's six points to you in all. So far the contest is quite close! Rest tonight. You've earned it. We'll meet back here at eight tomorrow morning for day two of *Can You Beat a Billionaire?*"

He waited a beat and made a slicing motion with his hand. Immediately the cameras shut down and the crew backed off. Madelyn stepped forward, startling Bella, who hadn't seen the woman arrive. She found herself glancing down at Madelyn's feet. Nope, no stilettos this time. Madelyn wore a pair of top-grade hiking boots, however, that probably set her back several hundred dollars. Bella wished she had a pair like that.

"The crew's campground is a quarter mile up the path," Madelyn said in her usual clipped tones. "You are forbidden to enter it. Your campground will be observed and filmed at all times during the night, including a remotely operated camera within your tent which we will switch on once you are changed for sleeping. You will want to observe a certain amount of modesty—in other words, sleeping in the nude is out.

"Bella—Adrienne, here, will look at your ankle. We'll get that fixed up and give you an insert for your boots that should help. The audience wants competition, not cripples. Good-night to both of you. See you bright and early tomorrow morning." Madelyn turned, trailed as always by Ellis, who flashed them both a smile and a thumb's-up, and headed down the path.

Bella allowed herself to be ministered to and she and Evan took turns in the tent changing into more comfortable clothes. It was still fairly early in the evening, however, and the sun remained above the horizon.

"What time do you think it will set?" she asked Evan as they lounged near the campfire. The crew had faded away down the path, except for a single cameraman and assistant.

Evan considered the sky. "Eight, eight thirty maybe?"

"I'm not sure I can stay awake that long."

"There's no rule says you have to."

He was right. Except for the point where she was competing to win the money she needed to keep her business afloat, she was essentially on vacation. There was nothing more she could accomplish tonight. She leaned back and gazed upon the valley spread beneath them, with its flashing silver band of water traversing through it. Up here, it was hard to focus on her problems back in Montana. Hannah and the volunteers would have all the animals fed, exercised, and back in their pens for the night. She hoped no emergencies had cropped up, or if they had that her brother had been able to handle them.

She missed the animals—their noses butting against her hands as she wandered among them, the way they were always happy to see her, no matter what. Their native optimism.

She could use some of that. Evan was proving to be a true competitor, and if she was going to win she needed to focus all her attention on her goal.

Which meant a good night's sleep.

"I can't keep my eyes open anymore," she said.

"I'll take care of the fire and be in soon. Don't hog all the covers."

She repressed the anxious feeling that tightened her gut at his words. "I'll leave a corner for you."

She visited the bushes some yards from off the path and awkwardly washed her face and brushed her teeth with some of her drinking water. Soon she was in the still-warm tent with the sleeping bag unzipped and spread lightly over her. Despite the hardness of the ground and the earliness of the hour, her eyelids were drooping closed when Evan unzipped the tent flap and stepped inside.

Instantly, she was wide-awake again.

The tent was so small he had to crawl on his hands and knees to get inside of it. She heard him rustling around before she felt the sleeping bag lift and the warm bulk of a man slip in beside her. Every nerve ending she possessed went on high alert as he wriggled closer and spread the sleeping bag back over the two of them.

"You good?" he asked.

"Uh...yeah," she said.

"We're set," he called out and she frowned when she remembered that the remaining cameraman was supposed to install a small, remote camera inside the tent. She stifled a curse as the tent flap unzipped again and a man's hand reached in and hooked something to a fabric loop in the ceiling. That must be the camera. She glared at it for a moment before pulling the sleeping bag high around her shoulders despite the heat.

The heat that was increasing moment by moment with Evan's bulk pressed against her.

"Do you have to be so close to me?" she snapped when she couldn't stand it anymore.

"Where am I supposed to go?" he asked, a hint of humor—strained humor—in his voice.

"Just—don't touch me."

He laughed and moved half an inch away from her. "How's that?"

"Not good enough." She moved this time, and almost immediately came up against the fabric of the side of the tent. She wriggled back and encountered Evan again. "For God's sake, isn't there more room on your side?"

"Not really." This time he sounded chagrined. "Guess we'll just have to deal with close quarters."

She sighed heavily but lay still and closed her eyes again. It didn't help that the sun was barely down. Evan turned, which pressed him even closer to her. She was aware of every single place their bodies touched, even if they were modestly dressed, as Jake put it. Evan was muscle all over. For a billionaire, he was actually pretty hot. She wondered if women threw themselves at him all the time and nodded to herself; of course they did. Handsome and filthy rich? What a combination.

Did he ever wonder about people's motives? How did he protect himself from everyone who wanted to use him for their own gain? He came across as very self-contained, and she wondered if that was merely a defense mechanism he had to use to survive.

Had he always been a billionaire? Yes—Hannah showed her an article about him that said Mortimer Innovations had been in his family for generations now, so he must have grown up knowing that he could always have exactly what he wanted.

What did he want?

The question brought a rush of heat to her body that she tried unsuccessfully to squash. More than once today she'd been convinced that he wanted her. Ridiculous. He must be surrounded by beautiful women all the time. She wasn't anything special. Cute. That's the word people used to sum her up.

She'd always been cute, from when she was a child trying to keep up with her older brother to when she'd spent her high school years competing with girls like Lacey Taylor, who wrapped all the cowboys from the nearby ranches around her little finger.

Cute and broke.

The thought depressed her and she turned to her back. Now her shoulder was pressed against Evan's.

"I thought you'd be asleep by now," he said, his deep

voice rumbling through her and setting her senses alight.

"I thought you'd be asleep. What's keeping you up?"

There was a long pause and just when she thought he wasn't going to answer at all, she felt his arm move and his fingers touched hers, under the covers. They slid between her own and he squeezed her hand.

Her breath caught in her throat and she didn't move. His thumb traced across her palm softly once, twice—a caress so small, yet so intimate it made her tingle all over. He squeezed her hand again, then let go, and she felt the loss. His admission—for that's what it had to be—unnerved her and set her on fire all at the same time.

She fought the urge to roll over and press herself against him, all too aware of the video camera rolling just a few feet above their bodies. Besides, he was her enemy—her opponent. His goal was to force her to marry him and to tie up her time for a whole year, while she lost everything that really mattered to her.

Still, his nearness was a powerful aphrodisiac, especially to a woman who hadn't seen any action since…well, since the last president was in office.

*Close your eyes and go to sleep. Don't even think about him,* she told herself. Easy to say. Harder to do when Evan announced his presence with every breath he took. He was obviously still awake, too. Was he thinking about her?

Desperate to squelch her rising libido, she pictured Misty, a small, wiry dog who'd been dumped at the clinic recently, half-starving, with the worst case of mange she'd ever seen. The poor dog stunk when she'd first handled her, and shrank away from Bella as if embarrassed about her appearance. Who would look after pets like Misty if she lost? She couldn't let Evan distract her. Turning her back on him, she closed her eyes tightly and began to count sheep.

AS BELLA'S BREATHING evened out beside him, Evan stared at the stupid camera hanging from the roof of the tent and counted the number of ways he'd screwed up today. Somehow Bella had cast a spell on him and he'd lost the ability to think rationally, while she made use of each of his blunders to catapult herself into a stronger position. When he'd taken her hand beneath the covers just now, a spark of desire had lit up his whole body, yet she remained unmoved.

Several times today he thought she returned his interest, especially on the zip line platform, where he'd come perilously close to kissing her, but now he wasn't at all sure he'd read her right. Maybe she was playing him like a fiddle—teasing him to a fever pitch of wanting, while she laughed at him all the way to the bank. It would be just like a woman to want to humiliate him that way.

Well, she wasn't going to win—no way. He was two points ahead of her and he'd pull further ahead tomorrow. Heck, he would be at least five points ahead if he'd kept his mouth shut at the archery range. No more mister nice guy, he promised himself. He'd show Bella his true colors tomorrow.

Still, as the minutes ticked by and his eyes remained

open, Evan grew more and more uncomfortable. He hated confined spaces—even tents—and while he could sleep in one just fine when he was on his own—as long as the flap remained open—it was too much to bear having Bella pressed against him—in more ways than one.

She turned him on, for one thing, but her presence also made it hard to breathe. In fact, the longer he stayed inside the tent the less oxygen there seemed to be.

Shit. He recognized this tightness in his chest and the feeling that the walls were about to cave in and smother him. If he didn't get outside—pronto—he would head into a full-fledged panic attack. He didn't need that broadcast over national TV.

He quickly threw the sleeping bag back and made a big show of wiping his brow and peeling his damp t-shirt from his chest a few times, to indicate he couldn't stand the heat. Nothing unmanly about getting too hot, he thought as he struggled to the front of the tent and unzipped the flap. He exited it gratefully just as the sun finally set. Heading back to the campfire, which he'd carefully put out a half-hour before, he leaned against a rock and settled in for the night.

# Chapter Six

BELLA SLEPT MUCH better than she'd imagined she would, but when she pushed herself to a sitting position in the morning and felt the coolness of the sleeping mat next to her, she realized that was partly due to Evan not sharing the tent with her. When had he left? God—had she snored so loud it drove him out? That was an embarrassing idea. None of her previous bed partners had complained about her snoring, however, so maybe it wasn't that. Maybe he was an early riser.

Pushing her way outside a moment later, she realized that wasn't the answer, either. Evan lay sound asleep near the ruins of their campfire from the night before, and looked like he'd been there for some time. She remembered his fingers wrapping around hers so intimately. What had driven him away?

*Don't even think about it,* she told herself. Instead she waited as a crew member came and dismantled the tent camera, then took the opportunity to change inside it before Evan woke up. Back outside, she checked her heel. It looked far better than it had last night, and the insert she'd been given for the back of her boot should help, too. She wondered what surprises this day would bring.

She decided to stretch some of her stiffness away while she waited for breakfast. Evan wandered past, back from his own visit to the bushes. He looked worse than she felt—like he'd aged ten years overnight—but she wouldn't underestimate him. If today's contests were as badly skewed toward his strengths as they were yesterday, she'd be in trouble. Her right arm twinged from the unusual activities of drawing bowstrings and throwing beanbags. Still, stretching felt good. Thank goodness for all those yoga classes over the years.

"Love this view!" Evan proclaimed from behind her as she pushed up from a prone position into downward dog.

He'd better mean the valley, she thought, willing herself not to drop back to the ground. When she shifted into a new pose, however, she saw he most definitely wasn't looking at the vista below them. She faltered, but continued with her routine.

*He's just trying to make me nervous. I can't let it work.*

Still, a few minutes later she gave up trying to reclaim the calmness she'd felt at the beginning of her stretching. Evan's frank perusal of her body sent waves of heat through her until she wobbled in her poses. Best to stop before she keeled over and hurt herself. She joined him at the firepit where a crew member fed her coffee and a breakfast burrito. Mmmm. Maybe today wouldn't be so bad.

Three hours later, however, she conceded that today would probably turn out to be worse. She, Evan, Jake, and a platoon of camera crewmen and assistants stood on the banks of the Athabasca River while a woman named Jessie outlined basic kayaking safety procedures. When she was done, Jake took over.

"Welcome to day two of *Can You Beat a Billionaire*. Bella, Evan, I hope you slept well?"

"Like a baby," Bella said. She thought she was getting the hang of this acting enthusiastic thing.

"Evan, we noticed you were rather restless during the night. Any specific reason for that?"

A muscle in Evan's jaw twitched. "I like sleeping out under the stars."

"Without a mattress pad or even a sleeping bag?" Jake widened his eyes theatrically.

"I like roughing it."

Jake shrugged theatrically, and returned to his spiel. "You've already hiked for several hours. Your first challenge this morning involves kayaking. You will need to use strength, skill and accuracy to collect five plastic fish along the kayaking route we've made for you on the spectacular Athabasca River. Notice the poles." He waved at the river behind him where a series of differently colored poles stuck several feet out of the water. "Keep the yellow stripes to your right and the green stripes to your left and you'll stay on track. If you leave the course you are disqualified. You may not turn around at any time. Put your fish in the nylon pouch attached to your kayak. Each fish is worth one point. Do you understand?"

"Yes," Evan said.

"Yes," Bella echoed. The river water seemed to be traveling awfully fast, however. How were they to control their kayaks with one hand on the paddle and grab a fish from a basket with the other? This was all too similar to yesterday's beanbag toss—only worse.

Much worse.

"Evan, you reached the challenge ahead of Bella, so you go first," Jake said. "Good luck!"

Bella wasn't sorry Evan was to go ahead of her, even though he'd only beaten her to the river by a few steps. They'd hiked together for the most part, talking little as the day warmed up and they worked the kinks out of their muscles. Too much of her time was spent considering the way he'd furtively squeezed her hand last night under the covers. What had he meant by it? And why had he abandoned the tent halfway through the night? It couldn't have been comfortable sleeping outside without a sleeping bag.

When he approached the river, Jessie handed Evan a wetsuit and ushered him toward a makeshift changing room the crew had rigged up nearby. A few minutes later, Bella watched him squeeze into the kayak and Jessie snap him in. The woman made him practice rolling the kayak and flipping himself back to vertical several times, and Bella was relieved to see six other men and women joining him in the water in their own kayaks. Apparently there would be plenty of help should something go wrong out on the river.

She bit her lip as Evan fought the current to get away from shore. A guide kayak led him upstream far enough so he could turn around and get going in the right direction before he reached two bright red poles that demarked the starting point. The current grabbed the kayak immediately and whisked him down the course. The poles which marked the sides must be farther apart than they looked from the banks, because he didn't seem to be struggling to stay between them. He was struggling, however, to head towards the first container of fish, and to her surprise, he missed it all together.

"Harder than it looks, eh?" Jake said.

"Yes—it must be."

Evan paddled like mad and managed to snag the next fish, and the next one. He nearly missed the fourth container, but with a last desperate struggle and heave, he snagged one, nearly lost it, managed to hold on and shoved it in the bag, too.

"Damn it—miss!" she yelled, forgetting for a moment she was on camera. That wouldn't look very good. She sighed. No sense even wondering if Madelyn might not choose to air that—of course she would.

But she whooped aloud as Evan did miss the last one. He'd been heading straight for the container when his kayak jerked away from it, nearly unbalancing him. She had to remember the current went funky there.

"Three points for Evan. Looks like a challenging course, Bella. Are you ready for it?" Jake asked.

She was getting sick of his smarmy television-announcer tones, but she answered clearly, "Yes—I'm all set!"

She wished it was true. She wasn't afraid of a river like she'd been of the zip lines yesterday—she'd actually gone whitewater river rafting before, which seemed much more dangerous than this—but seeing Evan flailing around told her the current was very strong and she knew she might not make it through the entire course without being pulled right past the boundary poles. Plus, she had to make up some lost points, or Evan was going to get too far ahead of her to beat.

*You can do this*, she told herself as she struggled into her wetsuit. *Evan may be stronger, but he's also heavier. You don't need to be as strong as him to stay on course.* She had no idea if that made any sense, but it sounded good.

She allowed Jessie to help her into the kayak, her courage lasting right until Jessie made her flip it. She went over just fine, but she struggled mightily to get back up and was gasping for breath by the time she managed it.

"You all right?" Jessie asked.

"Yes." What else could she say?

"Do it again."

"What?" She had to be kidding.

"Again—I can't let you out there until you know how to flip and recover." The stocky blonde stared her down.

Bella sighed but flipped over again. This time she came up rightside more quickly, but the effort it took made her arms ache and she hadn't even started the course yet.

"You'd better try that one more..." Jessie began but Madelyn appeared on shore.

"We're behind schedule. Move it!"

Apparently even Jessie was afraid of the director, but the woman's expression was uneasy as she said, "All right, get out there."

Bella paddled unsteadily out to a position far upstream of the starting gate. She wanted to stall for time and recover from her exertions and the cold slap of ice water on her face when she'd gone over, but fighting the current to stay in place sapped her energy too much. Best to just get this over with.

Evan had missed the first container. She had to get that fish. She decided to overcorrect, get as close to the guide-poles on the right-hand side of the course as possible and allow the current to bring her back to the container. She turned the kayak, drifted to the starting point, and paddled for all she was worth to the right. Her strategy worked, except when she judged it time to ease up and let the current take her, it swirled her around and she was nearly facing backward when she got to the container. She just managed to fling her arm out and make a wild grab as it went by.

A fish!

She stuffed it in the nylon bag, grabbed hold of the paddle again and drove for the second container. The current seemed weaker now and she saw why Evan had an easier time getting the next several fish. Unfortunately, she got too cocky and overshot the fourth container. She hung on for a moment, paddling backward furiously before she remembered the rule against going back for fish. She had to give in and let the current drag her forward again.

The final container was where that tricky current jerked Evan away at the last moment. How could she get past it? Since the container sat right at the edge of the course, she couldn't try to pass it on the far side—she had to approach it in the same way Evan had. All she could do was count on her ability to dig in and fight the current.

With little hope of actually accomplishing this, she paddled toward the end of the course. When she approached the final container she put on a burst of speed, digging her paddle far into the water as she got close. She felt the current grab the kayak and realized why Evan hadn't been able to overcome it—she felt like a giant hand had closed on the prow and yanked her off course. With desperate strokes she paddled in the opposite direction—she still had a shot. The current jerked her around and she gave up fighting it. Instead she hurled the paddle away and lunged toward the container. Her right hand closed on the hard plastic shape of a fish as she overbalanced and hit the water, the cold shock of it forcing the air from her lungs.

She windmilled her arms, but her body was still snapped into the kayak, and without a paddle she had no way of righting herself. She thrashed impotently, the coldness quickly dulling the strength in her limbs. She could see the sunlight on the surface of the water above her, bisected by the dark line of the kayak, but she had no way to reach it. The skirt still clung to her. She knew she was supposed to do something to release it—pull something—but she couldn't stop thrashing long enough to do so. She had to get out, had to...

...*save Caramel, had to reach her before the awful thing happened, had to stop her from dying, stop Cyclone from dying, stop her family from losing their land*...

The kayak jerked, something plunged into the water next to her and fought with the snaps on the seal that held her in place. Hands grabbed her arms, her shoulders, and the next thing she knew she broke the surface and air seared down her throat and through her lungs. She coughed, spit, and cried out as she was pulled atop another kayak unceremoniously. Seconds later she was hauled to shore.

Lying on the banks of the Athabasca, she let tears run down her face without shame. She'd discovered one thing was worse than losing her job and her fight to save her animals.

Losing her own life.

"SHE'S GOT A FISH!" one of the crew members cried out. "Look—she got the fifth fish!"

Evan scraped a hand across his stubbled jaw and turned aside in the hopes all the cameras were trained on Bella, newly rescued from the river, and wouldn't catch him wiping his eyes.

*She'd nearly drowned.*

Hell, he wasn't one to cry. He couldn't remember the last time he had, so it freaked him out to find water seeping from the corners of his eyes now. He couldn't believe how Bella attacked the kayak course, like she'd been born to the sport. She put his puny efforts to shame. He preferred land sports to water ones, but he'd kayaked before and he thought he knew what he was doing. The variances in the current completely threw him off, though. Bella must have watched his efforts and learned from them.

*The lovely, vibrant woman who'd shared his tent last night—part of the night—had nearly drowned.*

He wasn't prepared for the pain that thought brought him. If she hadn't been breathing when they rescued her... If she wasn't lying on the shore now, responding to her rescuers questions...

He couldn't even imagine how he'd feel.

Evan crossed his arms over his chest, not knowing what else to do with his hands. Thank God everyone was focused on Bella right now because he was making a fool out of himself. Over a woman he barely knew.

He couldn't remember feeling like this.

He couldn't remember feeling...

Evan dragged his attention away from that direction and refocused on his adversary. Because that's all she was—an adversary.

And she was one hell of an adversary—going for the last fish like that, throwing away her paddle, for God's sake. Or was she just reckless? She'd managed to hang on to the darn fish, too. He shook his head in disbelief. She'd made up two points in this challenge. He had to beat her good on the next one.

*Beat her good.* Hell, he sounded like his father.

A wry laugh escaped him. Bella was practically un-conscious, lying on the shore near the water. She might be out of the contest for good and he was plotting his strategy to win. The acorn surely didn't fall far from the tree.

He didn't want to beat Bella. He wanted to scoop her into his arms, press his ear against her chest to hear the heartbeat that would confirm she did indeed live, and cover her with kisses from her lips to her...

He turned his back on the river—on Bella—and struggled to get himself together. Whether or not she was beautiful or vibrant or wonderful or took his breath away, or any of the other trite things men thought about the women they wanted, she was still his enemy. She still stood between him and a dignified—well, somewhat dignified—way to maintain control of his company.

He was glad she was alive, but he still planned to crush her in this game.

A ragged cheer escaped from the camera crew, and he turned back around to see two of them helping Bella to her feet. She walked under her own power up from the bank toward him. Jake appeared by Evan's side. "She's still in it, thank God."

Evan shot him a quizzical look.

"Can you imagine the expense of finding a backup competitor now? Starting all over?"

No, he couldn't. In fact, the thought left him cold. He didn't want another competitor—he wanted Bella. He wanted to win this competition and he wanted Bella for his wife.

No other woman would do.

Evan watched her approach.

He wanted Bella? He wanted to spend a whole year with one woman? He waited for the surge of claustrophobia the thought should bring, but it didn't come. Bella was beautiful, kind, smart... real. She wasn't plastic, like all the California girls were—too beautiful, too grasping—and she wasn't like his mother, either, always demanding he stay close, always preventing him from doing what he wanted to do. Bella was independent. Best of all, she didn't want anything from him. The women he usually dated wanted to control all of his cash and they wanted to control him, too.

Still, he'd been plenty claustrophobic in that tent last night, so he hadn't done some mental turnaround in the last twelve hours. He was still Evan, and he doubted anything could make him comfortable with a long-term relationship—even Bella.

Best to keep her at arm's length.

Jake kept the point score announcement ceremony short and simple, while Bella shivered in the blanket the first aid worker wrapped around her shoulders. All too soon, it was time to move on.

Evan followed the crew toward the SUVs, knowing something had changed today—something in his heart—and he was going to have a hell of a time changing it back again.

## Chapter Seven

B ELLA WAS GRATEFUL they didn't have to hike to the next challenge. As she rode in the backseat of one of the SUVs next to Evan, the dull ache from the raw spot at the back of her ankle couldn't compare to the pervasive tiredness in the rest of her body. Evan seemed subdued as well, but maybe watching your opponent nearly die would do that to you. Back at the river, the show's physician had checked her out thoroughly and declared her fit to continue. She wasn't sure she agreed with his diagnosis. More than anything she wanted to lie down and go to sleep.

She must have slept a little, for the next thing she knew the SUV came to a stop and a bustle began all around her. Evan opened the door and climbed out, and Bella forced herself to wake up and survey the activity. They had pulled up near a square wooden structure with a green metal roof. The camera crew was busy getting its gear together and Madelyn came into view, as polished as usual, barking orders at everyone.

"All right, sleepy time is over," she said, ducking her

head in through the open door of the SUV. "Chop-chop, let's go."

"Where are we?" She climbed out of the vehicle as Madelyn pulled back. "Oh," she added as she spotted the small boxy green metal cars attached to cables going up the side of the mountain in front of them.

"The Jasper Tramway," Madelyn said. "A seven minute ride to 7700 feet." She smirked as Bella's face fell. "Don't worry—it's perfectly safe." Her tone said it wasn't anything of the kind, but Bella squashed the panic rising in her gut. A tram was far safer than a zip line and she'd done just fine with that yesterday.

"What's the challenge?"

"You'll find out when we get to the top."

"When's lunch?" Evan materialized by her side and as usual, Bella felt the stirrings of desire. Good to know a dousing in cold water hadn't put out that flame. If anything it had sharpened it.

"Soon," was all Madelyn said before stalking off and shouting to a cameraman.

"How are you doing?" Evan asked her. Glancing up, she noticed several cameras trained on her and stifled a sigh.

"Fine. Tired." Shoot, she wasn't supposed to admit that to him.

"I'll bet. It really scared me, seeing you go under like that. It's a good thing they had extra personnel out on the river with you." He touched her arm gently. "You know, I want to win this thing, but if you die in the process it kind of spoils things for me."

She looked up sharply, caught his grin and melted a little inside. "I guess so." Usually his closeness unnerved her, but this time she felt herself draw strength from his presence. He was so calm and sane in the midst of the craziness of the film shoot, and in a way he was her ally—the only other person around who wasn't part of the crew. "What's up with that marriage thing anyway? Why not marry someone you love?"

He shrugged and looked away. "I don't love anyone enough for that."

"Really? No steady girlfriend?"

"Hell, no." He laughed and glanced at her sheepishly. "That kind of came out wrong. I'm not the settling-down type of guy, but in order to maintain control of Mortimer Innovations, I have to be married by the end of the month, and I have to stay married for a year."

"You couldn't spend a little of your billions and just buy a fake wife?"

"Nah, I'm too cheap for that. If I win this thing I get you for free," he said, laughter glinting in his dark eyes.

"Wouldn't it be simpler not to spend five days galli-vanting around Jasper?"

"I suppose, but it would be less fun. I guess if I lose, that's what I'll do."

"Why not just do it to begin with?" she pressed.

He glanced away from her, then back, "This is going to sound bad no matter how I phrase it, but it's the truth. I've always known women aren't dating me—they're dating my money. They're dating the possibility of becoming Mrs. Billionaire. I learned very early on that women are experts at pretending to love you when you have something they want. I also learned that they're experts at sinking their claws into you and not letting go, even when you want them to. My competition would have a field day if I bought a wife and I doubt I'd be able to shake the woman when the year was up. She'd claim she was truly in love when we married, and say that I'd duped her about my intentions, and the courts might take her side. After all, I'm just a nasty billionaire."

"Wow," Bella said. Poor little rich guy, indeed. The desire she'd felt a moment ago melted away under the cynicism of his words.

"I told you it would sound bad."

"I don't want to meet the women you hang out with." She took a step back from him.

"No, you don't." He watched Madelyn usher a herd of crew members into a tram and send them up the mountain. The director scanned the area and headed their way. Evan frowned. "Look—I know there are good women out there, but I'm so messed up at this point I won't make a good husband no matter who I'm with. So I'm doing it this way. If you lose, you've already agreed to sign an airtight prenuptial agreement. You'll get an all-expenses-paid yearlong vacation among the high rollers of the business world, with accommodations in the best hotels and homes on the West Coast. We'll throw in some travel to exotic locals, and I promise I'll always be a gentleman. It'll be great, I swear."

*It'll be great? Was he for real?* Bella laughed derisively. "You are unbelievable. You think you can tell me that sad little story and I'll just stop competing and join you in false matrimony? Hello—I'm here to win five million dollars because I'm about to go broke and lose my business. There are animals depending on me—real, live creatures who have no one else to turn to, and who are going to die if I don't win. I'm not rolling over and playing wifey, Moneybuns. I'm going to win this thing!"

"Did you get that?" Madelyn snapped at Paul the cameraman as she strode up to them.

"Sure did." Paul scratched his stomach.

"Excellent. Great television. Bella, Evan, come on— your turn in the tram."

Bella's rising anger at Evan's insensitivity drained away as she trailed after Madelyn to the small, green metal car. Engrossed in evaluating how she really felt about riding in one of these things, she felt rather than saw Evan fall back. Madelyn noticed, too.

"Keep up. What's the matter with you?" she snapped at him.

"I'd prefer to hike up," he said. Bella thought he looked a little pale. Had her words hurt him that much? She doubted it. Something else must be bugging him.

"You'd prefer to hike up?" Madelyn put her hands on her hips. "Well, I'd prefer to get this television show filmed sometime in the next century. Get in the tram!"

"No."

Bella raised an eyebrow. Evan didn't like the tram, either? Was he afraid of heights? That made no sense; he'd been fine on the zip line the previous day, and didn't he say he liked rock climbing?

"What do you mean, no? I said get in the tram and I mean it, mister—we have a schedule to keep." Madelyn stepped forward menacingly.

"No."

Biting back a smile, Bella waited for Madelyn's response.

"Are you forfeiting the game? Ellis—get Legal on the line!" she called, and leaned in toward Evan with an icy look. "You have ten seconds to decide, Mr. Mortimer. Contestants must participate in every contest or they forfeit and lose the game. Five…four…three…two…"

Bella held her breath. Was this it? Was she about to win five million dollars, all because Evan wouldn't—or couldn't—get on a tram? She glanced over the small metal contraption again. Small. Was Evan claustrophobic?

Of course he was—he couldn't stay in the tent with her, either.

She turned back to him just in time to see a muscle in his jaw ticking like crazy before he opened his mouth and said, "I'm not forfeiting. Fine, I'll ride the tram." He stalked off toward it and disappeared around the back end. A moment later Bella could make out his profile through one of the large windows.

He didn't look happy.

A smile curved her lips. Time for her to make some headway—she wouldn't let this opportunity slip through her fingers. Forgetting her own qualms, she decided to put his to very good use. Whatever the next challenge was, it obviously was going to take place on top this mountain. She needed to make sure he was thoroughly freaked out by the time they got off that tram.

EVAN KEPT HIS fingers wrapped tightly around the railing as the tram filled with passengers. Bella squeezed in beside him and various crew members took up the rest of the space with their bodies and equipment. He could feel them using up all the oxygen. Already the metal walls pressed back upon him and they hadn't even left the ground. The only thing he had going for him was the knowledge that the ride was only seven minutes long. He could stand anything for seven minutes.

Bella pressed up against him, as if the crush of bodies gave her no other choice. She leaned into him heavily and although normally he'd relish the feeling of her soft breasts pressed against his arm, right this moment it felt like someone had tossed a woolen blanket over his head and was about to smother him. The image of his mother flashed into his mind, rushing to pull him into her arms just when he'd been about to escape outside to play with his friends. "No, Evan, stay with me. Mommy needs you."

He brushed the memory aside and stared out the window as the tram lurched forward.

*Breathe. Just breathe. In. Out. Empty your mind.*

Bella slipped an arm around his waist and pressed closer. "You know sometimes they overload these little cars," she said conversationally. "They don't mean to, but they have to make as much money as possible, so they make sure to get as many people on as they can. Sometimes they only count the number of people—not their weight. North Americans are getting heavier all the time, so even though 10 people might have fit just fine in here a century ago, they don't really fit now, do they?" She crowded him against the wall.

Evan wanted to push back. In fact, he wanted to shove Bella as hard as he could against the other riders. A sheen of sweat coated his hands and the back of his neck and he was beginning to find it hard to breathe. "Back up a little, would you?" he managed to ask instead.

"What?" She crowded even closer. "This is just like riding in a really crowded elevator, isn't it? Do you ever worry about elevators stopping in between floors and you'd get stuck and you'd have to wait for hours and hours until someone came along and rescued you?"

Hell, getting stuck in an elevator was his worst fear. He never took elevators if he could help it. He passed off his obsession with taking the stairs as part of his dedication to staying fit. "Good practice for climbing mountains," he always said just before he disappeared into the stairwell of a high rise. Luckily he was too rich for people to question him too closely.

"Imagine if the tram stopped. It could be days before we were rescued. We'd have to take turns lying down to sleep while the others stood up."

Days? He dragged his gaze away from the spectacular mountain scenery outside the window and looked down at her, finally catching her evil grin. "It isn't working," he ground out.

"What isn't working?" she asked innocently, pushing him farther into the wall.

"You're not scaring me."

"I think I am," she laughed. "You're really sweating."

Damn it, she was right—he was practically dripping. "So I don't like small spaces, so what?"

"So, it's kind of pathetic, Moneybuns. This is just a tourist attraction." She draped herself over him. "A really, really small and confined tourist attraction."

This time he did push her away, firmly but not too roughly. No need to make a spectacle of himself while the cameras were rolling. "Enough. I know I'm impossible to resist, but you're going to have to control yourself until you get to the top. Once we're there, I'll be happy to indulge your every fantasy." Out of the corner of his eye he saw the upper station come into view and breathed a sigh of relief. A couple more moments and he'd be done with this ride from hell.

With any luck they'd hike down.

EVEN SCARED TO DEATH, Evan was hot. Once he succumbed to his claustrophobia he stopped complaining about the hordes of money-hungry women who threw themselves at him on a daily basis, and she was able to remember why she'd found him so attractive. The fact that billionaire Evan Mortimer had an Achilles heel made him all that much more interesting. What had happened to make him so antsy in small spaces?

Bella filed out of the tram onto the top of Whistler's Mountain, no relation to the famous ski resort far to the southwest, as Madelyn pointed out. The air was noticeably cooler up here, even in the broad sunshine, and the view took her breath away. She only glanced at the upper station, which looked to contain a restaurant as well as a gift shop, before she turned to face the valley spread out below them and the jagged mountains that marched in every direction off into the distance.

Canada had so far exceeded her expectations, she had to admit. She'd heard about Banff and Jasper from many of her friends and family members—since Montana bordered Canada, the park was a popular vacation destination for Chance Creek's citizens—but their descriptions and even their photographs didn't do it justice. For one minute all her worries about the show, Evan, her animals and business slid away and she let the light breeze and thin air refresh her. She wished she always had this view in front of her to remind her of the infinite wonder of the world she inhabited. Somehow, in the day to day of life and work, it was all too easy to forget.

"Pretty spectacular, isn't it?" Evan said, coming up beside her.

"It sure is. Feeling better?"

"Much. No thanks to you."

"You deserved it," she said tartly.

"Look, I never meant to imply that your goals in winning this contest are any less worthy than my goals," Evan said.

"Yes, you did," she retorted.

"Well, I guess I did," he admitted. "But I want you

to know I do admire your work."

"I wish I could say the same." She wasn't going to fall for his charm again. She'd watched him turn it on and off too many times.

"Oh, yeah? Is your filing and appointment system computerized?"

"Sure. Everyone's is," she said. "So what?"

"Mortimer Innovations has five patents that pertain to that software. Do you use the new, longer-lasting lightbulbs?"

"Uh-huh."

"We helped develop them. Do you care at all if people in Africa have access to clean drinking water?"

She just looked at him.

"We're a major backer in a plan to deliver simple, low cost technology to a thousand remote villages in the next three years. How about disease control…"

"I get it, I get it. You're a saint and we'd all be lost without you," Bella said, waving him off.

"All I'm saying is I'm not a bad guy, Bella. I want to retain control over Mortimer Innovations because I have a vision for the company—one that values improving conditions for human beings all over this planet above stockholder profits. Unfortunately, if I don't get married I'll lose control over the company and my brother will take charge."

"Let me guess; your brother is the devil incarnate and he'll use his super-powers for evil?"

"Something like that," Evan said. "Let's just say his belief in the bottom line trumps everything else. I'm in an incredible position, Bella—I can affect millions of lives for the better."

"Or my life for the worse," she said and walked away.

EVAN STARED OUT of the mountaintop restaurant's huge windows without seeing the incredible panorama spread below them anymore. His first attempt to impress Bella and get her thinking positively about the possibility of marrying him for a year had failed utterly because once again he'd forgotten she wasn't one of the legions of women back in California throwing themselves at his feet in order to get hold of his money. He wanted to tell her more about what his company could do—why she should look at it as a force for good rather than just another enormous corporation—but if he thought she would be wowed by a list of patents and inventions, he was highly mistaken.

He needed specifics. He needed to prove that his need to maintain control over Mortimer Innovations was just as important and valid as her need to keep control over her veterinary clinic. If he could introduce some doubt into her mind about who deserved to win, he could wrap up this contest in no time. Who could have guessed the little vet from Montana would prove to be such a competitor?

Or maybe he was just getting soft.

*If you're not a winner, you're a loser.*

His father's favorite saying. Damn it—he wasn't going to be a loser in this competition. He'd walk off this show with a wife on his arm contractually bound to be where he wanted, when he wanted. Mortimer Innovations was his—no one else's—and it was going to stay that way. He'd already set up a series of labs and think tanks around the country to provide guidance for ways Mortimer Innovations could lead the United States into a golden age of sustainable technology production.

He noticed Bella picking at her food and wondered what she was thinking about. Probably her precious animals. Didn't she realize the world was overrun with pets? No amount of money could solve that problem permanently. Still, as he watched her finally raise a bite to her mouth, he found himself memorizing the shape of her lips and all his thoughts of business strategy slipped away. She'd make someone a wonderful wife. She was kind, thoughtful, full of energy. She was the kind of woman who would be a true partner to her husband, bringing her own thoughts, ideas and plans to the marriage.

He had no experience with that.

His mother had been a pampered invalid as long as he could remember, and now he wondered how she came to play that role. He'd have to ask Amanda to do some research. What if he'd had a mother like Bella, a mother who wasn't afraid to step out of her door, leave her community, and head out into adventures? A mother who encouraged him, rather than tried to hold him back? He frowned, considering this. Between his mother and father, his childhood was by no means ideal, but it had pushed him in the right direction to become the man he was today. So was it all bad? He was determined, strong, competitive to the extreme, refused to be held back by others' fears... an excellent businessman.

Maybe he should thank them for being so messed up.

*Yeah, right.*

"Okay, people, finish up," Madelyn said. "Time for the next challenge."

Bella met his gaze and rolled her eyes. He grinned despite himself.

*Here we go again.*

THEY STOOD AT the end of the wooden boardwalks that traversed the ground around the upper station. The cameras rolled as Jake gave his spiel. "This contest is different than the previous ones in that it does not require any strength of body to win. Instead, it requires a sharp eye and quick reflexes. The summit of Whistler's Mountain supports a diverse ecosystem of creatures. You have fifteen minutes to find some of these creatures and photograph them. You'll earn a point for every different species you photograph."

Bella tuned Jake out as he shifted into a spiel about the digital cameras they were going to use in the contest. Obviously some company had paid a mint for this particular product placement. Instead she adjusted her hat and covertly studied Evan. She didn't buy his earlier argument that he deserved to win because his company couldn't do all the wonderful things it did for the world unless he was running it, but it had changed her perception of him, just a little. Maybe being a billionaire didn't stop you from being human or caring about other human beings. It didn't stop him from having irrational fears just the same as everyone else, did it? She stifled a chuckle as she pictured his white-knuckled grip on the handrail inside the tram. Poor Evan. Poor little Money-buns.

She was still going to beat him.

She accepted a laminated card that showed a variety of species of mammals and birds that made their homes on Whistler's Mountain, and a compact digital camera whose workings proved nearly identical to her own. Taking her place next to the white-taped starting line someone had made near the end of the boardwalk, she waited for Jake's "Go!" before plunging off it onto the rocky summit of the mountain itself, heading in the opposite direction that Evan took.

With the thud of her camera crew's boots behind her on the rocks, she quickly realized what the true challenge was going to be in this contest. Gritting her teeth, she kept up her pace until she got a good distance from the crowds near the upper station, and slowed to a walk. She took a moment to peruse the laminated card, absorbing the types of critters she might see, rolled it up and shoved it into her pocket. From now on, she needed to keep her eyes peeled.

As she scanned the barren, rocky ground of the summit, she began to think this challenge was a joke. No sensible animal would make their home here, and even if they did, they'd hide until all the people left.

Except—what was that?

A scurry of movement stopped Bella cold and she crouched, as if that made her less visible on the barren mountaintop. She waved a hand behind her, hoping the camera crew understood she wanted them to stay still, and inched forward. There. Some kind of furry little beast ran around the rocks. She pointed the camera, clicked, and swore as she realized she still had the cap on. Before she could try again, the critter was gone.

Stifling another curse, Bella pulled out the laminated card. Was that a marmot? A glance over the pictures reminded her that birds counted for the challenge, as well, and she scanned the sky, scrambling to lift her camera when she spotted a black dot flying past. It took several moments to zoom the camera and find the bird again, but she snapped the photo and captured it successfully. She had no idea what type of bird it was and she didn't care. One point.

An intake of breath from Nita had her alert again. The marmot was back. This was almost too easy, Bella thought as she composed the picture and snapped it. Two!

She stood up again and scanned the barren rock all around her, but no other animals came into view. Slowly, she began to walk. As minutes ticked by, her jubilation slipped away, replaced by panic. How many photos had Evan taken? Was he strengthening his lead?

She followed a trail farther away from the upper station, combing the ground for signs of smaller critters hiding among the rocks. Her camera ready in her hands, she stepped as quietly as she could, wincing every time one of the camera crew's boots scraped against stone.

More minutes passed and her fingers gripping the camera became as sweaty as if she was running a race. Dammit, where were all the animals?

Wait a minute, what was that?

Bella froze, lifted the camera, and focused on what at first appeared to be a rock. This rock, however, had an eye. She took the picture, focused again, zoomed in closer and took a second shot. Satisfied, she moved toward it for a closer look.

The bird erupted from the ground in a flurry of wings, and Bella shrieked, nearly dropping the camera. Behind her, Nita and Paul, normally quiet as church mice, laughed out loud. She turned on them, but after a moment's anger had to laugh, too.

"Scared me to death," she gasped, knowing they were still getting all of this on film.

She only had a couple of minutes left, however, so she got back to scanning the ground and sky for more signs of life. When she came upon a spider, she took a quick picture although she figured it didn't count. She also snapped another bird, but had the sinking suspicion it was the same one she'd photographed before.

When Madelyn hollered from the boardwalk that their time was up, Nita and Paul ushered her back, giving her no time to try to find one more animal. She stalked back over the rocks toward the director and tried to shake the heaviness pooling in the bottom of her stomach. If she didn't take the lead today, she figured she might not ever pull ahead in this competition.

Jake stood right where they'd left him and as she approached, Madelyn held out her hand for her digital camera. She took out the memory card and plugged it into a laptop computer, which had been rigged up to a larger screen. Evan joined them, his jaw a rigid line. Maybe he didn't find much to photograph either, she thought with a rush of relief.

"Bella, let's see what you found here on top of Whistler's Mountain, in Jasper Park," Jake said. She'd become used to his stilted way of talking, knowing that when the show actually ran, each day would be broken into two episodes complete with many commercial breaks, after which the viewers needed to be reminded of what was happening and where the contestants were. Out of sight of the cameras Madelyn pressed keys on the keyboard and her first photo popped up on the large screen, a fuzzy image of a black bird in flight. A man Bella didn't recognize whispered in Madelyn's ear and she quickly typed something. Jake glanced down at the PDA in his hand, then looked straight at the camera. "Ah, a Cooper's Hawk, common to these parts. Excellent. That's one point!"

She let out the breath she didn't know she'd been holding.

"Second photo. A yellow-bellied marmot—very common on top of Whistler's mountain and throughout the park. That's two points. Let's see what's next. Oooooh," he let out an exaggerated sound. "Excellent shot, Bella. That's a ptarmigan—very hard to spot when it's camouflaged against the rocks. Well done—three points!"

Bella cringed, knowing what would come next. She wasn't wrong.

"Oh, dear. Spiders are not mammals, Bella. I'm afraid this photo doesn't count." Madelyn flipped to her final photo, and an intense whispered conversation erupted between her and the man beside her, whom Bella now assumed was a local biologist. Madelyn typed furiously at her keyboard and Jake glanced down at his PDA again.

"While this photo shows the Cooper's Hawk very clearly, the show's producer has determined it to be the same bird you photographed before, Bella. I'm very sorry," he didn't look sorry at all, "but we can't award a point for that shot." He shook his head. "But three points is a fine effort! Now Evan, let's take a look at your photographs."

EVAN CONSIDERED TOSSING the camera at Jake—*let's see how good your reflexes are, buddy*—but decided he'd better hand it over the normal way. He balled his hands into fists as he waited for Jake to pass it to Madelyn, and for her to fiddle around with the equipment until everything was connected.

The screen next to Jake remained blank.

Jake half-turned to the screen, one hand pointing toward it, ready to launch into his host-patter as soon as Evan's first photograph came up, but after several long moments, he began to fidget.

"What's the holdup, Maddie?" he said, finally.

"I'm not finding any images. What the hell did you do to your camera?" She straightened from her laptop and glared at Evan.

"Nothing. There are no pictures."

"No pictures?" Jake repeated. "I don't understand. Maddie, I don't understand what's happening here."

Only by sheer force of will did Evan refrain from smashing his fist into Jake's face. He hadn't seen a single animal—not one, single animal, and he'd become so obsessed with finding one, that he obviously hadn't spent enough time looking up into the air, because he hadn't seen the damn bird Bella photographed, either. Instead, he'd gotten angrier and angrier—sure this was some sort of trick the network had played on them—until he'd come back and seen Bella's stupid marmot and ptarmigan.

"Evan, where are your pictures?" Madelyn demanded.

"I have none. There were no animals on my side of the mountaintop. None. Not a single one!" He didn't realize he was advancing toward Jake until the man's smirk was a foot in front of his face. "What the hell did you guys do—send your goons to scare them all away?"

"Okay, Evan—calm down. It's just one challenge," Madelyn said, shoving the laptop into Ellis's hands and trying to push between Evan and Jake. "Look—I get it. Tensions are high, the contest is close and you like to win, but you can't win every time, can you?"

"Like hell I can't!" He knew he was making an ass

out of himself but he didn't care. No way was he going to lose this show. No freaking way. Not with an audience of millions. "This contest was fixed. You don't want Bella getting too far behind, so you rigged things against me. Don't think you're fooling anyone, because you're not. It's all fake!"

"Sore loser."

Evan spun on his heel to face Bella, who stood with her fists on her hips.

"What did you say?"

"Sore. Loser." She enunciated the words carefully. "You're really showing your true colors now, Mr. My-Innovations-Will-Save-The-World. Gee, you're such a humanitarian. You really care about other people's well-being, don't you? One thing goes wrong for you and you're ready to use your fists to get your way. Forget about the sore part—you're just a loser."

*Loser.* His father's voice echoed in his mind.

Evan saw red. "I might be a sore loser, Bumpkin, but when this show's over, I'm going to be the billionaire and I'm going to own you for a year. Then who'll be the loser? Huh?"

"Okay, okay, contestants," Jake said. He stepped forward to reclaim center stage. "Bella gains three points for this challenge, Evan zero." He paused a minute to let that sink in, his smirk back in place. "Evan, you end Day Two with a grand total of eleven points. Bella..." His smarmy smile broadened. "You have taken the lead with thirteen."

Bella whooped and jumped up and down in place.

"Yeah! Kiss my ass, sucker!" She waved her hat around and did a sort of wriggling dance that almost caused Evan to smile.

Almost.

His scowl resumed its place by the time she replaced her hat and stopped celebrating. When Jake cleared his throat, he reluctantly turned his attention back to the man.

"Evan, you'll be thrilled to hear the two of you won't take the tramway back down Whistler's Mountain. Instead, you'll hike down to give you more time to enjoy the spectacular scenery and stretch your legs. Here are maps to your campsite for the evening. We have a special surprise for you two tonight."

Evan grabbed the proffered map and stalked toward the trail down the mountain without looking back. He was done playing the chump in this contest, and he wasn't waiting for Bella to keep up with him. As far as he was concerned, she was just a pawn in his strategy to get control of Mortimer Innovations for good.

## Chapter Eight

BELLA HUNG BACK for a minute before she grabbed her map and followed after Evan, still shocked at the change that had come over him when he lost the challenge. Even his camera crew hung back, reluctant to be the next targets of his rage. Sure, he'd been annoying before, but this was different. She didn't like the way he'd tried to bully Jake and Madelyn, and she didn't care at all for the tone he used to address her. She monitored her feelings as she began the descent, hearing Nita and Paul take their places behind her. Her chest was tight, shoulders ached and she was finding it hard to breathe evenly. All her body's normal stress signals.

In her family emotions had always been kept under wraps, all the more so after the day Caramel died, so when someone yelled or cried or even laughed too loud—it made her want to run away and hide. She'd never stood up to anyone the way she just stood up to Evan, and she couldn't understand why she suddenly found the gumption to do so. Maybe because she'd cheated death this morning? She felt like she could take on anything and survive.

In fact, even if she lost this stupid television show and couldn't return to Chance Creek for a year, she bet there was still some way to help the animals in her care. She could make an on-air plea during the last show for volunteers to open their homes, or to donate money. The producers had to give her some time to settle her affairs, didn't they, before they shipped her off to become Mrs. Mortimer? She'd do whatever it took not to euthanize a single pet at the clinic, and even while she was stuck in California she could do something to help other animals. Evan couldn't need her 24-7 and he was a moncy guru, wasn't he? She could learn from him and the people around him how to raise money—real money—in order to help spay and neuter pets. Somehow, mired in the day-to-day details of her practice it didn't seem possible to do anything else but navigate from crisis to crisis, but that was stupid; she had all sorts of options.

Heck, she might actually win this thing.

Maybe getting angry was good for her, Bella thought as she strode down the track, feeling the tension begin to melt away from her neck. The possibility of losing her business was still devastating, but she'd survived a lot already. She'd probably survive that, too.

The fresh air must be making progress in her brain. Maybe Hannah had been right all this time; maybe getting away from her business once in a while could help her get a new perspective on her problems.

Could she begin to get her message across to viewers

even before the contest was over—that her clinic needed help? She would have to be sly about it; she had a feeling Madelyn would edit out overt calls for donations. But what if she mentioned the clinic during the exciting moments she knew Madelyn had to keep?

That ought to keep everyone off balance, she thought with a grin. Feeling lighter on her feet than she had since she landed in Jasper, Bella continued down the track with renewed vigor. If she played her cards right she could solve the clinic's problems no matter what the outcome of the show.

EVAN KNEW HE must be setting a record pace for the descent of Whistler's Mountain. His camera crew was hustling to keep up with him, judging by the muffled curses and skids of shoe leather on stone he kept hearing behind him.

He didn't care. He was furious with Madelyn, furious with fate, and most of all furious at himself. How could he screw up a stupid photography shoot, when there were obviously animals and birds all around him? How could he be such a stupid loser?

Loser.

His father had loved that word. His business associates were losers, his squash opponents were losers, anyone who didn't earn seven figures or more a year was a loser. In his father's world there were two kinds of people: those who counted and those who didn't. Each time Evan screwed up, he knew he skated closer to the line that separated him from the unwashed hordes.

Well, he counted now. Even his father would have to admit that. He was a billionaire for crying out loud and long before he inherited the majority shares, he'd brought millions of dollars of profits to the family business. He was a winner. He had been for years, and with his father's death the last person to question that was gone. He had a clean slate.

Except now he was screwing up again.

He walked faster. So he'd blown one challenge—one stupid challenge that depended on luck, not skill, mind you. He'd work his way back into first place and he'd stay there.

And if he couldn't do it through strength and skill, he'd intimidate the hell out of everyone until they handed him the victory.

Evan stopped dead.

Chris and Andrew stumbled to a halt behind him and for one long moment everything was still. Evan scanned the valley that still unfolded beneath him, fringed in all directions by forbidding, snow-topped mountains. A breeze tinged with the breath of arctic winter played across his face and dried the sweat from the back of his neck. Quiet reigned. True quiet.

And in it Evan heard the voice of the conscience he no longer knew he had.

He sounded just like his father with his emphasis on winning at all costs. Just like the man who'd made his childhood miserable and turned his mother from the pretty girl he'd seen in photographs to the querulous clinging woman who'd kept him locked to her side.

What had winning gotten him? An empire? An amount of money in his bank account he couldn't spend no matter how hard he tried?

A life of unending loneliness?

He sat down heavily in the center of the track, ignoring the whispered conversation among the crew behind him.

"What's he doing?"

"Shh!"

Slowly, he pulled the water bottle from his daypack and took a swig.

Then he began to laugh.

Had he really thought he could get away from his past just by burying everyone who'd been a part of it? His mom and dad were gone—*great*—and he thought that was going to set him free? It obviously hadn't, because here he was acting like his mother could still stifle him at any moment and his father still watched him like a hawk for any sign of failure.

When was the last time he simply acted from the heart?

He couldn't answer that.

Here he was—*a billionaire*—locked in competition with a little cowgirl veterinarian from Montana who just wanted to feed her kittens, and he was acting like he was personally in charge of storming the beaches of Normandy. When had his perspective flown out the window? He could buy and sell Bella's business ten times over. He could buy a hundred wives.

What was wrong with him?

For one awful moment his laughter hitched on a sob and he thought he might lose his grip right here on national television. He refused to do that. He pushed himself heavily to his feet and turned around.

Chris and Andrew scuttled off the path and several moments later Bella strode into sight. She faltered when she saw him and slowed to a halt.

Holding his hands out before him as if to show he wasn't armed, he simply said, "I'm sorry."

She didn't look convinced.

"Really, Bella. I don't know how to explain what happened up there except to say that competitiveness is an occupational hazard in my business and sometimes I don't know how to shut it off. You might not believe this, but that's not me—not the real me, anyway."

"It doesn't matter what I think of you, does it?" she said slowly.

He was struck again by her wholesome beauty, a kind he didn't often see among the women in his social circle. She didn't need makeup or surgery to create the illusion of prettiness. Bella defined prettiness, just as she was.

She defined other things, too. Honesty. Compassion.

"It matters to me. Come on—can we walk together?"

She still eyed him warily as they went forward side by side, and he decided not to press his luck. No need to fill up the silence with chatter, anyway. His own insights were still too new to share and he didn't want to pave them over with platitudes about the scenery. He figured when either of them had something real to say, they'd say it.

Their silence stretched ten, then twenty minutes, so when Bella finally spoke up, it startled him.

"Do you know anything about fundraising?"

"I know who to call if I want investors," he said. "That's probably not what you mean, though."

"No." She looked pensive. "I think I need to make some changes when I get back home—regardless of whether or not I win. I don't think I'm running the Chance Creek Pet Clinic as well as I could."

He remembered joking with Amanda about her lack of business skills back in San Jose. "You really have two businesses, don't you? A normal veterinary office whose clients pay for the care you give their pets, and an animal shelter that relies on donations?"

She looked at him in surprise. "Yes, that's it exactly. Except the shelter doesn't get enough donations. Chance Creek, Montana is a small town and most of its population lives on the ranches which surround it. They're hardworking people, but ranching doesn't pay all that well. Not everyone has money to give."

"But you're interested in learning more about fundraising."

"I am. You're right—the Chance Creek Pet Clinic pays its way, but the Chance Creek Animal Shelter needs all the help it can get. We have loads of cats and dogs that need good homes, and other animals unfit for adoption that simply need enough food to eat and room to run around. How would you suggest I raise money for the Chance Creek Shelter?"

Evan narrowed his eyes. Was it his imagination or was she giving that very shelter a plug on national television? Maybe she didn't need all that much help with fundraising after all, but he knew that Madelyn could easily edit out those sentences. Best to sandwich it between footage she couldn't afford to cut. He reached out and took Bella's hand, holding tight when she made to yank it free. He knew both cameras had zoomed in to capture the motion, so he hurried to say, "I'd start by building a website that told all about the Chance Creek Shelter's mission, with plenty of photographs of your facility and the animals who live there, some information about each specific goal, and a way for people to donate online. Do you have a favorite animal?"

Bella smiled although she was still trying to disengage her hand. He gave it a sharp tug, trying to send her a message. Leaning close to her ear, he whispered, *play along*, without moving his lips. She looked at him askance, but he was sure she heard what he said when she stopped pulling her hand away.

"I love all the animals that come to stay at the Chance Creek Shelter in Montana, but I love Rusty the best. He's a mutt who was dropped off on my doorstep a few months ago with a damaged paw. He must have stepped into a trap, because two of his toes were nearly ripped off his foot. We did emergency surgery that turned out to be highly successful and today he can run and jump like he was never even injured. I swear Rusty lets me know he loves me every time he sees me, and the gratitude in his eyes and the way he's so happy and so playful now just makes my day. I miss him."

"I bet he misses you, too. I'll tell you what. You get that website up and running and I'll be the first one to donate to the Chance Creek Shelter." He smiled at her.

Bella smiled back, somewhat uncertainly. He wondered if Madelyn would cut all that, or if their unexpected hand-holding would be enough to make her keep it in the show? Hell, why risk it? Evan stopped, pulled Bella close and kissed her square on the lips.

He meant it to be short and sweet, but when her body slammed against his and his arms tightened reflexively around her, he didn't want to let go. He slid one hand up her back and under her curls to cup her head, while his other hand remained at her waist, pulling her close. She made a surprised noise and he deepened the kiss, groaning when her arms slid around his neck. She was answering him, kissing him back with as much fervor as he was her.

"Bella," he whispered against her neck when he finally pulled away. "Sweet, sweet Bella."

"CUT!"

Bella leaped back out of Evan's arms when Madelyn's strident voice cut through the mountain air. One hand to her throat, she fought to get her heart rate under control. Evan and the camera crews looked just as surprised to see her here, but Madelyn was as cool as always, dressed in pin-neat dungarees and sparkling clean hiking boots, paired with a short-sleeved button-down blouse that looked newly ironed.

"You two are supposed to be competitors, not fuck-buddies!"

Bella cringed.

"Hey," Evan said. "Watch your language."

Madelyn fixed him with a look that could melt tar off a roof. "Watch your hands, mister—and your lips. Don't think I don't know what you're up to. Trying to convince Miss Just-Off-The-Turnip-Truck over there to think you're falling in love with her so she'll throw the contest and waltz off with you into never-never land? That's not how this show works!" She turned to Bella. "We research our contestants carefully, did you know that? Did you also know that Evan Mortimer here has never dated a woman for more than two weeks before dumping her? And once they sleep together he doesn't even spend the night. Very nice, Mortimer." She gave him a disgusted look.

"That's the man who's kissing you, Bella. That's the guy who wants to win this contest so bad because he's too cheap to pay a woman to be his wife for a year. That's the guy you're going to live with day in, day out for three hundred and sixty-five consecutive days—and nights—if you lose. A man who's so selfish he can't even be bothered to sleep through the night beside the woman he fucks. Are you going to fall for that?"

Bella glanced at Evan, heat rising in her cheeks. He had turned away and stood staring into the distance, a muscle twitching in his jaw. He didn't deny any of it.

She let out a shaky breath. If Madelyn hadn't come along, she would have fallen for it hook, line and sinker.

His touch made her hum with excitement and his lips on hers transported her away from her daily life into the possibility of a future in which she was worthy of love.

But she wasn't worthy of love, was she? Or respect. Or anything else. She was just Bella—the one who always screwed up. The rancher's daughter who was terrified of horses. The veterinarian who couldn't even keep a roof over the heads of the animals who depended on her.

She shook her head at Madelyn and pushed past her, tears clouding her eyes. A powerful, successful man like Evan Mortimer wouldn't think twice about using her to get what he wanted. He sure as hell wouldn't fall in love with her.

Barely three minutes later, she rounded a bend in the path and realized how Madelyn had found them while remaining so spotless. They were down the mountain and here were the SUVs. She climbed into the nearest one, slid down in the seat and closed her eyes.

"YOU REALLY THOUGHT you were going to get away with that?" Madelyn asked, fixing Evan with a beady glare.

"I wasn't trying to get away with anything," Evan said tiredly. He wasn't sure why he bothered—it wasn't like Madelyn would understand.

"I know you better than you know yourself, Mortimer," she snapped, stepping forward to put a finger in his face. "You may think you've found a woman you can truly love, but you can't escape your nature. I guarantee that if I make you share a tent tonight, you'll be crawling out of there before an hour is up. You are physically incapable of staying with a woman."

Evan narrowed his eyes. There was a lot of venom in Madelyn's voice for someone who had only known him a matter of weeks. "Why do you care so much what I do with Bella?" he asked cautiously.

Her eyes widened and her nostrils flared. "I know men like you—selfish, self-absorbed men who don't realize the good thing they have even after they toss it away. You are not screwing up my show, Mortimer. Get out there and fight like a man!" She stomped off back down the trail and he followed her more slowly, wondering how he could possibly repair the damage she'd just done to his budding relationship with Bella.

Behind him, Chris and Andrew were whispering, and although he hadn't been paying attention to their conversation, one phrase carried clearly and nearly brought him up short.

"Of course she wants him to win; the network doesn't want to shell out another five million bucks."

He masked his surprise as a stumble and kept going, hoping his camera crew hadn't realized he'd overheard them. Madelyn wanted him to win? Was that why she was so angry?

The network didn't want to spend another five million, eh? He knew they'd already had to pay one contestant the money this season. So despite the debacle up on the mountain, the show was actually stacked in his favor—not Bella's.

Somehow that knowledge didn't sit well with him.

The kayaking contest had nearly killed Bella. Just how far was Madelyn willing to go to get the result the network wanted?

Mulling over these questions and more, he continued walking. Soon the trail widened and he realized they'd made it down the mountain. Madelyn showed him to a different SUV than the one Bella was riding in and moments later the vehicle whisked him away to a new destination.

He labored to sort out everything that had happened. The elation he felt on the mountainside as his revelation overtook him was long gone, decimated by Madelyn's devastating recap of his prior love life, and the knowledge the show might indeed be rigged. Bella hated him more than ever, despite his attempt to help her promote the Chance Creek Pet Clinic and Shelter.

How to get things back on track?

He leaned back and considered this. What were his final objectives? He learned long ago that the best way to accomplish anything was to start with your goal and work backward. His first goal was to secure his control over his company. He'd prefer for Bella to be his wife for the year, but if it meant she'd hate him for all eternity there were other options. His second goal was to prove he wasn't like his father. He wanted to show that he could be a good loser and that he understood other people's dreams and aspirations were just as important as his.

His third goal was not to let Madelyn control the

outcome of the show. If she stacked the contest against Bella, he could very well lose Bella for good. On the other hand, if he decided to throw the show and overtly tried to lose the challenges, both women would catch on, and he'd lose just the same. Madelyn would charge him with breaking his contract, and Bella would hate his guts.

Where did that leave him? Should he try to win and use the year with Bella to change her mind about him? Somehow he didn't think that would work.

No, if he really wanted Bella in his life, he had to lose, and convince her to marry him just the same. Which meant he had to lose in such a way he looked like he was trying to win.

Okay, that was confusing.

He shook his head at the craziness of his situation, and puzzled on through the rest of it. From now on he'd make Bella go first when it came to the challenges so he'd have time to plan how best to lose inconspicuously. He needed to act angry when he lost, too—but not so angry he turned Bella off even more than his temper tantrum on the mountaintop had. He had to lose gracefully but realistically.

Hell, if he pulled this act off, he would deserve an award.

And if he didn't pull it off, he'd lose Bella.

## Chapter Nine

SEVERAL HOURS LATER, Bella slipped into the steaming pools of the Miette Hot Springs. They'd dined well but silently at a picnic area along the road while the cameras rolled, and were whisked here as an end-of-the-day treat. The hot water felt terrific, even though the evening was still warm. Her muscles relaxed almost immediately and after a day which had included a near-death experience and a kiss that rocked her to her toes, she was grateful to rest against the side of the large pool and merely float.

Unlike some hot springs she'd visited in her youth, these weren't smelly little pools of sulfurous water. The Miette Hot Springs looked like any other public outdoor swimming facility, except the water was so deliciously hot—it felt like taking a bath under the open sky.

"Bella."

She opened her eyes at the sound of Evan's voice. "Leave me alone," she groaned.

"I will in a minute. I just want to say that Madelyn's right—we need to finish this contest before anything else happens between us. She's right about what she said about me and the women I've dated, too. I'm not good at relationships. Hell, I suck at them. There's a reason for that, though. I don't feel like explaining it on camera, but maybe someday we'll have the chance to talk privately about it. I hope so." He swam a little closer. "My life is hectic. You wouldn't believe how hectic it is. Taking a couple of days off without a computer or even a phone…" He made a face. "It's like I'm seeing things clearly for the first time in years. And I don't like what I see. I need to make some changes."

"What does that have to do with me?" She tried to sound sharp, but in truth she was surprised. He sounded like he'd had a similar revelation to hers.

"Not much—not at the moment." He smiled wryly. "We're competitors and I still need a wife. I want it to be you. So I'm going to do my best to win this thing."

"So am I," she said, but his words made her insides dance with some emotion she couldn't even fathom. He wanted her for his wife? That sounded close enough to real desire to make her sink into a swirl of feelings best left unlooked at. She leaned back against the edge of the pool. "I don't want to be your wife. I want to be rich enough to make a difference to the animals who depend on me."

He held her gaze long enough she felt the heat of it down into the deepest places within her. What was he telling her with his eyes? That he truly wanted her? That his kiss was for real? She was afraid of what her own gaze betrayed about her—that his kiss swept her right off her feet, that if he swam any closer she'd meet him halfway and betray herself and her furry charges for just a few more moments pressed against him. A smile curved his lips again and she knew he must have seen some of that in her expression.

"Fair enough," Evan said. "Our cards are on the table. You know what I want." He paused, his smile widening. "And I know what you want. May the best man win."

"Best woman," she called out after him as he swum away.

But she had a feeling he won that round.

THE WARM GLOW within Evan stayed with him until the SUVs dumped them at another campground—this one on flat ground. He stood next to Bella and eyed the small pile of equipment. She bent to pick up the tent.

"I think this is even smaller than last night's," she said.

"Yep." Damn Madelyn.

She handed him the single, rolled-up sleeping mat. "Here—you might as well take this since I get the tent."

"What do you mean?"

"We both know you can't sleep all night in something this small—not with me beside you. That's it, right—why you don't stay with women through the whole night? They give you claustrophobia just like small spaces do?"

He hesitated, rattled by her insight, but shook his head. "Whatever. I'm sleeping in that tent tonight."

"I'm not sleeping outside!"

"I didn't say you were." With more bravado than he felt, he flopped the ground cloth down, took the tent away from her and pulled it from its protective sack. He popped out the tension poles and threaded them through their sleeves. "Do those ends, will you?"

Together they lifted the tiny structure into position on top of the ground cloth.

"That's got to be a one man tent," Bella said disgustedly.

"Yep."

It was getting dark, but well after they'd both brushed their teeth and used the nearby outhouse they sat on logs around an empty fire pit, saying little. The day crew packed up and left, and the night cameraman installed his tent-cam, and retreated to the edge of the clearing, his assistant in tow.

Was there any chance he'd make it through the night in that...cocoon...pressed up against Bella? Just the thought of climbing into that little orange nylon excuse for a tent made his hands sweat. He regretted now he'd never taken Amanda's advice to find a shrink—a therapist—to talk about his claustrophobia. Maybe if he had he wouldn't be sweating like a pig right now.

"I'm turning in," Bella said finally. She crossed the campground, took off her boots and left them neatly side by side to the left of the door flap, before bending to crawl into it on her hands and knees. For several minutes he heard her rustling around. Then all was still.

Ten minutes later, he finally worked up the courage

to approach the tent himself. Mimicking Bella, he shucked off his shoes first, and bent to unzip the flap. Taking one last deep breath of air, he pushed himself into the small opening.

It was worse than he thought.

Even on hands and knees his back scraped up against the fabric ceiling and the whole tent shook as he inched his way to a prone position beside Bella. She held up one side of the sleeping bag and he slid beneath it, almost instantly tossing it off him again as the familiar suffocating feeling descended on him.

He heard Bella's exhaled breath. "You really have this claustrophobic thing bad, don't you?"

"Yeah. Pretty bad," he wheezed.

"Are you going to be okay?"

He curled onto his side, his back to her, arms crossed over his chest. "Probably not."

"Look, you don't have to prove anything to anyone. You can sleep outside." She sounded like she'd prefer it.

"I kind of do," he said, fighting to keep himself from tearing the tent apart with his bare hands—anything to get air into this tiny space. Any second the fabric walls would wrap themselves around him, tightening until they'd squeezed every inch of air from his lungs. He didn't think he could stand it for another minute. But he had to.

"Why?"

"Because it's true—I find it just about impossible to spend an entire night with a woman. It's…really screwed things up for me. That's not how I want to be."

He felt her turn to face him, felt a tentative touch on his back. "If you have a phobia, it can take time to overcome. You don't do it all at once."

"What do you know about it?" Her hand felt good on his skin. She stroked him lightly and he wondered if she knew she was sending streaks of heat straight through him to his groin.

"Sometimes I work with people who are afraid of animals—usually dogs. There's a counselor in town who calls me up and I bring a really gentle dog to her office when her patient is ready for it. At first I stand with the dog near the patient—just for a minute or two. In later appointments I bring the dog closer. Finally the patient touches the animal. It's not all at once—it happens over time."

Her touch mesmerized him, and in a moment he wouldn't be able to leave the tent without shocking their national audience. He reached for the sleeping bag and covered his traitorous body. Thankfully, Bella didn't stop her ministrations. "So you're saying I should only stay in the tent for a few minutes."

"I'm saying you shouldn't feel bad if you can't overcome a lifelong phobia in a single night." She caressed his back, his shoulder, his bicep, running her hand up and down his skin until he wanted to turn over, scoop her into his arms and make love to her until the sun came up.

But he couldn't. For one thing, there was a camera ten inches above his head capturing all of this, and it was bad enough the whole world would know about his phobia when these episodes aired; they didn't need a front row seat to his lovemaking, too. For another, he never struggled to stay in bed with a woman while they were having sex. It was afterwards, when they snuggled up and he felt their desire to snare him forever, keep him tied to their sides, like his mother had all throughout his youth.

He thrashed to a sitting position. Bella's hand fell away from him. "Sorry," he said. Damn it, he could do this. He had to do this.

"It's okay, Evan. Everybody has issues. You aren't any less of a man because you're claustrophobic."

So why did he feel like a worm when he pushed his way out of the tent and went to sleep outside on the ground?

THE PANG OF LONELINESS she felt when Evan fled the tent unnerved Bella. She supposed it was natural to bond to someone you'd just spent two straight days with— especially while being filmed the whole time—but she was surprised by the depth of his claustrophobia. While it had been funny on the tram, and giving him a hard time had definitely paid off in spades when she gained three points in the next challenge, watching him struggle against his fears right next to her in the tent made his pain too real to ignore. Evan obviously had demons. She wondered what made him so afraid to be close to people.

When Madelyn had taunted him about his inability to spend the whole night with a woman she thought he'd face her down by bragging about his conquests and claiming indifference to cuddling after the deed was done, but now she saw this wasn't about machismo at all. Evan was afraid—no, terrified—of being close enough to a woman that she might take advantage of him when he was vulnerable. He couldn't spend the night with a woman because that would expose him utterly. He couldn't fall in love with a woman and get married in a normal way because that would literally tie him down and he couldn't bear to be restrained or confined in such a manner.

She knew the textbook definition of claustrophobia, of course, but had always considered the fear to be based on a physical state. She understood why Evan freaked out in the tram car, for example; it was an enclosed space he could not leave while they were en route.

There was another aspect to Evan's claustrophobia, though—he was just as afraid of close connections with people as he was of close quarters. If he couldn't even date a woman, what did that mean for his other relationships? Did he have close friends? What about his family?

Strange to think that someone as rich and successful as Evan could be as damaged as someone as poor and dumb as her.

She woke hours later tangled in the sleeping bag. When she unzipped the tent flap, the cool air was a welcome antidote to her groggy mind, but when she looked at the sky, she groaned. It didn't take a weatherman to know they'd see rain before the day was done.

"Morning," Evan grunted at her as he returned from the campground outhouse. He looked disheveled, and when a crew member handed him a cup of coffee, he accepted it and paced to the far side of the fire pit to drink it alone.

"GOOD MORNING, CONTESTANTS!" Jake said with an enthusiasm that made Evan want to belt him. What, exactly, was good about it? He'd barely slept for the second night running, and he was so stiff he felt like he'd aged a decade. Worst of all, rain was coming. Stomping around all day and getting soaked wasn't his idea of fun. "Today we have a new type of challenge that starts now and will run for most of the day. You'll each need one of these babies," Jake handed them each a state-of-the-art GPS unit, "and a set of directions. You'll be on your own today, however. You'll each travel to your next destination by a different route." Evan scowled. How was he supposed to clandestinely help Bella win if they weren't even in the same place? "Along the way you'll use your GPS units to discover ten geocaches. Each one will contain directions to the next one. You have until sundown to get all ten and navigate your way to the next campsite."

"What if we don't?" Bella asked, looking at her GPS unit worriedly. Evan cursed inwardly. He'd used the things a thousand times—if she'd never used one before, he'd have a hell of a time not beating her ten times over to the final destination.

"Don't worry, your GPS unit comes complete with a homing beacon. If you don't find us, we'll find you, but any geocaches you dig up past sundown won't count toward your point total." Jake flashed his trademark smile.

Bella didn't look reassured.

"It's not that hard," Evan said, reaching out to show her. "You just push these buttons to set..."

"I can figure it out," Bella snapped at him.

Whoops. That's right—he was supposed to be *clandestinely* helping her. "Sorry. My bad. So, are we all set here? Can I get going?"

"Here are your first coordinates." Jake handed them each a small, plastic-coated card. The show must spend a mint on lamination, Evan thought. "And here's a shovel. It just might come in handy today."

It took Evan all of two seconds to program the co-ordinates into the GPS, stow the shovel in his daypack, and head off in the right direction. He made a show of rushing out of the campground but after a quarter mile slowed down. "No need to hurry," he said aloud for the benefit of the cameras. "She doesn't even know how to program the thing." He sat down on a handy log, untied his shoes and retied them, as if he'd done a poor job the first time around. Afterwards, he set off at an ambling pace punctuated by frequent stops.

He might be in for a boring day, but at least he'd lose.

ONCE SHE GOT the hang of the GPS, it wasn't hard to stay on track. Bella decided the product placement of the units was probably more important to the show than making this challenge particularly hard. It made sense when she thought about it. The company that produced the GPS units would want them to seem easy to use and accurate. If she got lost, they'd look bad.

As she moved along the trail she checked the unit from time to time to see if the dot that represented her was indeed getting closer to the dot that represented the first geocache. Yep, right on target. She'd stuck the little shovel through the flap of the day pack where it was easy to carry, but definitely made the pack heavier than on previous days. Ten geocaches seemed like a lot. She wondered just how much hiking she'd need to do before the day was over.

*Evan was right; they ought to bill this show as a weight-loss vehicle*, she thought some time later as she reached the spot where her GPS told her the first geocache would be. Her clothes definitely felt bigger today, and the muscles in her legs were more defined.

She looked around the little clearing for a sign of where the geocache was hiding. Was she supposed to just start digging? A few months ago, a little boy at her clinic with his cat had regaled her with a story about geocaching with his family. According to him, the canisters he'd found were hidden—not buried—so people could find them, open them up, sign a log and possibly retrieve a prize, then hide them again for the next seeker.

This was different, she told herself. No one else was going to look for these geocaches—just her. Of course Madelyn would make it difficult by burying them.

She spotted an area where the dirt looked different

from the rest of the ground—like it had been disturbed recently—and started digging. Moments later she heard a satisfying thud and bent down to push the rest of the loose dirt away from the metal canister buried in the ground. She pulled it out triumphantly, unhooked the lid and dumped out a laminated card, a stuffed animal that vaguely resembled the marmot she photographed the previous day, and an energy bar.

Hey now, if the geocaches all contained treats, she was on it!

Bella stuffed the marmot in her daypack, programmed the new coordinates into her GPS and unwrapped the bar. This was going to be a cinch.

"COULD YOU GO any slower?" Chris said behind him.

Evan turned around. "You're not supposed to talk to me, remember?"

"The camera's off. So what gives?"

"I twisted my ankle." Hell, he'd made a huge production of it back there after he'd found his third geocache in the first half-hour of the day. He'd been limping ever since. Was this guy dense?

"Twisted it, yeah. You'll get an Emmy for sure for that bit of acting."

Anger tightened Evan's jaw. "Look, I don't need your…"

"Fine, fine. Stop talking to the camera and get a move on," Chris said.

"You're the one holding me up now," Evan said, but he resumed his hike, going just a bit faster. Losing points today was going to be harder than he thought. How was he supposed to fake getting lost when the trail was so clearly marked and the GPS took him right to the caches?

He wondered how Bella was faring. Surely she'd have to have found at least five or six by now. He was moving at a snail's pace. If she was walking as fast as she normally did, she'd have a big lead on him.

As long as Madelyn hadn't stacked the odds against her in some way.

Evan stopped in his tracks and Chris swore behind him. Could Madelyn be using their separation as a way to sabotage Bella? Was her hike longer, or her caches buried more deeply? What if Madelyn gave her the wrong coordinates and led her astray completely?

He couldn't think of any way to find out.

Except….

"I'm beginning to think you guys have it out for me," he said out loud.

"What do you mean?" Chris said. "You know you're not supposed to talk to us, right?"

"I mean, what's with the tiny tents? What about the gondola? What's next—a night in a cave? It's obvious you guys know I'm claustrophobic, and you're using it to make me lose the contest."

"You're only losing by a couple of points," Andrew pointed out. "If you hurried up a little bit, you'd make them up in no time."

"How? If Bella's course is as easy as mine, she'll get full points, too."

"Dude, if you don't hurry up, you're not going to get full points," Chris said.

"Dude, no matter how slow I go, I'm going to finish this course before noon. Obviously today isn't the day you're going to screw me over. But tomorrow...I bet tomorrow Madelyn's got something up her sleeve that will totally mess with me."

Andrew snickered. "You're not the one who needs to worry about that."

Chris elbowed him. "Shut up, man."

"Sorry." Chastened, Andrew put a hand on his hip and addressed Evan. "If I were you, I'd just do my best to complete every challenge as quickly and carefully as I could. Don't worry about Bella."

"Whatever." As he resumed walking, Evan hoped his act fooled them, but he was worried about Bella. More worried than he'd been before, in fact. If Madelyn felt no compunction about using his worst fears against him, even though she wanted him to win, what might she do to Bella?

What was Bella's worst fear?

And where was she now?

"THIS CAN'T BE RIGHT," Bella said for twentieth time as she bushwhacked through thick underbrush, following the GPS directions to her next geocache. She'd found the first four easily enough, but her new coordinates took her right off the trail and into the woods.

She should have known they wouldn't all be that easy. The show wouldn't expect viewers to watch two episodes of the contestants simply walking down a trail. Still, this was brutal; she needed a machete to get through this undergrowth.

A half an hour later, she was hot, sweaty, and no closer to the cache if her GPS was to be believed. She shook the gadget, convinced something was wrong with it. Shouldn't she have reached the next one by now? She squinted at the sun that was climbing higher in the sky by the minute, peeking out through billows of ever-thickening clouds. Evan was probably far ahead of her by now, even if his route was as rough as hers. He knew how to operate a GPS far better than she did, and she was beginning to think her earlier successes were simply luck.

"Maybe you should stop for lunch," Nita said, startling Bella. She'd become so used to the two silent crew members trailing her, she'd forgotten they could speak.

"I wanted to find five caches before I stopped," Bella said, but she longed for a break. "Ten more minutes. If I don't find it, we'll take a rest."

Another half-hour later, there was no cache in sight and Bella wanted to throw the GPS unit into the next creek they crossed. The thing was worthless. She should have found that cache five times over by now.

"Eat something," Nita said gently, pointing her to sit on a fallen log. "You'll feel better and think better, too."

"You two aren't supposed to talk," Paul said.

"Give her a break, can't you?" Nita said. "She's having a tough day."

Something about the way she said it made Bella look

sharply at the camerawoman. What exactly did she mean by that?

*That you're having a bad day, Miss I-Can't-Use-a-GPS-To-Save-My-Life,* she told herself. Surely there wasn't anything more to it.

She didn't have a phobia of geocaches, after all. Madelyn had no way of knowing she'd be a failure at following directions. Now, if the challenge included riding horses, she'd know Madelyn had it in for her.

No, today it was her own stupidity tripping her up. As usual.

She'd always been the one who caused trouble in her family; the one who ruined everything. She'd been responsible for Caramel's death, hadn't she? Responsible for Cyclone's death and the hard months that followed, ending in the sale of half her family's ranch.

Plus there was her fear of horses. Her refusal to go anywhere near them again despite her mother's attempts to help her get over it. One day Sylvie had led her to the corral, where a sweet-tempered mare stood ready to be ridden. Bella's protests hadn't stopped her, but her father spotted them from the barn and he put an end to the session with a quick burst of words: *Get her away from there! She's got no business around horses. I can't afford to lose her; she's the only one I've got.*

His words had hit her like a slap to the face. He cared more about the mare than he did her and he thought she'd kill any horse she got near, for heaven's sake. She'd run into the house and cried for an hour.

After that, her mother kept her away from the ranch

as much as possible. With no money for activities, she hit on the idea that Bella could make herself useful to elderly Maggie Silverton, the local pet veterinarian. Maggie, in turn, was grateful for any help she could get. A gray-haired, soft-spoken, gentle woman, she took Bella in every afternoon after school and all day on weekends. Bella wasn't sure how she'd have survived her teenage years without her.

Her father acted as if she had died along with Caramel and Cyclone. He focused on Craig as the worthy heir to his diminished kingdom. Together they plotted how someday they'd recoup the lost land and restore the Chathams to their former glory.

Bella kept her head down and learned to be invisible. While her parents scrimped and saved to make up any gap between Craig's scholarships and grants and the cost of his education, she'd never once discussed the cost of hers with them. A top-notch student—all those afternoons working on her homework under Maggie's gentle tutelage paid off—she'd still needed to take out loans to fund the final years of her veterinary education.

At least she knew she had a job waiting for her with Maggie, and when Maggie had passed all too soon, she'd been shocked to find herself the sole beneficiary of her elderly friend's will. Maggie was the only reason she had a clinic and shelter to run, and now she was losing it.

She wasn't worthy of the old woman's trust. Wasn't worthy of anyone's love.

She jerked to her feet, her lunch spilling to the ground. She had to win this thing.

"Bella?" Nita reached out a hand, but Bella batted it away. Blinking back tears, she grabbed her pack and the GPS, leaving her lunch scattered on the ground. She had to move, had to walk and keep on walking, until she left those memories far behind.

"Bella! Wait!"

She didn't slow down.

She couldn't.

And if Madelyn tried to put her on a horse, she'd just crumple up and die.

## Chapter Ten

"**W**HAT ARE YOU doing here?"

Evan, Chris and Andrew all swiveled to see Bella crash through the brush at the side of the trail, followed closely by Nita and Paul, who didn't look at all happy. Bella's hair was tumbling down around her shoulders, and a smudge of dirt streaked her forehead. She looked like she'd been crying, or maybe fighting hard not to cry. Evan's stomach squeezed. Evidently, while he'd been taking it easy, she'd been working hard.

*On what? These geocaches couldn't be any easier to find.*

"Damn it, we missed the shot!" Chris said, and he and Andrew raced to get their equipment set up again and rolling as a drizzling mist of rain began to fall.

Bella faced Evan down. "Why are you on my trail?" Her voice was thin and high, and he thought she might break down into tears any second. What the hell had happened to her out there? He wanted to pull her into his arms, but now was not the time.

"This is my trail," he said, holding up his GPS. "You sure you know how to work that thing?"

She scowled down at hers fiercely. "I think mine's broken. It keeps blinking on and off and giving me new directions."

"Let me see that." He swiped it from her hand along with her laminated card and went to work pressing buttons and checking the coordinates she'd put into it.

"Hey! Give it to me! I don't need your help." She made a grab for it, but Evan turned his back on her, engaged in figuring out what she'd done. He ignored her when she shoved him—he was quite a bit heavier than she was; she couldn't budge him and she obviously needed his help. "Give it!" She whacked his arm this time. Evan held fast. "I said, give it!"

She locked her hands around his wrist and pulled hard. Evan pulled back, aware she was nearing the breaking point, but wanting one more minute to look over the GPS. If he could just help her, everything would be fine. "Hey, I almost figured it out…"

"Let go!" Bella dug her heels into the now-slick dirt track and pulled with all her might. Suddenly, Evan caught sight of the camera crew, all four of them ranged in front of him, their expressions blank with shock, the heavy mist dampening their hair and clothes. He realized how all of this must look—like he was helping Bella against her will. Which of course he was, but the viewing public—and Madelyn—weren't supposed to know that.

He let go.

Bella slipped and landed on her butt with a yelp of pain, and the GPS flew from her hands, landing with a harsh crack that spelled the end of her search for her geocaches.

For one long moment, silence reigned as the rain began to patter down in larger drops. Then Bella leaped to her feet and charged him. "Where is it? Where'd you put it?"

Mortified by what he'd just done, Evan had no idea what she was talking about, and he stumbled backwards as her hands searched his Jacket pockets, patted down his clothing and finally delved into his pants pockets, uncomfortably close to his groin.

"Hey!"

But she already had his GPS in hand.

"Bella—wait. Don't...."

She hurled it against the closest rock where it smashed with a satisfying crack.

"Turnabout is fair play, right?" she demanded. "Right?" She glared at him through the damp tendrils that framed her face, waterdroplets dripping from their ends.

Damn, she was furious. Did she think he'd broken hers on purpose?

"Madelyn's going to be pissed, you know." He swiped a hand through his own wet hair to push it back from his face.

"That's not my fault!" She met his gaze, eyes wide, and he knew she was picturing the director's reaction to this chain of events.

"Think about it. The GPS maker has to be a sponsor of the show."

With a wild groan, she covered her face with her

hands. "Shit."

Chris cleared his throat. "I'll give Madelyn a call. See what she wants us to do." He stepped away down the trail a bit and the rest of the crew trailed after him, forming a semicircle around him as he pulled out his cell phone and hunched his shoulders to keep it safe from the rain. Evan sat down on a nearby boulder, ignoring the dampness that soaked through his pants, and motioned Bella to join him. She did so, slowly, her reluctance evident on her face.

"What do you think she's going to do?" she asked.

"Oh, I bet she's got a hundred more GPS's with her. We'll probably have to start all over again. Tell me," he said, then leaned back and peered down at her as a raindrop slid down the bridge of his nose, "what's with you not being able to take the slightest bit of help from me?"

She snorted and folded her arms across her chest. "Help? Like you weren't going to mess my GPS all up and program the wrong coordinates in it? Right—you're such a saint you were going to help me win those millions."

"I could beat you handily, even if I did show you how to work the GPS, you know," he said. She was close enough she brushed his arm when she shifted her weight, and the touch reminded him of her earlier onslaught, the way she'd searched his pockets as if he belonged to her.

He'd like to belong to her.

He shrugged that errant thought away, but as he

searched for something else to say, he couldn't help reaching out and wiping a drop of rain from her face.

She turned in surprise. "What are you doing?"

A glance down the trail told him the crew were still occupied, Chris gesticulating as he talked into his cell phone. "This." He leaned down and brushed his lips over hers. He'd wanted to do that for twenty-four hours. Her small cry of surprise made desire surge within him, and he laced an arm around her, pulling her in close as he kissed her again.

She didn't fight him. It was as if for one second she acquiesced in his attempt to forget the show, the crew, the rain, and their separate lives, and decided to enjoy the moment. He deepened the kiss and her lips parted, allowing him entry. She snaked a hand up to his shoulder and encircled his neck, pulled him down and matched his hunger with her own.

A silence behind him alerted Evan that the crew must have seen them, and he pulled away. Bella sucked in a breath at his sudden removal.

"Sorry," he whispered. "They're watching, aren't they?"

She glanced over his shoulder. "Just setting up their cameras."

As if in silent accord, they leaped apart, Evan to pace the trail and Bella to retie her damp shoelaces. A muttered curse from Andrew told him the crew hadn't managed to film them. He caught Bella's eye and winked. When she smiled back reluctantly, he thought the sun must have just dawned.

FIVE MILLION DOLLARS was slipping through her fingers and she was smiling like a fool because her enemy had kissed her.

Bella turned back to her hiking boots and tied the wet laces with shaking fingers. Thank goodness the crew hadn't captured that searing kiss on camera. Was it the long days in the fresh air, or the disturbing nights in the cramped tent with Evan, then alone when he made his break for wide-open spaces, that made her feel so off-balance?

*I'm tired and at the end of my rope, and he took advantage of me,* she told herself. *If he wins this contest, he'll get the right to take advantage of me for an entire year.* Her smile vanished and her throat constricted. She would not think of the sexual implications of that statement. Bad enough she'd lose her veterinary practice and all the animals in her shelter if she didn't win. Not to mention the fact she'd have to move to some city where she knew no one, and be at Evan's beck and call for a year. What would she do when he didn't need her? Just sit at home with her hands folded in her lap, waiting for his phone call? Who would care for the rest of Chance Creek's pets and strays? Suddenly, she understood what Evan's claustrophobia must feel like. She dropped her head in her hands and waited for the rushing sensation to ebb away.

"You okay?"

Evan dropped a hand on her shoulder and she flinched away. "I'm fine." But she wasn't. This was her chance to get a lock on the lead, and so far she'd proven an idiot at using her GPS. What would she do when

Madelyn unleashed the big guns at her? It was obvious the woman somehow knew about Evan's claustro-phobia—how else to explain the tiny tents and gondola ride? Did she know about Bella's terror of horses? Would she exploit it?

Just the thought made her stomach roil.

"Need some water? You don't look so hot." He crouched beside her and lifted a hand as if to check her temperature. Bella surged to her feet.

"I'm fine."

"Okay. All right—just trying to help." He stood up, too, and backed away, hands held out to placate her.

"How many times do I have to tell you I don't need help?" She knew her voice was rising with each word and knew the cameras were focused on her, too, catching all the drama, but she couldn't stop herself. "I'm a capable, grown woman and I don't need anybody interfering in my life—especially you. Just leave me alone!"

"Cut!" Madelyn stalked around a bend in the trail, followed as usual by Ellis and several other crew mem-bers, and Bella had the horrible sensation that the woman might have seen more than just the drama. Had she seen them kiss? She hoped not.

The director faced them. "I'm glad you guys are sal-vaging something from this travesty. You two have got to be the lamest excuses for contestants that I've ever had on this show. Evan, you realize Bella wants to walk away with five million dollars and leave you hanging? And Bella, you realize that Evan wants to make you his *wife*," she emphasized the word like it was dirty, "for a full year? You two are contestants. You are mortal enemies. Your job is to win. So why are the two of you behaving like losers?"

Bella stood absolutely still, afraid to catch Madelyn's attention by the slightest hitch of breath or dart of eyes. If the director got too angry at them, she'd dig deep into her bag of tricks to punish them. That meant she'd find a way to throw horses into the mix if she somehow knew about Bella's phobia.

Madelyn shook her clipboard at them. "Lucky for you guys I have two more GPS units. It's well past noon and the two of you bozos have managed to find less than half of your geocaches. Less than half." She pointed first at Bella, then at Evan. "I know you two can barely find your way out of a paper bag, but as an added incentive to try to complete this course, I'll give the first one of you who locates all ten caches dinner at the Little River restaurant, the finest in Jasper. Dinner and a hot shower, not necessarily in that order."

Bella did glance at Evan this time, at his dripping hair and clothing. The path was turning into a slick river of mud under their feet and in his eyes she saw reflected her own greedy desire to win this prize. Real food? She was there. After the ups and downs of the last few days she needed a dose of normalcy.

Madelyn fished two new GPS units out of her pockets. "Here you go." She handed one to each of them, along with replacement cards for their directions to the next cache. "May the best contestant win."

This time Evan didn't try to help her program her

coordinates into her GPS. With a glance at Madelyn Bella couldn't decipher, he only hesitated a moment before he punched some buttons on his own gadget and jogged off along the trail. Bella didn't waste time analyzing the disappointment she felt as she watched his receding back. Instead, she focused on her own GPS, programming her set of coordinates into the little machine and hurrying off in the direction it indicated. She thought she had the hang of it now.

At least she hoped so.

## Chapter Eleven

W HEN THE HEADLIGHTS of an SUV heralded Bella's arrival at their campsite, Evan's shoulders slumped with relief. He had managed to finish the course by midafternoon, and had been whisked off to a motel for a hot shower—actually a hot shower, followed by a long, hot bath, followed by a nap in the luxurious comfort of a king-sized bed—after which he joined Madelyn for a steak supper with several glasses of wine, and returned to their campsite feeling clean, refreshed, and more rested than he'd been in days.

Only to find Bella still hadn't finished the GPS course. While the afternoon's rain had tapered off, and the setting sun appeared in between long streamers of scudding clouds, apparently she and her increasingly furious camera crew were still stomping around the wilds of Jasper.

The base crew was tracking their movements and Madelyn had just decided to send in a rescue team when Bella changed course and made a bee-line toward camp.

"Bet Paul finally wrestled that thing out of her

hands," Evan said to Madelyn, standing next to the portable table she'd set up as a workstation.

"She's stubborn, all right." Madelyn cocked an eyebrow. "Stubborn enough to win this thing if you don't watch out. Ellis, send someone to pick them up."

The contented feeling drained right out of him. Damn it, Bella was supposed to win—and he was supposed to be helping her—so why had he rushed off to find the geocaches like a hound of hell was chasing him all the way?

Madelyn smiled, and the good feeling deserted him all together.

She knew.

This was Madelyn's way of telling him she wasn't going to let him throw the contest. A shower and a good meal—a bribe guaranteed to make him forget all about his good intentions? What else did the old bat know?

That he was claustrophobic, for one thing. Why else shove him and Bella in a tiny tent together every night? Why else force him into the gondola up the mountain? Granted, he was sure Jasper National Park was one of the show's sponsors, so of course they'd showcase the best the park had to offer, but he knew Madelyn relished the double purpose of that challenge.

She probably predicted her two contestants would develop a mutual lust, too. Why wouldn't they? They were both young, single, easy on the eyes, stuck together for days on end battling fatigue, hunger and fear.

Was he even really attracted to Bella, or had he been cleverly coerced into feeling something for her?

That thought made him squirm. No, he decided, he hadn't been coerced into anything where Bella was concerned. He found her to be beautiful in a fresh, sunshiny way, intelligent, caring, but spirited, too. When she rested her gaze on his face, it was like a beacon, drawing him in. Being her adversary in this contest heightened the rush when he snatched a kiss from her lips. She would fight him to the death—he knew that with utter certainty—and yet he knew, too, that given a chance she'd fall into bed with him just as fast as he'd fall into bed with her.

If he let her win, she would have the money she needed to run her clinic in high style, and once the show was over, maybe she'd consent to date him—to get to know the man, rather than the billionaire. Maybe they'd fall in love.

Maybe they'd get married someday.

Or maybe she'd turn her back on him and walk away for good, because if he lost he'd need to find another wife—a woman willing to marry him for a year in exchange for money.

Evan paced away from Madelyn's table toward a fire one of the crew members built in the center of a ring of rocks. He shoved his hands in his pockets and nudged a stone with his foot. As a millionaire in her own right, beautiful Bella would be besieged by men, all wanting a piece of her pie in more ways than one.

Why would she cool her heels for a year and wait for him? So far he'd shown himself to be arrogant, self-absorbed, a lousy loser, and incapable of even sleeping in the same tent as her for an entire night.

But if he won, on the other hand, he could spend an entire year convincing her he was a stellar guy.

An SUV pulled into the campsite, and Bella exited the vehicle.

"You made it," Madelyn said acerbically as Bella approached the fire.

"Yep." Still damp from the rain and shivering, she huddled close to the flames' warmth, not looking at either of them.

"Glad to see you're safe," Evan said.

"Sure."

Her face looked strained in the firelight and Evan scanned the campsite for food. "Where's her dinner?" he demanded.

Madelyn snapped her fingers and Ellis rushed up with a covered aluminum foil container. "Here—I tried to keep it warm," he said.

Bella accepted the tin and a plastic fork from him without a word and crossed to sit on the far side of the campfire. The crew began to pack it in for the evening, loading their equipment into the SUV. Madelyn conferred with Ellis, both of them hunched over their little devices.

Evan went to set up the tent, taking extra care as he spread the sleeping bag and plumped the pillow. Bella deserved better than this tonight, but there was nothing he could do to change their accommodations. In a couple of days the show would end and he would shower Bella—his new wife—with luxury.

Because he'd changed his mind again. He'd love to help Bella keep her clinic—hell, he'd do everything in his power to see that she did.

But he couldn't take the chance that she might walk away from him.

## Chapter Twelve

"ALL RIGHT FOLKS, gather up," Madelyn called. A new SUV pulled into the campsite and Bella sighed when Jake stepped out. The crew hastened to put the finishing touches on his makeup, set up his easel, and light the tiki torches stuck in the ground at angles behind it until their light pushed away the gathering shadows. Natalie, the makeup woman, swooped in for a quick touch of powder on Bella and Evan's faces, and swooped away again.

Bella stood up with a groan and handed the remains of her dinner to Ellis, who came to escort her to her position. She was sore and stiff after her day bushwhacking through the wilds of Jasper. She'd never felt so defeated.

"It's been another exciting day on *Can You Beat a Billionaire*," Jake said jovially, but she had the feeling he was stretching for his enthusiasm today. It hadn't been very exciting at all—at least except for the steamy kiss she'd shared with her sworn adversary, and the camera crew hadn't gotten that on film. The show made from today's footage would feature lots of shots of her stumbling around lost in the woods. By the time Paul yanked her GPS away and showed her exactly where to go she'd lost all desire to fight him.

"Evan, you've obviously used a GPS before," Jake said in his oily way.

"Yes, I do quite a bit of hiking and rock climbing, so I rely on GPS units often," Evan said.

What a self-satisfied prick.

"Bella, I take it you're not as familiar with GPS units?" Jake turned his thousand watt smile on her, and she fought to keep the greasy, cold food she'd just consumed from coming back up.

"No," she said tightly. "I've never used one before."

"Tough break." Jake nodded sagely. "Evan, you found all ten geocaches handily, completing the course with plenty of daylight to spare. Bella, you had more difficulty. What happened after you found the fourth cache?"

"I got lost," she ground out. Seriously, did he have to rub it in? It wasn't like the audience wouldn't just have watched an hour of footage of her scratching her head and walking in circles. She was tired. She was wet. She wanted nothing more than to crawl into her sleeping bag and forget this whole day.

Except that kiss.

"You got lost," Jake repeated. "What a shame. Well, you did eventually manage to find six geocaches, and you did—eventually—make it back to camp. I'll leave you two to get some shut-eye in a minute, but first let's look at our totals. Evan, you currently have 21 points. Bella," he drew the moment out and she was sure all the cameras were focused in tightly on her face, "you have 19."

She blinked. Nineteen? And Evan only had 21? They were only two points apart!

"You are only two points behind Evan," Jake said, as if he'd read her mind. "And you still have two days in which to take the lead. Four more contests." He leaned forward, his face a mask of seriousness. "Four more chances to find out—*Can You Beat a Billionaire!*"

"Cut!" Madelyn called. "Okay, people, pack it up. Let's go get some rest. We've got a fun day planned for the two of you tomorrow." She smiled her vicious smile and Bella fought the urge to lash out at her. Obviously, that wouldn't do any good.

Soon she and Evan were left alone with their usual skeleton crew of cameramen, and she was instantly all too aware of Evan standing only a few feet away.

"Ready to hit the hay?" he asked.

*No*—she thought with a shiver of anticipation. After that toe-curling kiss this afternoon she wasn't sure what he'd try next. On the other hand, it wasn't like he'd stay in the tent with her anyway—he never did. "Sure," she said aloud. Still, as she made her way into the bush to brush her teeth and heed a call of nature before she slipped into the tent to change, excitement twirled her innards into knots.

Would he kiss her again?

She hoped so. No—she hoped not! Especially not

with the stupid camera hanging down from the ceiling. Was there any way to cover the damn thing? The night time cameraman watched their every move on his monitors, probably hoping desperately for some action. It must be boring as anything watching two people sleep night after night.

Rather, one person sleep and the other make a break for the open air.

She snuggled down under the single sleeping bag, exhaustion aching in her limbs. Surely she'd clocked enough miles today to warrant a good night's rest. Even as the thought crossed her mind, however, the tent shivered and Evan poked his head through the flap, shouldered his way inside and immediately swallowing up every speck of extra space. He crawled to the mat and got under the covers as well, but instead of lying down, he turned on his side, opened his overnight bag and pulled out shirts, jackets and even the rain slicker the show had provided each of them in case of inclement weather.

"What are you doing?" she asked.

He spread the clothes in layers over the top of them. "It's cold tonight, what with all the rain today. I thought we could use some extra warmth. What've you got?"

Under cover of the sleeping bag he squeezed her hand. She didn't exactly understand what he was trying to convey to her, but she slowly sat up and dug in her own pack. Together, they spread the remainder of the items, until they were covered in a mound of clothes. Evan was right—it was a little cold tonight, but it wasn't that cold. They would be roasting under all these layers soon.

Evan lay down, and Bella followed suit. He nudged her, giving her a little push, and she went with it, turning to her side, her senses on high alert for what might happen next. Now she was staring at the wall of the tent, Evan's bulk behind her. He turned, too, in the same direction, and she felt his breath stir the hair at the back of her neck.

For a few minutes, all she could hear was his steady breathing. He was so close to her, she could feel the rise and fall of his chest as well. He snuggled in, shrugging the covers higher up over their shoulders, then their faces, until she was afraid he planned to smother her. She was warm, all right. In fact, she was beginning to sweat.

Then he touched her.

He settled one hand on her hip and a blaze of heat suffused her, concentrated in the area between her legs. Her breathing hitched as he traced a path up toward her waist and down again. Even though a pair of yoga pants and a t-shirt still separated their skin, she bit her lip at the sudden need his light caress stirred within her.

She leaned back, ready to turn toward him, but his hand stilled on her hip and he whispered, so quietly she barely heard him, "Don't move. Let me do it."

She stiffened. *Let me do it.* Like she would let him boss her around. But before she could push him away, he whispered, "You'll get your turn. Can't wait."

He couldn't wait? She released a shaky breath and

her tension slid away at the thought of touching him wherever she wanted, knowing he was powerless to stop her—that he relished everything she did, but that she was in control.

She liked being in control. It was the only way she knew how to keep her inner voices in check—the ones that told her what a failure she was, that no amount of animal lives she saved could make up for Caramel, or Cyclone, or the loss of her family's home.

*Stop it.*

She forced herself to breathe as Evan continued to stroke her lightly. Struggling to clear her mind of the guilt that had plagued her all her life, she focused on Evan's hand, traveling up and down, up and down.

Why was feeling pleasure so hard for her? Why did she always fight it? Did she think that would help anyone—Caramel, her parents…?

She gasped as his hand traveled an inch higher and brushed the underside of her breast. It suddenly occurred to Bella that she was fighting all the time. Fighting her memories. Fighting her feelings of inadequacy. Fighting the thought that she could never atone for her past failures.

But here and now the challenge was not to fight. The challenge was to simply accept the pleasure Evan brought her with each stroke of his hand.

What if she gave in? Truly gave in—just for tonight; she still planned to win this contest—and let him have his way with her body since she ached all over to be with him?

Well, why not find out?

She took a deep breath and let it out, holding perfectly still as Evan's hand inched higher, cupped her breast for just an instant, and slid away again. This time he found the hem of her shirt and slid his fingers beneath it. His hand was warm—so warm—and his fingers felt so good against her bare skin. She wanted to groan out loud as he slipped up to cup her breast again, but she was all too aware of the camera dangling right above them, and bit it back. Evan squeezed her nipple and she felt warmth pooling between her thighs, the ache there building with each step of this sweet torment.

Now his motions were smoother, his explorations widening to include her other breast, her stomach, both her hips, and—just once—the place she wanted his touch the most. He inched closer to her until the length of him pressed against her. She felt his hardness and longed to turn over and do some explorations of her own.

Letting all conscious thought go, she reveled in feeling his touch. Her skin burned under each stroke. The heat inside her built until she wanted to writhe in bliss.

Underneath the covers, Evan lifted his hand to tuck her hair behind her ear and kissed the back of her neck. Each breath he expelled made her shiver until she wanted to laugh and gasp with pleasure at the same time. Keeping still, she moved her hips, the better to feel his hardness against the curve of her bottom. She was rewarded with a gasp and an almost-stifled moan.

"Slowly," he murmured, barely audible. "Remember

the camera." He pushed her t-shirt high over her breasts to bare her from collarbone to waist, and carefully began to roll down her pants. She bit her lip as his hand began stroking her thighs, hips, and then touched her between her legs.

She was on fire. Buried underneath layers of covers and clothing, she was slick with sweat and desire, and when he began to swirl his fingers over her folds, stroking her to further heights, she knew she wasn't going to last long.

She edged her own hand behind her and found his hip. She searched for the waistband of his boxer shorts. He quickly guided her to it, then returned to his ministrations, and gasped when she pushed them down and reached around to grasp the length of him.

"I have protection," he breathed in her ear.

She knew what he was asking. "Yes," she said. "Hurry."

His hand slipped away again. There was a rustle as he dug in his bag, a sound that could only be his teeth tearing the packaging of the condom, and a few jerking movements, and he was back again. Now he pressed against her firmly, reached around to stroke her, and together they moved into position. Just the pressure of him against her made Bella want to cry aloud. In a moment she would come no matter what he did; she wanted him inside her before that happened.

"Please," she breathed.

With one arm beneath her, wrapped around her waist, and the other cupping first one breast, then the other, he shifted her hips exactly where he wanted them, and pushed into her from behind.

She bit back a cry. He opened her inch by inch, filling her, sparking every nerve ending in her to life, until she blazed with sensation. He began to move, slow strokes at first, then gathering steam as they slickened with the motion. She'd never felt so alive, so burned up with wanting, longing, desire, and—oh—more, she wanted more...

Evidently still aware of the camera, Evan kept his motions smooth. He didn't piston into a frantic frenzy, but pumped long and hard, in and out, until she thought she'd tear the sleeping bag to shreds. He squeezed her breasts, pinched her nipples, and rained heavy kisses down on her neck and shoulders. Just when she thought she couldn't stand anymore, he dipped his hand between her legs, and stoked the fire within her to a roaring flame.

"Bella," he whispered, a warning and a sound of wonder.

She surged over the edge, wave after wave of ecstasy and release rushing through her. He stiffened behind her then pumped into her again, and she knew he was right there with her, his stifled groans and the jerk of his hips the only outward show of his completion. When they'd shuddered to a stop, they rested together and he kissed her again. Moments later he eased out of her and she missed him immediately. He turned away and she knew he must be cleaning up the evidence of their encounter. Would he leave the tent now? Surely, he'd make a break for the open air after this claustrophobic coupling. She readied herself for his departure, bracing herself for the sick betrayal she knew she'd feel, but he turned back and wrapped an arm around her again.

"I don't know if I can stay here all night," he whispered. She could just make out his words. "I really have a hard time with small places, but I want to stay. I want you to know that."

"It's okay. I understand."

"If I leave it has nothing to do with you," he said again. "I mean it, Bella."

"Okay." She rearranged her clothing, already sleepy, his words easing her fears. *This is just a fling, anyway,* she told herself drowsily. *It's not like I'm going to marry the guy.*

Her eyes snapped open.

If she didn't start winning challenges soon, she would be marrying him.

Desire suffused her again at the idea of doing this night after night with Evan; their lives joined together just like their bodies would be. She glanced at him from under her eyelids.

Would he be up for another round right now?

## Chapter Thirteen

H E WAS SLEEPING in the desert under a bear skin rug.

Evan stretched and immediately came in contact with something solid, warm, and damp. Something…human. He was far too warm, himself. His head ached and while he wanted to open his eyes, he knew the sun would burn him blind the minute he did. Still, after another moment wondering where the hell he was, he cracked one eye, then the other.

He was in a tent.

The orange nylon fabric stretched above him, broken only by the camera dangling from a strap sewn to the ceiling. The sun blazed outside, warming the tent's interior like a greenhouse, the heat compounded by the sleeping bag and heaps of clothing still piled on top of him.

At least he was naked beneath the covers, otherwise he'd be worse off than he was now. Where were his boxers? He turned to look at the person still sleeping beside him, got one glance of Bella's blond hair spilling over the covers and remembered everything.

*Wow*, he thought, falling back against the pillow. What a night. Not only had they made love within inches of the rolling camera—a feat hotter than any other sexual experience he could remember—but he'd managed to sleep all night in the tiny, claustrophobic cocoon Madelyn deemed a tent.

He waited for the feeling of panic to envelop him, but it never came. He ran a hand over his stubbled jaw and bit back the smile threatening to spread over his face. Headache be damned, he felt good. He felt really good.

He could get used to waking up next to the fiery, stubborn, lovely woman sleeping beside him, and if he played his cards right these next two days he'd get at least a year to convince her to make it a full time gig. Maybe it was insane to think he'd found the woman for him after only three days, but he felt sure about this in a way he hadn't felt sure about anything that had to do with a woman before. He felt around with his toes, found his boxers wadded up near the base of their bedding and tried to surreptitiously pull them on. Crawling out from under his covers, he pulled on a pair of sweats, stuck the evidence of last night's shenanigans in his pocket and headed out of the tent to the bushes where he hoped to dispose of it.

Aware he desperately needed a shower, he disappeared into the forest, doing his best to clean himself thoroughly once he was away from prying eyes. He was still damp when he returned to the campsite, but felt a good deal more presentable.

Soon Bella pushed her way out of the tent and headed for the woods, as well, carrying a small bag of
toiletries with her. When she returned, he caught her
gaze and winked. She flushed, but said nothing, making
her way to the logs around the dead campfire to await
breakfast. He wished they were alone, and he could show
her just how alive he felt this morning, and just how
anxious he was to pick up where they'd left off. They'd
made love not once, but twice, Bella surprising him with
her desire for a second round.

Heck, he'd better stop thinking about it, or the whole
world would figure out where his mind was at. These
sweatpants weren't going to hide anything.

He turned away and thought about his last business
lunch with a particularly boring member of the Board of
Directors of Mortimer Innovations until his ardor cooled
and the evidence of it disappeared. He turned back just
in time to see the influx of SUVs that heralded another
exciting day of *Can You Beat a Billionaire.*

"Let's get cracking!" Madelyn called. As Evan and
Bella slowly approached, she tapped her foot. "And let's
get one thing clear today. We're not having a repeat of
yesterday's yawn-fest. I want some action. I want competition. I want something my viewers have never seen
before!"

Evan tried not to look at Bella. Failed.

Her cheeks flushed pink.

"Today we have two challenges that pit you in direct
competition. Maybe that will get your competitive juices

flowing. And since the two of you have become such good friends," she emphasized the last word with a smarmy inflection that made Evan stiffen—had they betrayed themselves in the tent last night? "Let me remind you of a few things." She glared at Evan. "You won't get the wife you need if you don't get yourself together. And Bella," she pointed to her, "kittens."

"Kittens?"

"Fluffy, sweet, helpless, *dead* kittens."

Bella jerked and a glance told him Madelyn's words had hit their mark, undoing all the goodwill between them since their interlude under the covers.

"Eat your breakfast, grab your gear, and we'll take you to the start of this day's hike. Get going and give us some good television," Madelyn said.

TODAY SHE'D TAKE the lead, Bella told herself as she munched a carrot muffin and tried not to watch Evan doing warm up lunges to get ready for the day's hike. Every time he moved, though, his sweatpants moved with him, molding themselves to his muscular thighs and incredible ass.

Last night was incredible, she had to admit. Truly incredible. Although in the light of day she couldn't believe she'd basically consented to having sex on national television. Twice. Had the camera been able to make any of it out? So far no one had said anything, or acted weird around them, except Madelyn's one remark about them being such good friends.

She hoped like crazy there was nothing to see on

those recordings.

Would they do it again tonight?

Biting into her carrot muffin, she struggled to concentrate on the events of the day ahead. More hiking first, obviously, followed by head-to-head challenges.

When it was time to set out down the path, Bella realized she felt terrific. After their shenanigans the previous night, she'd slept soundly, and her feet and muscles weren't as sore today as they had been yesterday. She felt stronger than when she'd started the show, and she kept finding herself humming as she walked along.

Evan walked behind her, and she could swear she heard a snatch of melody from him now and then, as well. As the morning went on she stopped worrying about what the future would bring and decided just to enjoy the day.

And she did enjoy it, up until the point she rounded a bend in the trail and came upon their first challenge.

"Oh, my God."

A pond lay ahead of her, but that wasn't the problem. Stretched over it like twin suspension bridges were two thin strips of a metallic material about ten feet apart. They couldn't be bridges, though. They were too narrow, for one thing, and they lacked any railings at all.

At intervals alongside each of them were five posts that reached high above the bridges. Dangling from them were more of the stuffed animals that seemed to be this show's trademark.

"Do we have to walk across those?" Bella asked the crew member who strode up to greet them.

"Yep," he said. "I'm Louis, by the way. You get a point for each stuffie you grab."

"That shouldn't be hard," Evan said.

"Once you fall off, you're out," Louis said.

"That won't support my weight," Bella said, pointing to the nearest bridge.

"Sure it will. It's an aluminum alloy; tough as anything. You don't have to worry about it breaking; you just have to worry about staying on it."

Bella bit back an oath and approached her bridge slowly, willing Evan to go first so she could learn from his mistakes. With a glance in her direction he did so. Sliding one foot out on to the narrow span, he fought for balance as it tipped and swayed. "Hell," he said.

He tried again, inching first one foot, then the other, out onto the bridge. Swaying and swiveling, he fought to keep upright. He'd almost made it to the first pole when the bridge tipped and his arms wheeled for balance. He hung on for an instant before he landed with a splash in the water below.

Bella shrieked, then clapped a hand to her mouth and hoped no one had noticed.

"Keep going," the crew member yelled to Evan, pointing toward the far shore. Evan struck out with an overhand crawl and reached it a few seconds later. His camera crew skirted the perimeter of the pond and joined him on the other side.

"Let's see what you can do!" Evan called back to Bella.

If she had her way, she'd follow the cameraman's

example and walk around the pond. Still, she couldn't do worse than Evan had.

She approached her bridge with caution, but decided not to emulate Evan. He'd inched his way out and gotten nowhere. Instead, she'd move as fast as she could and try to reach the first pole and cling to it while she retrieved the stuffie. Even one animal would help her catch up to him in points.

Standing on the pond's bank, she took a deep breath, fixed her eyes on the prize and dashed forward.

Her foot slipped and a split second later she hit the water with a tremendous splash. Coming up soaked and sputtering, she heard Evan's laughter from the far side of the pond. "Swim for it," he called out and beckoned her on.

"Well, that's going to make some riveting television," Chris was saying to Andrew when Bella staggered out of the water. "You think we should call Madelyn?"

"And spend the rest of the day waiting here while someone rebuilds those to be more stable?" Andrew said.

"Hell, no," Evan said.

Chris shot him a dark look, but after a moment he agreed. "Let's keep moving."

They'd only walked a half-dozen steps, however, before the roar of helicopter rotors had everyone turning in their tracks. As they watched, the helicopter touched down on the far side of the pond and Madelyn hopped out, followed closely by Ellis.

"Shit," Chris said.

"Double-shit," Andrew said.

"Are you trying to kill me?" she hollered as she stalked around the perimeter of the pond, Ellis trailing her as fast as he could. "Are you collectively trying to give me heart failure? That's not television; that's a train wreck!" She puffed up to them, out of breath and flustered in a way Bella had never seen her. "No, scratch that—a train wreck would make great television. That was as watchable as leaves rotting on the ground! Now get back there and do it again!"

Bella just stared at her. So did Evan. What had happened to the perfectly-in-control director?

"Madelyn…?" Chris said. "Everything all right?"

"No, it's not all right. The producers are livid. First yesterday's fiasco, now this. We're over-budget, our ratings nose-dived last quarter…"

"Madelyn, calm down. It's going to be okay," Ellis said, catching up and trying to hand her a cup of coffee.

"No, it's not!" She batted the coffee out of his hand and it splashed to the ground. She pointed to Evan and Bella. "You heard me! Get back on those bridges."

"No," Evan said. He stepped in front of Bella in a protective gesture which she appreciated given the crazy look in Madelyn's eyes.

"Ellis! Get me Legal…"

"I'm not bailing on my contract; I'm just saying those bridges are impossible to cross."

"Baloney!" Madelyn said. She whirled on her assistant. "Ellis, cross that bridge."

Bella looked to Ellis with the rest of them, assured

the assistant would do just that. He always jumped when Madelyn barked an order. But instead, he took a deep breath and said, "He's right, Madelyn. We both saw what happened; the bridges aren't stable enough."

Madelyn's face grew paler and the scarlet of her cheeks intensified. "Cross. That. Bridge." She punctuated each word with a stab of her finger.

The rest of them held their breath, mesmerized by the director's rising tones. Ellis stood his ground, his dark eyes inscrutable, before he extended his hand toward her. "I'll cross it when you cross it."

Bella blinked. She didn't think the assistant had it in him. But as he and Madelyn glared at each other, a thought insinuated itself into her mind. There was more going on here than met the eye. This wasn't just a contest of wills between boss and underling; something else sparked between them.

Lust.

Were Ellis and Madelyn a couple? Bella raised an eyebrow at the thought. Or...did Ellis want to be a couple, but Madelyn remained unconvinced?

Ellis was daring Madelyn; daring her to climb down off her director's high horse and roll in the muck with the rest of them. Bella couldn't believe he thought she'd do it.

But to her surprise—and everyone else's, judging from the collective intake of breath—Madelyn took his hand and allowed him to lead her back around the pond. Bella trailed after them, tugged as if by an invisible cord.

She had to see this.

Evan followed close behind her, and they stood together as director and assistant took their respective spots at the beginning of each bridge.

"Not stable enough, my ass," Madelyn hissed at Ellis.

"We'll see, won't we?" He set a foot on his span and sent a ripple of motion down the strip of metal.

"We certainly will." Madelyn set a foot on her own bridge. "Ready. Set. Go."

Bella didn't know what she expected to happen, but the sight of Madelyn and Ellis lurching out over the slippery, wobbling metal spans, then simultaneously losing balance and pitching headlong into the pond brought her hand to her mouth to cover a shriek of laughter. She dashed to the side of the pond, ready to wade in and help them back out of the water.

But when Madelyn broke the surface and found her footing, she didn't head for the bank. Instead, she launched herself at Ellis and bowled him over as he stood up, so both of them sunk beneath the water again.

"What the hell?" Evan said from behind Bella.

They came up locked together this time, Madelyn pounding her fists into Ellis's chest. "We're going to lose the show. I'll be back on daytime television. I can't do that!"

"It'll be all right. It's going to be all right, Maddie," Ellis said, taking what she dished out.

"Shit," Nita said. Beside her, Chris and Andrew stood with slack jaws, their cameras forgotten.

"I think we should give those two a little privacy," Evan said slowly, taking Bella's hand. She allowed him to tug her back the way they'd come just minutes before, still looking over her shoulder as Ellis pulled the director to him, wrapped his arms around her, and kissed the top of her head.

Footsteps behind them told her the camera crews dutifully trailed along behind.

"That...was a little weird," Bella said, finally finding her voice.

"Sounds like this show is really in trouble," Evan said.

"What kind of trouble? I thought it was a popular show." She sat down heavily when they reached the far bank, her clothes still sopping wet and uncomfortable.

"Money trouble. They've had to pay out too many times recently, I guess."

"Oh." Bella stopped twisting the fabric of her shirt to wring out the water. "So if I win..."

"If you win, the producers might give Madelyn the ax."

She thought back to the GPS unit and all the time she'd spent wandering around the woods. Had that been Madelyn's doing? Or was she really just lousy with directions?

"Can I win?"

He seemed to understand exactly what she meant. "I think so."

"You think so."

He shrugged.

Back across the pond, Ellis led a sopping Madelyn out of the water and toward the helicopter. Soon its rotors whipped up a whirlwind of dust and water as it lifted off.

"Now what?" Bella asked.

Chris answered. "On to the next challenge."

## Chapter Fourteen

THE REST OF THE MORNING'S hike was far from comfortable. Her wet clothing chafed her thighs and arms as she walked. Water oozed out of her shoes with every step. By noontime her shirt, cami, and bra were dry, but her pants remained damp and she held no hope that her feet would ever be dry again.

Still, when they paused to eat, she untied her shoes and stuffed half of her dry outer shirt into each one, hoping it would draw some of the water out of them. She peeled off her socks and draped them from nearby branches, then looked down at her pants.

"Go ahead—take 'em off," Evan said with a grin. "We won't mind."

Pursing her lips, she decided to keep them on. She sat down, stuck out her legs to catch as much as the sun as possible, and ate a sandwich.

"I hope the next challenge is a little easier," she said.

Evan laughed. "If it isn't, I bet they're working hard to modify it. Like Chris said—it isn't good television if we can't even score a single point between us." He lowered his voice. "How're you doing?"

She felt a blush creep over her skin, even though he hadn't mentioned what happened the night before. She knew he was asking after more than her physical condition. He meant how was she doing emotionally, and she liked him for that.

"Good. I think."

"You think?"

She shrugged. "I have to win this, you know. No matter if I…" She bit off her words, realizing what she was just about to say. *No matter if I'd like to lose.* A glance his way told her he'd heard her loud and clear.

"Same for me, you know." He said, taking a long drink from his water bottle. "I'm not in the habit of forcing women to marry me."

"Really? I figured you forced at least ten women to marry you every day before lunch."

"Then divorced them again before dinner? Yeah, billionaires do that stuff all the time."

"What do you do?" she asked. "I mean I know what your job is, but what do you do for fun?"

She wished that two cameras weren't recording every minute of this conversation. If only she and Evan were hiking alone, spending time together because they liked each other, not because they wanted to beat each other in some inane contest.

"I like being outdoors, so I run, hike, do a little rock climbing when I can. What about you? What's your favorite leisure-time activity?"

"Leisure time? What's that?" She laughed ruefully.

"Actually, before the shelter got so out of control, I used to like to go dancing. I haven't done that in a long, long time."

"Dancing? Like at a bar?"

"Yeah—line dancing, mostly." She glanced sidelong at Evan and caught him smirking. "What?"

"Line dancing? Does anyone do that anymore?"

"Are you kidding? It's huge!"

"In some circles," Evan intoned and laughed aloud.

"Jerk." But she didn't mind his teasing as much as she used to. Maybe only country people line danced; that didn't mean it wasn't fun.

"Don't you take any nights off work?" he said. He was sitting so close she could reach out and touch him. She wondered what the camera crew would do if she took Evan's hand.

*Lots of close-ups.*

"Not really. There's too much to do."

"You can't live like that," he said, turning to her. She read genuine concern in his eyes and her heart warmed.

"I don't know what else to do."

"Bella, you aren't responsible for every animal in the world. You can't be."

"Yes, I can." She knew he was right, but something within her refused to let that thought take hold. "I feel responsible for them all. I can't help it."

"Why?"

She glanced his way. "What do you mean?"

"Why should you be responsible for all the animals and not someone else? What about the rest of us? Aren't we responsible, too?"

"Well, sure, but I...I'm more responsible." It sounded crazy. It was crazy. But she'd never been able to shake the feeling, not after what happened to Caramel, not when she'd caused Cyclone to break his leg so he had to be put down, too. Saving animals was the only thing she did right.

"Why?"

She shook her head, wishing she'd never opened her mouth. "It's not important."

"Sounds pretty important to me if it's made you responsible for every pet in Montana," Evan said, nudging her with his shoulder.

She wished she could recapture the lighthearted feeling she'd had just a moment ago. Wished he'd do more than nudge her. She wanted to run her hand down his arm, to clasp his fingers in hers and lean in and give him a kiss. Anything to deflect this conversation from its inevitable end.

A glance told her he wasn't going to let her change the topic. She'd tell him the simple version, the one she told everyone who asked why she became a veterinarian. Leave the rest for another time...some other time that would hopefully never come.

"We had a dog when I was a kid. A lab named Caramel. I loved that dog." For a moment, memories overtook her. "We all did," she went on, straightening up. "My parents, my brother, Craig, and I."

Evan packed away the remainder of his lunch slowly, giving her time to tell her story.

"When I was ten I was playing with her in back of the house. My brother was helping my father and the other men with the horses. My father needed to take a stallion to another spread to stud. They were loading him into the trailer."

She'd relived this particular memory way too many times, but it never failed to bring tears to her eyes. "I wasn't supposed to be there at all. I was never allowed to play out back when the men were working, but I liked the attention. I didn't want to stay out front, away from the action. Craig was there helping. I wanted to be a part of it, too. Or at least to be close to it."

"What happened?"

"The stallion spooked. The next thing I knew he was rearing over me. I should have been killed. Caramel barked. I probably screamed. My Dad was yelling. I don't know what happened next. Except the stallion crashed and broke his leg. Then something hurt Caramel. She took off like she'd been hit…"

Bella broke off. *Like she'd been hit.* Something twinged in her subconscious. A memory she couldn't quite access.

*Like she'd been hit.*

She saw her father dash between her and the stallion. The stallion twisted away in alarm, and fell with a shattering crash. Caramel barked. Her father's face went red with fury. His lifted his arm.

Bella shook the memory away.

"I tried to go after her but a car came down the road much too fast…" she trailed off again.

"It was an accident," Evan said.

"If I had done what I was supposed to do, she would have lived."

Evan turned to face her. "That was what—twenty years ago? More? She would have died by now anyway, Bella. Accidents happen. Pets die. Horses die. You can't stop living your own life because of it."

"You don't understand," she said, knowing he truly didn't. No one did. No one outside of her family. Because that was only the beginning of the story. "I loved her and I caused her death. I was irresponsible, and selfish, and I didn't listen, and Caramel paid the price. Cyclone did, too. Everyone did." Despite her best efforts tears welled up.

Evan narrowed his eyes. "That's what they told you, didn't they? Your family? God, I can hear them say the words—your parents and Craig all blaming you. Didn't they take any responsibility at all?"

Bella stared at him. "But…"

"But what? I'm serious—you were ten years old. How hard would it have been for your father to scan the yard before he moved the horse to the trailer? How did the stallion get away from him, anyway?"

Bella blinked, astounded by the vehemence of his anger. "Horses are unpredictable."

"All the more reason he should have been careful." Evan leaned forward, his jaw tight. "And the fact that he dumped all his guilt on you sucks. Do you still see these people?"

She forgot the cameras around her and searched

Evan's face for the source of his anger. Was he really upset that her family blamed her? "No. Well… sometimes. My parents still live on the ranch. What's left of it. So does my brother."

"What do you mean, what's left of it?"

Bella's stomach twisted. "We had to sell half of it. My father had mortgaged it so he could buy Cyclone."

"So your father mismanaged his business and blamed you when it didn't pay off? Didn't he insure the horse?"

"I…I don't know. But it wasn't his fault he lost the land." *It was mine. Just like I'm losing my business.*

Evan stared at her, his eyes narrowed. "You don't know much about business either, do you? Tell me this. Do any of them ever help you with your shelter? How much time does your brother spend there?" He got to his feet and shouldered his pack. Bella followed his example, unnerved by the way this conversation had gone. Instead of condemning her, Evan was angry that her family had blamed her at all. She knew her own guilt over the incident was excessive. Still, Evan's reaction startled her.

"None. He hates it," Bella said. "Craig doesn't care for pets—he's a livestock vet. He never got over Caramel's death. He never forgave me for it. Anyway, he's busy." She followed him as he set out down the path again.

"Busier than you? Really? I find that hard to believe."

Watching him stride ahead of her, all too aware of his broad shoulders and powerful legs, Bella considered his words.

"I guess he's not busier; it's just his work is more important."

Evan stopped in his tracks and she walked right into him. He turned and caught her, and didn't let go even when she was steady on her feet. "Bullshit," he said. "His work isn't more important than yours. He takes care of animals that represent people's business. You take care of animals that people love. Your work is more important. You're important. How come you can't see that?"

"Because I screw everything up for people," she said. She bit her lip in anguish. Damn it, why did she feel the need to expose every flaw to his eyes? She liked Evan, and she wanted him to like her, so why was she trying so hard to make him loathe her?

Because she was used to being loathed by those she loved.

The thought hit her like a fist to her stomach. It was true. It was absolutely true.

She was used to it.

And the people she loved did loathe her. Craig, her parents…because of what she'd done. Because of what she'd made them do.

And now she was bankrupting her business—the one thing she'd ever gotten right.

She didn't deserve love.

Not until she beat Evan and used her millions to fix everything she'd broken.

WHEN THE TRAIL they followed broadened out into a

wide field an hour later, Bella stopped dead at the sight that greeted them. Evan, catching up to her, immediately saw why.

"Miniature golf?" Bella said, turning to him. She'd regained her composure somewhere along the trail, and Evan had recovered his equilibrium, as well. He couldn't say exactly why the thought of Bella's family blaming her for their dog's death burned him so much, or why he wanted to hunt them down and demand they apologize to her, but that's exactly how he felt. Couldn't they see she hadn't gotten over the loss, or the blame they'd heaped on her? A pet's death was traumatic to any child, but being told that she was responsible—and not letting up, even after all these years? That was unforgivable as far as he was concerned.

"I guess they really want us to score some points," he said as he looked at the curved green tracks flanked by windmills and pyramids and replicas of the Eiffel Tower.

"We should be able to handle this," she agreed. "It's just—I thought they were showcasing Jasper National Park. What does this have to do with Jasper?"

"Nothing," Evan said. "Maybe they're just trying to shake things up."

A crew member stepped forward and handed each of them a golf club and ball. He pointed Bella to one starting point, and Evan to another.

"These are par three courses. Sink your ball in the hole in three shots or less and you score a point, up to ten points for ten holes. The person who finishes the course first will win an extra point. Ready?"

Evan nodded and so did Bella.

"Start!"

Evan considered the course ahead of him. Despite the chance to win an extra point, speed wasn't the goal—accuracy was. He needed to play each hole carefully and methodically, and rack up the points. He'd never been an avid golfer; he hated getting stuck on a course for hours if his partners were slow or tedious. All too often he'd found himself in a foursome with two other perfectly decent human beings—and one complete asshole.

Not his scene.

He was reasonably athletic, though, and competent in other sports that required accuracy and control. This game should be a piece of cake.

He sunk the first hole in three shots and the next hole in two. After that he faced an uphill shot, through a gap cut into a Noah's ark, and into a hole placed near the far rim of the track. He lined up his shot, swung and took it, but the ball bounced off the side of the Noah's ark and rolled right back down to land at his feet.

A feminine curse to his right made him smile. Bella must also be facing a tough hole. Thoughts of their time together last night invaded his mind, leaving him aching to get the day's events finished so he could climb back into the little tent with her. He'd make her understand that her family was crazy and she was worth every bit of happiness that came into her life and more.

He took a second shot and missed again. Muttering a bad word, Evan cleared his mind of all distractions and prepared for another try.

"Woo-hoo!" Bella whooped just as he swung. He jerked around to see her dancing on an artificial green. His own ball rolled up the hill partway, hung there and rolled back down to bounce off his shoe.

"Damn it." He picked it up and walked to the next hole.

His concentration was shot, however, by Bella's continual shouts and laughter. She must be nailing the course the way she hopped around, pumping her fists over her head, slapping high fives with the camera crew and shaking her hips in a rather suggestive victory dance now and then.

"Quiet on the course," he called over to her finally.

"Why? Am I distracting you?" she yelled back, dancing around again.

Um, yes. He was distracted. Obviously her successes on the course had restored her good humor. She moved to a new hole and he turned back to his own course, only to be jolted mid-swing again by another of her high-pitched victory cries. She was doing that on purpose and it was working—he'd blown three holes now.

He got back to work and won three more, lost one, and won the final one. Six points in all and one point for finishing first.

"About time," Bella said.

He turned with a jerk and saw that she'd been waiting for him. Forget about that last point, but how on earth had she beaten him?

And what was her score?

Before he could ask her, Jake Cramer arrived on the

scene and with him a number of crew members who rushed to get ready for the day's closing wrap-up.

Evan exchanged a glance with Bella and both of them trailed over to where Natalie had hurried over to touch Jake up. He waved her away, and she turned her attention on Evan and Bella while Jake waited for another crew member to set his microphone up. Madelyn shooed Natalie away and Jake began his traditional patter.

"Another day has come to a close on *Can You Beat a Billionaire*, and it's been a tough one. Bella, what did you think of the day's first challenge?"

As the cameras swung to face Bella, she rolled her eyes. "Um, it was impossible."

"It did look difficult. How long do you think you managed to stay on the bridge?"

"One second?" she ventured.

"Try one-tenth of a second," Jake said happily. He swung around to Evan. "You've climbed sheer rock walls, Evan. Why was the bridge so difficult?"

Was the guy a total idiot? "Because it was thin, slippery and unstable," he said, glaring at Madelyn—cleaned up and back to her usual glowering, impeccable self—over Jake's shoulder as she gestured to him in wide circles. What the hell did that mean? Did she want him to turn a somersault?

"It was really exciting," Bella said, sounding anything but excited. Evan realized she'd interpreted Madelyn's signals—step up the energy.

"Yeah. Thrilling," he said. "That water was really…wet."

Madelyn smacked a hand to her forehead.

"Moving on to lunchtime. Seems like you two had a real meeting of the minds over your sandwiches. What were you talking about?"

Did he really have to go along with this? Evan wondered. "We were telling each other about our childhoods."

"Bella," Jake swiveled to face her. "Sounds like you lost a special pet. Do you want to tell our audience more about that?"

"Oh, come on," Evan said, stepping in between Jake and Bella. "You guys caught everything we said on film—do we really need to hash it all out again? I think our viewers are smart enough to get it the first time."

"Cut, CUT!" Madelyn yelled and strode forward. "You are walking on very thin ice, and any minute you are going to be in complete violation of your contract. Jake asks the questions, you answer them. Do I make myself clear?"

"It's all right," Bella said, flashing him a tired grimace. "I don't mind."

She obviously did mind, but getting himself thrown off the show wouldn't help matters any. He balled his hands into fists and shoved them in his pockets.

"Let's try this again," Madelyn said and stepped back behind the cameras. Jake repeated his question and Bella answered it in short, neutral sentences. Yes, she'd lost a pet early on and it prompted her to become a veterinarian. Yes, it was a very sad occurrence, but things like that happened in life—what was important was how you moved forward after them. Madelyn couldn't complain about Bella's answers, but Evan knew she must want to—this was television at its most banal.

When he finished grilling her even Jake looked defeated.

"Well, after this exciting day, the scores of our contestants are still closely matched. Evan, you began the day with 21 points. After the bridge debacle you still had 21 points. You did much better in this afternoon's miniature golf tournament, however, scoring 6 out of a possible 10, for a final total of 27 points!"

Bella made a face and Evan wondered if all her cheering and dancing had been just a ruse. Maybe he'd pulled ahead into a comfortable lead today. He sure hoped so. He wanted that year with her so bad he could taste it. Three hundred and sixty-five days of hot, languorous, mind-blowing sex with the most beautiful, sweet, tempting woman he'd ever met…

"Bella, you also fumbled the bridge challenge," Jake went on. "You started the day with 19 points and gained none this morning, either. But this afternoon you proved yourself a fair hand at miniature golf. How did you learn to play?"

Evan sighed. Couldn't the man get on with things and just announce her score?

"Golf was one of my family's favorite activities when I was growing up. I always lost back then, but I didn't mind because we were all together. I guess I remember more than I thought I did from those days on the course."

"You sure did. You scored an amazing 10 out of 10 points, and got the bonus point for finishing first. That brings your score to a grand total of 30 points. You have a three point lead!"

Evan's mouth dropped open in shock. Three points ahead of him? What the hell? Bella was dancing again, bouncing up and down with her arms upraised and her fingers fluttering. "Whooo!" she yelled and twirled in a circle. "Whooo—stray pets of Chance Creek, here I come, and you'll never go hungry or cold again!"

BELLA FALTERED TO a stop when she saw Evan's face. "Uh…sorry, just got carried away. You have to admit it's pretty cool I scored so high, though." Was he going to have another of his temper tantrums? She'd been through the ringer today, and though she'd regained her equilibrium, she didn't think she could take that.

"Yeah, really terrific," he said. "When's dinner?" he asked Madelyn, pushing past her.

"Evan," Bella said to his back. "Come on, what's the big deal? You don't really need to win this game anyway. You've got all the money in the world." Disappointment in him soured her stomach. She liked the man, but she hated this side of his personality. Why did he always need to win so badly?

"I don't need the money; I need a wife," he said, rounding on her. "That's why I'm on this show."

"You need a wife so you can keep the money," she said, "and let's face it, if push comes to shove you can just buy one off of any street corner."

"What if I don't want to buy one? What if I want someone in particular?" he challenged her.

Bella shrugged, taken aback by his vehemence. Obviously she'd hit a nerve and she'd better back off, let Moneybuns cool down for a minute. Funny, she hadn't called him the derogatory nickname for at least a day…since…

Her face warmed as she thought about their tryst. Evan was much more to her than an adversary now. He was someone she wanted to know. Someone she hoped to see more of, even after the show.

But would he want to keep seeing her if she won and left him high and dry?

"I'm talking to you," Evan said, following her as she turned and made her way to where crew members were setting out their dinners. Fish was on the menu today, with rice and some kind of vegetable mixture.

"I don't know what you mean," she said, grabbing a paper plate and loading it up with food.

"I mean, I don't want to spend a year with a stranger. I want to spend it with you."

"You already know I can't do that," she said, but her cheeks heated and Evan narrowed his eyes. Did her expression betray her regret? Had he guessed she was beginning to want to spend a year with him?

Hadn't she almost admitted as much at lunchtime?

"You won't regret losing, I promise you," he said, his gazed sliding to the camera crew hovering over them. "I…" he grimaced, obviously unable to say what he'd like to in front of them. "Bella, I promise."

## Chapter Fifteen

SEVERAL HOURS LATER, Evan stripped down and slipped into one of the twin makeshift showers the crew had rigged for a surprise for their last night out in the open air. They consisted of large, sun-warmed plastic bags of water hanging from trees and plastic curtained stalls for each of them.

It took Evan a moment to figure out the mechanism of the shower, but when he did the warm water sliding over his trail-dusty body felt wonderful. Off to his left Bella moaned in delight.

"Hey, what's going on over there?" he called out playfully. "Better keep it down or I'll come to investigate."

The thought made his body hum all over. Bella moaned again. For a second he forgot they were surrounded by crew members, some setting up for the night, others still training their cameras on the shower stalls, although they'd been assured they would not be filmed during pre- or post-shower dressing periods.

"That's it; I'm coming," he growled.

Bella shrieked when he rustled the plastic curtains as if he was tearing through them and he was disappointed he couldn't make good on his threat, but that wasn't possible—not while they were being filmed.

He hurried to wash the rest of himself before the water ran out. Still, when the water slowed to a drip and stopped all together, he wasn't ready for the shower to be over.

He dried himself on the towel he'd left right outside his stall and slipped out to pull on clean clothes. Making his way back toward the campfire now burning brightly, he met up with Bella. He walked beside her, and when one of the crew members dropped a camera, causing everyone else on the set to turn his way, Evan reached for her hand, squeezed it, and let it go again, his fingers trailing over her palm.

He hoped her answering squeeze was a promise of things to come. As much as he was determined to win this show, he wanted to make the most of what could possibly be his last night with Bella. He didn't think he could stand it if they didn't make love again. It was hard enough to imagine going back to life as usual after the show ended tomorrow.

She glanced up at him and smiled, a quick, intimate smile. He grinned in return, a lustful, wolfish grin, and making sure no one was looking, reached out and gave her ass a squeeze.

Bella squeaked and the camera crew around them swiveled her way. Biting back her laughter, she put her head down and hurried the remainder of the way into camp. She stowed her gear away, sat on a log near the fire, and made a big show of stretching and yawning widely.

Madelyn appeared just as Evan took a seat nearby.

"Okay, kids, we have one more day of filming—one more day to make this show a success. Your run with us may just about be over, but all of us," she waved a hand to encompass the crew members hard at work around them, "still need to make a living. We're counting on you to convince our network we need another season of the show. Think you can do that for us?"

"Sure," Evan said.

"Okay," Bella shrugged.

"We need drama, passion, chills, thrills—give us something we can work with." Madelyn surveyed first one and then the other. "I know there's something going on between you two. Sparks are smoldering, if they're not flying outright. How about you let them ignite tonight?" She waggled her eyebrows at them lasciviously, a sight Evan thought would haunt him to his grave. Time to put an end to that bit of speculation before she spooked Bella and their last night of passion became a bust.

"We'll provide all the drama you could want tomorrow during the contests," Evan said evenly. "I'm afraid you're wrong about the sparks, though. Bella will make me a perfectly adequate wife, but I don't call her Betty Bumpkin for nothing. I'm used to a little more...sophistication...in my bed."

He hoped Bella understood what he was trying to do,

and didn't take that personally. He stood up. "Speaking of bed, I'm going to hit the hay. Give me a minute then feel free to join me…Betty."

Madelyn turned to her, eyebrows raised high. "You going to take that lying down, Betty?" she asked, laughing uproariously at her own joke.

"Ha, ha. I can be sophisticated any time I want to," Bella said, meeting his gaze with a glint of humor in her eye. Evan relaxed a bit. "But a wealthy man isn't automatically an interesting man—or an endowed one. I don't think Moneybuns is packing much below the belt, if you get my drift." She arched an eyebrow at him, obviously saying, *take that!*

"Whoa—strong words!" Madelyn said. "Are you getting all of this?" She looked over her shoulder at the crew.

Nita gave her a thumb's up.

"I'm calling it a night, too," Bella said. "Early to bed, early to rise and beat the crap out of my opponent."

Evan headed out into the bushes to heed a final call of nature for the day, but Bella's last words stuck with him. He still had to beat Bella in this stupid contest and she was three points ahead of him. Somehow he had to throw her off her game, because now more than ever he was positive he wanted to win. He wanted a whole year with his sexy, little veterinarian to convince her she wanted to spend a lifetime with him.

How could he knock her off balance enough to take the lead tomorrow?

The answer brought a groan to his lips.

BY THE TIME Bella crawled into the tent and slid under the covers, Evan had already piled on all their extra clothes. He tugged her all the way under them and drew her into a long, hot kiss. When he released her, he lifted one of her hands to touch his mouth and she felt his smile. He kissed her fingertips, and made as if to turn her over. Thoughts of their previous night swirling in her head, she quickly complied and nestled herself in the crook of his arm.

His sensual onslaught began almost immediately. His hands slid up and down her body, finding her breasts, kneading them and squeezing them until she had to stifle a moan. He kissed the side of her neck and under her ear, nipped at her earlobe and pulled her even closer.

She could feel his hardness hot against her back and longed to have him inside of her, but she knew that would come in time. For now, she relished every stroke of his fingers over her skin and wondered how she would bear to part with him tomorrow night.

Maybe—just maybe—when she was a millionaire and the stray animals of Chance Creek were safe in her care, she could see Evan now and then. Maybe take a trip to California, or he could fly to Chance Creek. She tried to picture him in a cowboy hat and giggled aloud.

"Shh," Evan whispered and trailed one hand lower, finding the heat between her legs. Her eyes closed and she arched her back in a state of sensual overload as he dipped and swirled and stirred her to life.

She wanted him badly, bit her lip as she imagined him pressing into her, how she'd feel when she pushed back against him and they rocked together until their bodies exploded with desire. She smiled when a moment later he fumbled with something, and pressed against her core, his hardness already sending shivers of pleasure radiating through her body.

"Are you ready?" he whispered.

She nodded, knowing he'd feel the movement, knowing he'd taken care of protection, too. Thank goodness he'd had the foresight to bring some. He pushed farther inside her and the sensation made her want to cry aloud. She wished they were alone and she could give vent to everything she was bottling up inside her right now. Someday she'd make love to Evan and scream if he moved her to.

But she'd take whatever she could get right now, and she was getting quite a lot. Bracing his hand on her hip, he stroked into her and out again in strong, steady movements, stoking the fires inside her until she thought she might burst into flames.

She wanted to do so much more than they were able to do in the confines of these covers. She wanted to explore his whole body, taste him, touch him, experiment with every possible position until they found their favorites, stretch her boundaries—and his—with their sensual play.

She concentrated on the feel of him inside her, moved with him, pressed against him, lifted her ass to let him deeper inside. He sped up, reaching with his hand to cup her breasts again, playing with them, squeezing her nipples until she hovered just on the edge of release.

Just as he stroked in one last time, just as Bella started over the edge, her mouth opening in a silent cry, Evan stilled, pulled out with a jerk, and turned away from her and adjusted the covers as if they'd suddenly been exposed to view. Bella, shocked and bereft, turned with him.

"What are you doing?" she hissed into his shoulder. He clamped a hand over her mouth.

"I heard something. Someone's coming."

She lay still, her heart pounding, the juncture between her legs aching with pent up desire. One more second and she would have had the orgasm of her life. Couldn't whoever it was have waited just a little longer?

The seconds ticked by. Outside all was still. She was sure the beating of her heart was loud enough to wake the dead, but she couldn't hear anything else. She let several more minutes go by and said, "I think they're gone."

She hoped Evan would pick up where he left off. He'd have to backtrack a little to get her to the peak she'd so rudely been yanked from, but it wouldn't take much. Her whole body still tingled. Even her breasts ached for his touch.

"Evan?"

"Shhh," he said again. "I think there's a new camera. A better one," he whispered in a voice so low she could barely make out his words.

A new camera?

A better one?

What did that mean? Would her wanton behavior be

broadcast all over the United States? Could it pick up her breathless moans and writhing body even under their covers?

"I was so close," she whispered, hoping he'd have some idea how to finish things off. She couldn't stop now—not like this—she'd never sleep a wink. He had to be in a similar situation.

Right?

"Evan?"

His breathing slowed, evened out, and a few minutes later, she'd swear he'd gone to sleep.

How the hell could he sleep? Her entire body throbbed with need.

After several more minutes, Bella couldn't stand it anymore. Evan obviously wasn't going to come to her rescue, and his lack of follow-through was highly disappointing, to say the least. If he could roll over and fall asleep in the middle of one of the best sexual experiences of her life, he wasn't the partner for her, no matter how much she wanted him.

Frustrated enough she wanted to scream, she slid her own hand down under the covers to touch herself. It was a far cry from Evan's touch, but she knew she needed to relieve some of her pent up pressure if she was ever to sleep a wink tonight. She wriggled until her ass pressed up against Evan's thigh and her back touched the length of Evan's arm. It wasn't much, but she used his solid presence to fuel her fantasies. She closed her eyes and swirled her fingers against herself, picturing Evan back in position behind her, plunging into her again with his strong, steady strokes. In her mind, he moved faster and faster, cupping her breasts as he pressed in and out. She experimented with other positions in her mind. Evan above her, his body covering hers, Evan beneath her, holding her waist while she rode him wild and fast. It didn't matter what she imagined; it wasn't as good as the real thing.

But it helped, and when she came, she bucked against her hand, the shudders wracking through her until she knocked against Evan's thigh.

He slept through it all, and when she was done she hoped against hope that the camera hadn't picked up any of it. She felt better, the tension drained out of her, but as she curled up and shut her eyes, she wondered how Evan could be so cold.

It occurred to her she really knew nothing about the billionaire who slept beside her. Last night she'd hoped she'd found the one man who could set her on fire, but now she feared their lovemaking was a fluke, and that by tomorrow night she'd be all alone again.

She settled down and closed her eyes, but it was a long time before she slept.

## Chapter Sixteen

WHAT A COMPLETE and colossal failure.

Evan watched Bella crawl from the tent the next morning, looking as beautiful as ever, if a little drawn and tired. She shot him a glance and made her way out of camp to take care of her morning rituals. Evan debated crawling right back inside that tent and making use of her absence to pound out a good one. He was hard as hell this morning, a fact he was trying desperately—and failing just as desperately—to hide in his usual pair of hiking pants.

Giving up, he made his own way out into the bush, crouched among a cover of bushes and went to town. He imagined Bella in every position he could want to have her—some probable, some as impossible as his current situation. Finally he came in a shuddering spasm, washed himself as best he could in the water from his drinking bottle, set things to rights and took the long way back to the camp.

Better.

Kind of.

Stopping mid-plunge last night was the hardest thing he'd ever done. Bella had been so close to coming, and he'd been right on her heels, but in a stupid attempt to leave her dazed and confused, and shake her confidence during the challenges to come today, he'd pulled out before the event's conclusion. She'd certainly been confused, and she'd waited for some time to see what he'd do next, but when he'd pretended to fall asleep, she'd simply pleasured herself—and seemed to have a lot of fun doing it—and settled down to sleep.

Why hadn't it occurred to him that she'd solve her problem all by herself, leaving him hanging—hard as a rock—through the rest of the night? Bella had gotten plenty of sleep, but he'd gotten practically none, and when he did doze off, he'd had x-rated dreams that woke him up again before he got any satisfaction in them, either.

He was a mess—physically, psychologically—but he was more determined than he'd ever been in his life. He planned to win this contest and marry Bella, and spend the next year screwing the daylights out of her.

Except he'd make it a little more romantic after the first fifty or so times.

He spotted her at the breakfast buffet, selecting a muffin, her beautiful, curly hair spilling out under her trademark cowboy hat. She smiled at the woman behind the table, made a comment that garnered an answering laugh, and moved away.

That was his Bella. Sweet, charming, bringing light wherever she went. He bet she knew the names of all the crew. He was sure they were all rooting for her to win this contest. Probably the audience would be, as well. She was the underdog, of course. The beautiful, broke veterinarian.

And he was the merciless capitalist pig.

He didn't care. He was going to be the merciless capitalist pig that won the show and took home a wife.

As MADELYN GATHERED them in for the final day of filming, Bella was disgusted to find herself close to tears. The more she thought about it, especially given his furtive looks her way this morning, the more she felt sure Evan had planned last night's shenanigans ahead of time. He'd deliberately taken her to the height of passion, and pulled away—literally—and left her hanging with all that pent-up desire.

And the only reason he would do such a thing was because he wanted to win this contest so badly he'd do anything—even something so treacherous.

He'd used her—manipulated her like she meant nothing to him, like all their talks were worthless, the secrets they'd shared just so much information he'd extorted out of her with his velvet interrogations. He didn't care for her at all. He probably wasn't even attracted to her. It sickened her that not only had she told him some of her darkest secrets, but that she'd shared her body with him—she'd made love to him.

Only someone truly despicable would seduce her in order to triumph over her. And only someone truly stupid would fall for his trick.

Why would a handsome, accomplished, fabulously wealthy man who could have any woman he chose want her, anyway? What did she have to offer him? A bunch of homeless, mangy animals? A provincial, small-town outlook on life? A wardrobe of jeans and cowboy hats?

She was such a fool.

She caught his eye and glanced away again quickly, feeling her cheeks heat and wishing she could crawl into the tent and hide. Damn him—he knew everything about her now. He knew about her past and her dreams.

He knew every inch of her body.

He knew how to make her thrum with desire.

He knew how to drive her wild.

And he knew how to plunge in the knife and twist it until he'd cut out her heart. She'd fallen for a man who didn't exist. All the time they'd spent together, the laughter they'd shared, the pain they'd endured side by side—the craziness of this whole adventure—none of it was real.

Damn it—how was she going to get through this day? She blinked back the tears that threatened to fall. Wouldn't Madelyn love that? She was sure even now a camera was focused on her face. She couldn't slip—couldn't show for an instant how she felt.

She glanced at Evan again, despite her best intentions. He was watching her and his eyes widened when they met her gaze.

Shit! She was about to lose it. Bella dropped to her knees, untied one lace and wiped her cheek against her knee as she re-tied it more tightly.

"Bella?" Evan said, moving closer. For God's sake, was he going to make this even harder? Surging to her feet again, she hurried away.

"I've got to go pee," she said to the crowd. "Sorry, Madelyn—be right back."

She dashed off before anyone could focus on her and reached the bush before Madelyn could answer. Looking over her shoulder to make sure Evan hadn't followed—or one of the cameramen—she scrubbed at her face with the tail of her shirt.

She couldn't fall apart now. Not now.

*Kittens—think of kittens. Kittens hungry, kittens thirsty, kittens needing shots and food and care and cages and buildings to house them. Kittens, kittens, kittens.*

Taking a deep breath, Bella fought for control. She had to win. She had to. She couldn't stand to lose now, knowing Evan had used her, touched her....

"Come on, Bella," Madelyn hollered.

"Coming!" She wiped her cheeks again and told herself to smarten up. She had one shot at changing her life today. One shot to get the resources to save every stray pet in Chance Creek. No time for whining or crying or wishing for something that didn't exist.

Evan Mortimer was a jerk—a cold, hard, capitalist who cared nothing for animals or people.

Evan Mortimer had to be stopped.

She was the one to do it.

HE'D MADE BELLA cry.

Evan marched along the path toward their first challenge numb with shame and remorse. She'd let no tears pass her lids while the cameras were on her, but he'd seen that swipe of cheek against knee when she tied her shoe, and caught a glimpse of her face as she'd raced off into the bush for her second bathroom break.

He'd made her cry. He'd befriended her, teased out all her secrets, enticed her into his bed, made love to her, and made her cry.

He felt like crying himself.

What the hell was wrong with him? When had he stepped over the line from human compassion and become as big a monster as his father was? Wasn't the sole purpose of his life to steer clear of following in his father's footsteps?

Maybe it was impossible to run a corporation like Mortimer Innovations without losing your humanity. Maybe making decisions that affected hundreds—if not thousands—of other lives twisted you into some unrecognizable shape.

He wanted to scream with frustration, or better yet—bash his head against a rock. He wasn't like his father—he didn't manipulate people into doing his dirty work. He didn't play psychological games. He didn't ferret out information and use it against his adversaries.

Oh, who was he kidding? Of course he did. And he'd done it again—to Bella.

He'd made her cry.

He'd used a highly intimate moment to humiliate her—and he knew exactly how that felt.

*Taylor Remington.*

Hell, the name still made his gut twist. He'd dated her for a few weeks, thinking like usual that maybe she was the one to get him over his aversion to relationships. She'd befriended him at one of the first big conventions he'd attended on behalf of Mortimer Innovations. Lost among a sea of people, he'd been more than grateful when she sat down beside him during a panel discussion and made small talk effortlessly as they waited for the session to begin. Later they went to lunch, and met again for dinner. He hadn't expected it to go any further, but dinner turned into drinks and somehow they ended up back in her room.

His brand of claustrophobia made relationships with women all but impossible. Not the act—no, that was possible in a wham, bam, thank-you-ma'am sort of way. But Taylor wanted to cuddle afterwards. She wanted to talk about the future. She admitted she'd been looking for him since she arrived at the conference, eager to see for herself the handsome heir to billions.

The familiar tightening of the muscles around his neck and shoulders had warned him an attack was coming on. As she outlined her plans for them, including her intention to meet his parents when she moved to San Jose the following month, Evan panicked. He leaped out of bed and kept on running.

The next day he tracked down her number and apologized, but it was too late. Taylor went on a one-woman warpath, spreading lies about him to everyone who would listen.

His lack of sexual know-how.

The unimpressive size of his manhood.

His impotence.

He still burned with embarrassment when he thought about it. His father's money paid for a counter-campaign that erased her tweets, blogs, and forum posts when possible, or buried them with favorable replies. Suddenly he gained quite a reputation in the industry as a player and a stud.

But his father never let him forget it.

He believed the lies. He believed in Evan's inadequacy.

Why wouldn't he? Evan never brought home another girlfriend in the years before his father's death. Instead he lived with his dad's none-too-subtle gibes and kept away from women—far away—while the humiliation spurred him on to succeed in every other realm in his life.

He wanted to turn around and apologize to Bella, but he wouldn't do that to her on camera. He could tell she was barely holding it together—she refused to meet his gaze, or anyone else's, her expression stony, eyes on the ground. What should he do? Win the remaining contests and spend the next year making up for his crappy trick? He could buy her ten animal shelters, save every pet in Chance Creek, expand her services, hire her employees—whatever it took.

Or should he throw the challenges and lose gracefully so she could do all of that for herself?

Without him screwing up her life.

They burst into a clearing and Evan stumbled to a

stop, his jaw dropping open at the sight before him. A horse stood tied to a post at one end of a fenced-in field. Saddle and tack lay in a heap on the ground near it. A large sign detailed the proper procedure for saddling it, each step laid out complete with illustrations. A course of obstacles filled the rest of the fenced-in space.

Evan began to laugh. He shouldn't have worried at all about whether or not to throw this contest. He couldn't compete on horseback against a cowgirl who'd been riding all her life.

He had his answer—the universe had issued it loud and clear. Evan was going to lose by a mile. Bella would win, take the money, and leave his life forever.

## Chapter Seventeen

BELLA FOUGHT THE URGE to throw up. She knew her face was pale and waxy, and if anyone had touched her brow they'd find it damp with sweat.

A horse.

Damn it—that was a horse. Madelyn couldn't expect her to go anywhere near it.

Could she?

She could, if her eyes weren't deceiving her. The challenge was all too clear: saddle the horse, and ride a circuit of the course, guiding it over five obstacles. Bella's experienced eye told her none of the obstacles were difficult for an experienced rider. She wasn't an experienced rider, though. Not lately, anyway. She was probably the only woman her age in Chance Creek who hadn't been on a horse for twenty years.

And there was no way in hell she'd get close enough to one to saddle it, let alone climb on top of it.

Evan was laughing. Probably just another trick of his to throw her off. He called out, "Guess you'll take this one," over his shoulder as he stalked off toward the horse. He stood in front of the sign and read the steps one by one, and it wasn't until he moved to sort out the pile of tack that he looked back and noticed she hadn't budged. "Sorry, this might take a while, but I'll figure it out in the end. I may be beat, but I'm going to give it my best shot."

Terrific. She hoped he did figure it out, rode the course and got out of here. Hell, why was she even standing around here waiting for him? She hadn't been able to ride a horse in years; there was no way she could do it now.

She wouldn't score a point in this challenge, so she might as well head right on to the next one.

She walked forward, straight past Evan and around the corral, heading in the direction she hoped led to the next section of trail. Her vision blurred from tears and she picked up her pace. She was done for now. No way to win if she skipped a challenge entirely. Paul and Nita followed her, muttering to each other in confusion. If they moved in front of her they'd see she was one second from falling apart. She was so close to having enough money to finally right all her wrongs and now fate dished out this. She should have known better than to think she could win.

Memories beset her, flashing images of the day she'd ruined her family's lives.

*Caramel racing after the ball and bringing it back to drop at her feet.*

*Hugging the dog and burying her face in her fur.*

*The commotion behind her, Caramel's sudden barks.*

*Looking up. Seeing the hooves flailing above her.*

*Her father's shout: "Bella!"*

*His body flashing between them. The stallion twisting away in fear.*

*Hooves flashing, the horse's giant body falling. The sickening crack as its foreleg shattered.*

*Her own fear bitter in her mouth. Caramel twisting around their feet.*

*Her father's hand upraised.*

She blinked faster and picked up her pace some more, trying to leave those memories behind.

"Bella?"

Damn. She broke into a run, unable to control her tears any longer, the pain of her memories finally catching up to her. She'd vanquished that awful day from her mind for so many years, refusing to speak of it because nobody else in her family spoke of it.

"Bella, stop—where are you going?"

Bella ignored Nita's call and dashed onward, unaware of her surroundings. She was back on the family's ranch, back in the chaos of men running, the stallion falling, Caramel barking, her father watching his dream implode.

This time the voice was Evan's. "Bella." He caught up to her and pulled her to a stop. "What are you doing? Come back—ride the horse. It's okay—you're going to win fair and square, I can't complain. Bella?" Lifting a hand to trace the tears running down her face, his expression changed from laughter to concern. "What's wrong?"

"I can't…" She couldn't breathe for tears, couldn't

dispel the images from her mind. The dust kicked up by the horse's hooves, Cyclone's scream as his foreleg shattered.

Her father's face.

"I can't ride…I can't…"

And her brother wild with grief when he found her in the barn that night.

*It's all your fault*, he said. *Caramel's dead. Cyclone's dead. It's all your fault.*

"I can't…" Bella sobbed, her breath coming in great gasps. She clung to Evan, felt his arms go around her.

She couldn't save Caramel. She'd run and run but she'd been too late. She couldn't save Cyclone; his broken leg was his death warrant, and the destruction of her father's business. She couldn't save herself, either. She'd as good as died that same day, at least in her father's eyes. He'd never seen her again; she'd simply disappeared. No matter what she did, she couldn't fix it.

And she'd spent a lifetime trying to fix it. She'd spent a lifetime trying to save something—anything—to make up for what she'd done. But no matter how hard she worked, no matter how much she learned, no matter how much she *earned*—she couldn't bring Cyclone back to life. And everywhere she looked there were more animals—more suffering—more sickness—more neglect—animals abandoned, hiding, starving—animals *dying*…and she couldn't save them, she couldn't…

"Come on, Bella, you have to ride. You're going to lose if you don't."

Lose.

She was going to lose everything. Just like her father did.

Another image flashed before her eyes. *Her father dashing between her and the stallion, protecting her from his wheeling hooves. Cyclone crashing to the ground, the sound of his foreleg shattering.*

*Her father's dreams shattering.*

*Her father's face as he watched everything he'd worked for slip away.*

*Raising his arm.*

*Bringing it down on Caramel's back.*

Her father hit Caramel. Caramel ran into the street.

Bella staggered, blindsided by the realization. All this time she'd blamed herself for Caramel's death, because her father had blamed her. He barely talked to her since that day. Barely looked at her. Kept her awash in guilt and pain.

And it was all his fault. All his fault. Not hers. But he'd blamed her all this time.

Evan leaned in closer and dropped his voice. "Sweetie, it's going to be okay no matter what. Even if you lose I'll take care of you, I swear."

Bella's gaze snapped up to him. Her adversary. The man standing between her and the means to fix everything. Did he think she would fall for his scheme? Did he think he could manipulate her feelings and ruin her life, just like her father had? Were all men like this?

"You're the one making me lose," she said and shoved him. He stepped back, but recovered quickly and came at her again.

"What? Bella…"

"You tricked me! You've been tricking me all along!" Anger, thick and hot swirled up within her. It filled her until there was no room for sadness. No room for fear. If it wasn't for her father's manipulations she would have gotten over Caramel's death and gone on to live a normal life. If it wasn't for Evan's sweet-talk, his kisses and caresses and pretense that he cared for her, she'd have won this contest long ago.

"Bella, listen to me…" He gripped her arm.

"No! It's your fault! It's all your fault!" He'd slept with her for heaven's sake. Slept with her, and pulled out—just so he could win.

"Honey, it's not like that." He lifted a hand to touch her face and she stiffened with rage. He was calling her pet names? Now? Her clinic, her shelter, her chance to buy back her father's land was all slipping through her fingers and he was pretending he still cared?

Rage boiled up within her, choking her throat, burning her lungs, setting her aflame.

She struck him with every ounce of her strength.

The slap of her palm against the flesh of his cheek brought the set to a standstill.

Evan lurched backward, stumbled, caught himself. "Shit." He held a palm to his cheek.

Bella couldn't move. Stunned, she went cold, then hot, then began to tremble all over. What had she done?

"You hit me."

She'd hit him. She, who'd never hit anyone in her life, had slapped the man she loved.

She gazed at Evan, still rubbing his jaw, and knew it was true; she did love him. She'd fallen hard for the man in a record short time and now she'd ruined any chance she'd ever had to be with him.

Closing her eyes she bowed her head, wishing the ground would open and swallow her whole. Shame overwhelmed her. What kind of woman was she?

Her father's daughter.

Rocked by the realization, she put out a hand to steady herself, found nothing there. She'd lashed out just as he had—out of fury, out of frustration.

Out of fear.

In a flash she saw that day through her father's eyes. He was out of money, close to losing his business, losing his legacy. The horse's death was the final straw. Evan was right; the stallion should have been insured. But her father must not have insured him. In an instant it was all gone; the stallion's leg shattered, the chance to earn back his money vaporized, the chance to save his land lost for good.

Overwhelmed by his anger, he'd hit their pet, and Caramel—never treated like that before—had raced away to her death.

Evan turned back to face her and Bella ducked her head again, unwilling to meet his eye, not wanting to see the blame there.

*Just like her father.* He never looked her in the eye again after Caramel's death.

Now she knew why.

Not because he blamed her, but because he knew it

was his fault. Everything was his fault.

He'd blamed himself.

Speechless with understanding, she forced herself to raise her head. She didn't want to look at Evan—didn't want to see the blame in his eyes—but she had to. This was where her father stumbled. He could have apologized. He could have admitted his guilt and allowed her to forgive him, but he'd been so afraid that she wouldn't he never even gave her the chance.

She lifted her gaze to meet Evan's. "I'm sorry." The words were barely a whisper. "Shit. Evan, I'm sorry."

Evan made a kind of choking sound and she stiffened, afraid she'd done more damage than she first thought. No wonder her father hadn't been able to face her like this. Fear clogged her throat and twisted her guts—the fear that he'd never forgive her.

"I'm so sorry," she said again, her eyes filling with tears for what she could have had with Evan. A relationship. A marriage.

A life together.

Evan's shoulders heaved and he covered his face with his arm.

*Oh my God!* He was crying! Bella reached toward him. Stopped. Pulled her hand back.

"Evan? Are you okay?"

His shoulders shook. Around them, the crew shifted uncomfortably. Paul switched his camera off. "I can't film this, man. This isn't right."

"Dude, pull it together," Chris said.

"Evan…?" Bella touched him uncertainly.

He dropped his arm and Bella flinched back.

He wasn't crying.

He was laughing.

"You should have seen your face!" he said. "Oh, my God. Did you really think you hurt me?"

"I...I..."

"Bella. Sweetie." He swiped his arm across his cheeks and pulled her into an embrace. "Honey, I hate to tell you this." He kissed her hard on the mouth. "You hit like a girl."

EVAN COULD HARDLY breathe for fear this moment would end. He sat on one of the catering crew's ice chests, his arm around Bella who was snuggled up against him. Fifteen minutes after the slap heard round the world, as the film crew had already dubbed the incident, and she was still shaking. He wondered if she'd ever forgive herself for losing control. He'd forgiven her the moment her hand hit his jaw.

He'd deserved it for one thing. He kept treating her as if she was inferior to him. He acted like her worries were nothing to his, and that if she'd just let him take care of everything—and win—he'd sort out her little problems in no time flat.

What an idiot.

The camera crew was getting antsy, but he'd demanded they give Bella a cup of coffee and a donut before they went on with the challenge. He still didn't understand why she couldn't ride, but it was obvious she was terrified to try.

He wondered if Madelyn knew that when she planned this challenge.

Probably.

One part of him wanted to pretend he was terrified, too. Maybe they could both just skip it—get zero points like they had at the bridges yesterday—but when he mentioned the idea to Bella, she just shook her head no.

"All right, campers, what's the holdup?"

Evan winced as Madelyn's grating voice cut through clearing like a buzz saw.

"Who's up first?" the director demanded. "What's with all the cuddling?"

"I'm first," Evan said quickly. He wanted to give Bella some time to pull herself together. He got to his feet and paced to meet Madelyn, already missing the feel of Bella under his arm. He couldn't wait until the show was over and they could be together without the constant scrutiny.

"Take your place. We're well behind schedule. You have twenty minutes to complete the course," Madelyn said. "Ready. Set. Go."

Evan strode to the board that showed step by step how to saddle and prepare his horse to ride. He'd thought perhaps the show would have supplied a skittish steed that refused to stand still for the process, but Buttercup, as a crew member told him his mare was named, stood placidly while he yanked and tugged the saddle into place and fiddled with the reins. He relaxed a little. Even Bella shouldn't feel frightened of this gentle mare.

He felt an inordinate pride when he got everything situated and tightened all the straps. He'd never even attempted to ride a horse before, let alone handle its gear. He placed a foot in one stirrup, reached up for a handhold on the pommel and pulled himself into place, if not gracefully, at least successfully.

A look told him Bella watched him with her full attention. She bit her lower lip, her body completely rigid.

Again he wondered if he should try to lose.

No. The only thing to do was play this fair and square. Despite what Bella was going through, he wanted a year with her and he wanted to retain control of Mortimer Innovations. He'd help save those animals of hers and help set her up with a new clinic in San Jose if she wanted one. He'd spend the next twelve months showing her just how much good a few billion dollars could do in the world. Together they could be a force for change—both for humans and animals. Uplifted by that idea, he urged Buttercup forward into an easy walk.

The horse approached each obstacle as if she'd been trained for weeks on the course, and Evan pushed aside the uncomfortable thought that maybe she had. The mare traversed a small wooden bridge, wove through a maze of waist-high hurdles, stepped delicately through a jumble of broken logs and rocks, navigated into and out of a man-made ditch, and finally executed a small jump with Evan clinging to her back for dear life. He knew he wouldn't win any prizes for the elegance of his horsemanship, but he had made it through unscathed.

"Five points!" Madelyn called out. "A perfect score!"

Damn, couldn't she even pretend she wasn't playing favorites? Evan felt a blush creep up his neck as the camera crew shot looks at each other. Suddenly his elation at his accomplishment blew away like a morning fog before a noonday sun. Madelyn had made it easy on him. So how did she plan to make things difficult for Bella?

BELLA KNEW THAT she should be able to saddle and ride a horse like Buttercup with her hands tied behind her back, even if she hadn't ridden since she was ten. That didn't stop her stomach from twisting into knots as she stood up to take her turn. Nor did it stop her hands from becoming slick with sweat as she walked toward Madelyn and the tack area.

"Give Buttercup a good rubdown," Madelyn was saying to a crew member as she approached.

Rubdown? Why? Wasn't she going to get her turn at the course?

Bella watched as Buttercup was led away and spotted another horse being led forward. A much bigger horse.

A stallion.

Her fingers clenched into clammy fists.

Madelyn knew. Somehow she knew.

The director smiled. "Thunder's got some spirit to him—just right for an accomplished cowgirl like you, right Bella?

"That's not fair," Bella said.

"What's that? You want to forfeit this contest?" Madelyn said, her grin growing wider. "You want to become Mrs. Mortimer right now? I'm sure I can find someone to perform the ceremony. Ellis? Get me a minister on the line!"

Bella's eyes widened. "You should want me to win. Your audience loves it when the poor person wins!"

Madelyn just shrugged. "What's it going to be, cowgirl? You going to ride that horse or throw in the towel right now?"

Bella looked at Thunder, sidestepping and tossing his head as he was led to the start of the course, then back at Madelyn. She felt hollow, scoured and twisted by her fear. She wasn't sure she could even walk the twenty steps over to the horse, let alone get on him. But she had to, didn't she? She had to face this fear once and for all.

"I'll ride," she said.

Madelyn shook her head at her. "You don't know when to give in, do you?"

Stung, Bella wheeled away and walked a few paces off, trying to get a hold of her emotions. No, she didn't know when to give in. Otherwise, she wouldn't be in the financial mess she was today, she wouldn't be the self-proclaimed savior of all the pets in Chance Creek, and she wouldn't be on this stupid television show falling apart before the whole world.

"Bella, you don't have to do this," Evan said, approaching her again.

That was the last thing she needed; Evan nearby, all sympathy and open arms. She had to be strong. Had to keep her emotions in check. She searched for a reason to be angry and found it. Evan wanted her to give in. He wanted her to lose. He wanted his fake little wife, and the show was going to hand her to him. Damn it, she couldn't let that happen.

"Back off, Moneybuns," she snapped, brushing past him. "I'm ready," she called out. The crew member soothing Thunder and keeping him in place undid his lead and backed away. The horse stood by the tack area, but snorted uneasily. Madelyn had really picked a winner here, hadn't she? Bella thought angrily as her hands began to shake again. A real fireball, ready to throw her like she'd always feared.

But as Bella approached, Thunder quieted, and for all his initial jitteriness, she sensed a dignity about him. No doubt Madelyn had made sure to ruffle his feathers, but he wasn't a flighty horse.

Stepping toward him slowly, inch by agonizing inch, a song crept into her mind—one her mother used to sing to her when she was small and afraid of the dark. She found herself crooning it to Thunder, the way her mother had sung to her, back when her life was good.

Her voice was low and thin at first, just as shaky as her fingers, but she found it calmed her to be doing something—anything—amid this tense situation. She moved forward slowly, slowly, still crooning. Thunder settled even more and she stood still to let him catch her scent. She waited for him to bridge the last gap between them, her whole body quaking with fear, and after a long moment he did take a step. He breathed in her smell and nudged her shoulder with his nose.

His action brought tears to her eyes. The movement

was so gentle.

So human.

She took a deep breath and forced herself to move again, bending to pick up the heavy saddle. It wasn't easy to get it onto his tall back, and her fingers fumbled and slipped as she went through the process of tightening the straps. Once or twice she actually had to consult the directions the show had provided for them to make sure her memory hadn't failed her utterly.

"Ten minutes left," Madelyn sang out as she finished getting Thunder ready.

The knots in Bella's stomach tightened some more as she stepped back and looked the stallion over. So he had consented to let her saddle him. That didn't mean he'd be easy to ride. She'd overcome her fear enough to stand next to Thunder and work with him, but could she possibly ride him? Nausea rippled through her stomach as she thought of the last time she stood so close to a horse.

*The wheeling hoofs.*

*The crack of shattered bone.*

Afraid she really was going to lose the contents of her stomach, Bella turned away from him, a hand to her mouth. She couldn't do this. She just couldn't do this.

But when she glanced behind her and caught sight of Evan's knitted brow and Madelyn's triumphant smile, her resolve tightened.

She would do this.

Even if it killed her.

EVAN WATCHED BELLA PULL herself into the saddle and brace herself there on top of Thunder, as if the horse meant to pitch her off at any moment. The stallion sidestepped, but then held steady, and after a long minute, Bella's shoulders eased a fraction, and he let out the breath he'd been holding. She was going to be okay.

His confidence was premature, however. Only a few steps into the course it became clear that Thunder had sensed Bella's fear and was reacting to it. The horse danced nervously as he approached the first obstacle— an arched wooden bridge that should pose no problem.

Just as Thunder stepped forward onto the wooden rise, however, Bella gasped at his unsteady gait and the horse shied away, turning around back toward the start of the course.

"No points!" Madelyn called out. "Next obstacle."

"Wait a minute," Evan said, striding to her side. "She can try it again."

"Thunder's hoof touched the bridge; Bella gets one shot at each obstacle, just like you," Madelyn retorted. "Next obstacle."

He could see the set of Bella's jaw, but she didn't contradict the director. Instead, she urged Thunder back around, past the bridge to the maze of hurdles.

*Come on, Bella, just keep calm,* Evan found himself thinking at her. He still wanted her to lose, of course, but he wanted her not to lose too badly.

He didn't want her to feel afraid.

Easing Thunder into the close and twisting trail through the maze, Bella looked like she'd taken control, until Thunder got too close to one of the rails. She jerked on the stallion's reins and the beast shied away from the next turn. Bella scrambled to guide him in the right direction, but it was too late. He bumped one hurdle, panicked, and crashed right through another one. Bella gave Thunder his head and allowed him to dance around the packed earth ground of the course for a few seconds before reining him in and setting off determinedly for the third obstacle.

Evan closed his eyes. He couldn't watch anymore.

HER DREAMS WERE slipping right out of her fingers. If she couldn't get herself under control she was going to lose this contest right now. She couldn't blame Thunder, either; it was all her fault. The poor horse was doing his best, but she kept scaring him when he hadn't done anything to deserve it. She was sick with fear, sick at the memories that kept flooding back the longer she rode him.

So many years her family had wasted. So many years she'd felt hurt, alone and guilty.

"Ten minutes," Madelyn called out.

A pain so raw it made her bite her lip welled up inside her as she realized they were all in the same boat. Each and every member of her family still torn apart from that one awful day. Her father had waited for twenty years for her to forgive him; just as long as she'd waited to receive forgiveness from him.

A ragged sigh escaped her lips. No matter whose fault it all was, the time had come to end all of this sorrow and pain. It was time to win this show and buy back the land.

Time to put her family back together again. This was something she could fix, if she could just ride this horse.

Taking a deep breath she began to croon to Thunder again. She had no reason to fear him. The horse had no malice towards her—he was just confused by her fear, and starting to be afraid of what she'd do next. She had to convince him that she had confidence in him and that she wouldn't upset him again.

"You're a big, strong horse, aren't you, Thunder?" she murmured. "And you're a smart horse, too. You can do this course."

Thunder shifted beneath her and shook his mane.

"I trust you," she whispered. "I trust you to do your best, and that's all any of us can do."

She'd done her best since the day her family fell apart, hadn't she? Studying hard, building her practice, opening a shelter that took care of hundreds of unwanted animals... She'd done everything she could. Her father had done his best as well, saving what he could of the ranch. Even her mother had done her best, torn between them.

Some of the tension went out of her shoulders. She really had done everything she could, and if she failed, if she had to give up her practice, she wouldn't stop trying, either. She'd work to help animals for the rest of her life. Could she help her parents? She didn't know, but she'd try. She could reconnect with her mother. She could forgive her father. She could speak of the past with her brother. She could find a therapist and get help for herself.

Her gaze shifted to Evan and he nodded back at her. He wasn't a bad man either, was he?

Too bad they couldn't both win.

She returned her focus to the course ahead and guided Thunder toward the third obstacle, the random jumble of logs and stones. With Bella breathing deeply and remaining calm, Thunder stepped through the course with ease.

"One point," Madelyn said. She sounded disappointed.

Bella grasped the reins with more confidence now and urged the stallion toward the man-made ditch. She didn't like the look of it, but she let her resistance go and trusted Thunder to get her safely through. In a flash they were down and up out of the obstacle again. Bella smiled. They'd done it!

"Two points."

Only one obstacle ahead, a jump so tiny it barely deserved the name. She'd done jumps like this as a child, before she'd become afraid of horses. Still her heart beat hard in her chest as Thunder wheeled around to face it. As he started to pace toward it, building speed into a trot, Bella tightened her grip and fought for the same faith she'd shown during the last obstacle.

She had just managed to let go of her fear and put her trust in Thunder when a sound like a shot rang out through the air. Startled, Bella shrieked, and Thunder's pace hitched beneath her. He stumbled, recovered, jerked right.

Reared up in terror.

HELPLESS.

He was absolutely helpless to stop the disaster unfolding before his eyes. Why hadn't he stopped Bella from getting on that stallion? Why had he even played this stupid game? Because he didn't know how to love someone enough to find a wife the normal way?

Because he'd been too scared to love a woman?

Well, now he loved a woman. And as he watched that woman cling desperately to the rearing stallion, he knew he was going to lose his chance for a real marriage. A good marriage.

His chance for any happiness at all.

What was money, success, winning—*control*—compared to the love of the woman who was just about to fall and be trampled to death while he watched? Why hadn't he told her he'd save her animals if he won?

Why hadn't he lost and let her go?

He would never forgive himself if Bella died for his stupidity. Never forgive himself if he lost the woman he loved just as he found himself capable of loving at all.

"Bella!"

## Chapter Eighteen

S HE WAS TEN AGAIN, standing outside a corral, her mother pleading with her to just touch the mare. Just give her a pat.

"Sylvie!" Her father's voice boomed from across the yard. "Sylvie, what are you doing?"

"She's got to ride again, Walter. Otherwise she'll always be scared."

"Get her away from there! She's got no business around horses. Bella, get into the house!"

Shame suffused her at the anger in his tone.

"Walter!"

"I can't afford to lose her, don't you understand that? She's the only one I've got."

Something clicked in her mind. Bella opened her eyes. *I can't afford to lose her. She's the only one I've got.*

He hadn't meant the mare. He had plenty of mares. He'd meant his daughter.

He'd meant her.

Thud!

The jolt of Thunder's landing threw her forward and

Bella grabbed for his mane instinctively, opening her eyes to find the ground solidly beneath his feet. He shuffled to one side, still anxious, but as she held her breath he calmed down and came to a halt.

She'd stayed on the horse. She was alive. And she was loved, too. Her father loved her.

"Bella!"

She looked back and saw Evan reach the fence, throw himself up to grab the top rung and scramble to climb over into the corral.

Thunder shook his mane and ducked his head. She'd swear he was embarrassed by his bad behavior. Dazed, Bella slid off his back, nearly falling to her knees when her feet touched the ground.

Thunder whickered behind her. Pushed her with his large muzzle, once, twice.

*He's sorry*, she realized. *He's apologizing.*

"It's not your fault," she whispered to him. She caught his head in her hands and stroked his neck. "Someone scared you." Fear made people and animals do all kinds of awful things.

Evan and the rest of the crew raced up to mob her, their cries ringing in her ears.

"Bella! God, I thought I'd lost you!" Evan swung her into his arms, gripping her like he'd never let go.

"I wasn't sure I'd make it," she said, her voice unsteady. "I thought…"

"I know. Shh." He pulled her even closer, and kissed her forehead.

"All right, all right, enough of that," Madelyn said,

elbowing her way through the crowd that had gathered around them.

Evan let go of Bella and swung around to face her. "I can't believe you did that! You could have killed her!"

"What I did?" Madelyn faced him down. "I didn't do anything. One of the caterers tipped over a cart of trays carrying the crew members' lunch. Purely accidental."

Evan opened his mouth. Closed it.

Bella shut her eyes, wanting nothing more than this contest to be over. She wanted to go home. She wanted to see her family. "We have one more challenge, right? Let's just finish this."

Evan let out a breath. "Fine. An accident. But no more games. No more hiking, either. You drive us to wherever it is we're going. You got that? And feed us a decent lunch first."

"Okay," Madelyn drew out the word to make it clear she thought he was over-dramatizing the whole affair, and flounced away, shouting orders at the crew. Soon Bella was seated in a folding chair, a tin of lasagna perched on her lap and a sugary soda in her hand.

"For the shock," Ellis said when she initially demurred. "It'll help. Trust me."

"Are you okay?" Evan asked, taking a bite of his lunch. His gaze never left her, and she remembered the way he'd pulled her into his arms. How tightly he'd held her.

Evan cared for her, she realized. Really cared. She thought back to his earlier words; that he didn't want just any wife, he wanted her. This wasn't just about winning anymore for him. This was about winning her.

Did he really think the only way to get to know her was to win her hand in marriage for a year? Was he that insecure?

She peered at him from under her lashes. He was handsome, wealthy, powerful. She'd assumed he was egotistical, predatory and ruthless, too, but he wasn't, was he? He kept helping her whenever she had trouble. Although the trick he pulled last night was pretty predatory.

*The trick he pulled to try to win another three hundred and sixty-five nights with me.*

"I think so," she said. And for the first time in years, she thought it just might be true.


"OUR TWO CONTESTANTS are tied at 32 points apiece," Jake Cramer said in his oily television announcer voice. "After a thrilling morning, the entire contest comes down to this final challenge. Bella, Evan, whoever comes out the victor will win the entire show!"

"Can't wait," Evan said unenthusiastically.

"Whoo," Bella said.

Evan expected Madelyn to yell, "Cut!" and take all of them to task for their poor showing, but she just nodded.

"Get on with it."

"Your final challenge is a simple treasure hunt," Jake said. "Behind me you'll see some thick woods, the perfect hiding place for wild animals. And wild animals are what you'll need to find—stuffed wild animals, of course." He handed them each a stack of laminated cards showing photos of various animals that apparently might inhabit a northern forest—cougars, moose, brown bears, grizzly bears, and foxes. "Each of you will conduct your search in a fenced off patch of forest. You have twenty minutes to find your animals and carry them to the finish line, marked an equal distance from your hunting grounds. The first to reach the finish line with all ten animals wins!"

Twenty minutes and this would all be over. Bella would either be his to wed or his to woo. Either way, he knew he would build his life around her. He hoped she knew it, too.

As he followed a crew member to his starting position, he looked over to where Bella walked toward hers.

"Bella—even if you lose, you'll win. I promise!" he called out.

Jerking toward him, Bella shot him a look he couldn't decipher, and Evan knew with a jolt of fear she'd misinterpreted what he'd said.

"I mean…" he tried again, but Madelyn stepped in front of him.

"You aren't trying to rig this contest, are you, Mr. Mortimer? Because the contract you signed has some things to say about that."

Thwarted, Evan let the words he longed to say to Bella remain unspoken. He'd made himself clear earlier, hadn't he? She must know he meant to help her no matter what happened. "No, I'm not," he said to Madelyn.

"Good. Get ready." She nodded to Jake Cramer.

"Twenty minutes from now, we'll know who is going to win *Can You Beat a Billionaire*. Bella, will you take home five million dollars and save your veterinary practice and animal shelter? Or Evan, will you take home a new, blushing bride?"

Evan flashed a last look over at Bella, and took in her determined expression. She meant to win the contest. She'd take the money and she'd leave this nightmare behind. Would she associate him with the whole debacle? Would she even want to see him again afterward?

No.

Probably not. He'd hit on her, slept with her while cameras were rolling, left her in the lurch just when she opened up to him, and kept putting his own needs ahead of hers. The only shot he had was to win fair and square and afterwards open a chain of clinics and animal shelters to make up for it.

He braced himself, his laminated cards in his hand, ready to run for it the moment Jake gave the signal.

"Ready?" Jake said. "Set. Go!"

So she'd win even if she lost, would she? That was all fine and dandy because she didn't plan to lose no matter how much she liked the man. No matter how much she lusted after him. It might be nice to be Mrs. Evan Mortimer, but not like that.

In fact, she felt grateful for his poor choice of words because it yanked her right back to the present moment and the goal she'd come on this show to achieve. As much as she wanted to be with Evan, as much as she hoped they would find a way to be together after the show, no way in hell would she throw the contest. She didn't want to be a billionaire's wife.

She wanted to be a millionaire.

She couldn't save every animal, she knew that now, and she no longer wished to drive herself insane trying. Instead, she planned to make good decisions and ask for help. She would start by building a better animal shelter. Perhaps she'd extend her care to larger animals, too. And she knew the perfect person to help run a ranch for old or injured horses. Someone who'd wanted to expand his spread back to its original size for a long, long time.

Besides, if she and Evan were to have a future, it had to be as equals; two adults coming to a relationship because they both wanted to be there. No games. Neither of them holding power over the other. Five days wasn't enough to prepare for a life together, and when she got married she wanted it to be for good.

She tensed, waiting for Jake's signal, and when it came, she raced into her hunting grounds and got to work searching for animals.

She found the grizzly bear right away, tucked behind a cedar. A few minutes later, she located the moose in a clump of bushes. The rest of the animals remained hidden, however, and as the seconds ticked by, she began to panic a little.

She decided she needed a more methodical approach. Quickly moving to one end of the enclosed square, she began walking swiftly back and forth across it, covering every inch of ground. She found the black bear several minutes later, but it wasn't until she'd nearly searched the whole space that the fox turned up.

That left the cougar. She didn't have a watch, but she knew her twenty minutes must be nearly up. As tension tightened her shoulders, she returned to the search, quickly covering the rest of the ground. She couldn't find the last stuffed animal. Her panic surging, she moved to cover the ground a second time, knowing she couldn't possibly search it all again in the allotted time.

Damn it, where was that animal?

Desperately raising her eyes to the heavens in a plea for help, she spotted the answer.

The cougar rested in a notch of a pine tree.

Fifteen feet off the ground.

Bella began to laugh. Not the hysterical kind of laughter that quickly turned to desperate sobs. No, this was laughter, pure and simple.

Madelyn might know her well enough to realize stallions scared her to death, but the director hadn't done her homework as thoroughly as she thought.

She obviously had no idea how many kittens Bella had rescued from trees.

FOR ONCE EVAN had to concede that maybe the game wasn't stacked in his favor, because he was having a hell of a time finding those damn animals.

Or maybe it felt like it was taking forever because the end to this whole darn show was so close.

Every time his mind wandered he saw Bella in a

fairy-tale wedding dress, saw himself putting a ring on her finger.

Then pictured the two of them going to bed to celebrate their wedding night.

Pushing that highly distracting thought from his mind, he concentrated again on finding his remaining two animals. He had the cougar, the black bear and the fox, but the moose and the grizzly remained hidden somewhere in this tangled mess.

It wasn't until he decided to climb a tree and look down at the forest floor from above that he spotted the moose set high in the crotch of a cedar. Scrambling up to get it, he quickly noticed the dark lump in another tree that heralded the grizzly.

Mentally kicking himself for not thinking to look up sooner, he retrieved both animals and made a dash for the enclosure entrance. He bolted through it, head down, ready to make the final run for the finish line, when something crashed into him and spun away.

Bella!

He took in the scene in an instant; Bella's arms full of stuffed animals, Jake standing far off just visible at the finish line, Madelyn and Ellis arguing off to one side, the path they had to race along the dirt bank of a swift-running stream. He had no doubt it all made for great television. Tangled forest behind them, rushing water beside them. Ahead of them, sunshine and the finish line.

Bella glanced back at him and ran faster. Evan raced after her, determined to win.

Their pounding course brought them alongside the river, and he had a crazy, half-hysterical thought that maybe she'd push him in. The water wasn't wide, but the current looked powerful. Better keep his footing, and keep an eye on Bella.

Bella who was ten feet in front of him.

Bella who was going to win if he didn't get a move on.

Evan redoubled his efforts and in a second his longer legs brought him even with her. Another few steps and he took the lead.

"Damn it!" she swore and the pounding of her footsteps behind him told him she was doing her best to catch up again.

But just as he put on a burst of speed, he heard Madelyn shout as she grabbed something from Ellis and hurled it into the middle of the path.

BELLA RACED AFTER EVAN, her lungs bursting, her chest heaving for all she was worth to get more air. He was pulling ahead, edging forward, stretching the boundary between her and victory until it pulled taut.

Digging deep inside herself for her last shred of strength, she lowered her head and charged. Beside them roared a narrow torrent of water, and ahead lay Jake Cramer and victory.

Just as she threw herself into a flat-out run, moving faster than she'd ever dreamed she could, Madelyn grabbed a small, dark shape from Ellis's arms and shouted something:

*Police the creatures?*

*Excuse the killers?*

The raging torrent beside her made it too hard to hear. She didn't slow for an instant, however, not until a fluffy ball of fur landed in the dirt in front of them, streaked out across the track, and Evan stumbled, nearly hurtling himself to the ground.

Bella raced forward, unwilling to give her opponent an inch no matter what the circumstances. She was drawing even. She was pulling ahead!

Madelyn's words filtered through her subconscious:

*RELEASE THE KITTEN!*

The kitten who even now streaked toward the raging stream beside her. The kitten who was about to plunge over the bank to a watery death.

Save the kitten, or win five million dollars?

She dove for the black ball of fur even as the thought crossed her mind.

*What the hell?*

A kitten—a black ball of fluff no bigger than his hand—made a beeline across his path toward the foaming torrent beside them, and in an instant Evan knew exactly what would happen next.

Bella would dive for the kitten and save it. He would cross the finish line and win the show. He would have her hand in marriage for one year.

And for three hundred and sixty-five days Bella would hate his guts because once again his priorities betrayed his selfishness.

He didn't stop to think what he might be giving up. For the first time in his life, he thought only of someone else. Diving for the kitten, he scooped it up before Bella could even reach it, and in a feat worthy of a pro-sports greatest hits reel he scooped up Bella in his other hand and hurled her toward the finish line.

She landed with a thud in front of Jake Cramer, flinging her arms out to stop herself from rolling into him.

"We have a winner!" Jake crowed and reached down to haul Bella to her feet.

Evan sat in the dirt, raised the kitten to his face, and stroked his cheek against its soft fur.

The kitten licked his nose.

## Chapter Nineteen

"SERIOUSLY? YOU'RE still living in your trailer?" Rose Bellingham asked, leaning against the reception counter of the Chance Creek Pet Clinic.

"It's going to take a week or two until the money's deposited in my account, and I still have to figure out what to spend it on," Bella said. She could have answered the question in her sleep; the jewelry store salesclerk was the fifteenth person to stop by this morning to question her housing arrangements. At least the flow was down from yesterday, her first day back at work. She'd thought all of Chance Creek planned to come by and ogle the town's newest millionaire.

"So what was he like?"

"Who?" As if she didn't know.

"The billionaire! Was he an old geezer on the make?"

"No." Bella blushed, realizing what her vehemence betrayed. "No," she repeated softly. "He was actually pretty nice."

Rose exchanged a look with Hannah, who pretended to check over the day's client files, but was listening avidly.

"Are you going to see him again?"

"I don't know." It had never occurred to Bella that as soon as the closing point ceremony was over she'd be plunked into an SUV and driven straight to the Calgary airport while one of the show's legal advisors went over the huge list of do's and don'ts that would govern her behavior until the show aired. Someone had packed up her belongings and the minute she entered the terminal, she was led through a maze of security checkpoints and right to her gate.

She'd assumed Evan was in another car right behind her, but she didn't see him at the airport and when she asked, the legal advisor knew nothing about it. She couldn't believe they didn't get a chance to say good-bye or to make plans for the future.

But maybe Evan wanted it that way.

After all, he needed to race home to San Jose to find a wife, didn't he? Someone to marry him and secure his company. He'd told her time and time again he'd like her to be that woman, but she'd spurned that idea. So now she was alone.

Bella snapped her attention back to the clipboard she held in her hand. She had a number of appointments this morning, including cats who needed their flea shots and dogs that needed their teeth looked at. She was busier than ever. No time for boyfriends or fiancés or anything of the sort.

"What did he look like?" Rose asked.

Bella didn't look up. "I don't know."

"You just spent a week with him. You must know."

Something snapped inside her. "Of course I know. He was hot, okay? Totally, smoking hot."

"Brown hair?" Rose pushed.

"Yes." For heaven's sake, couldn't she leave it alone?

"Tall? Broad shouldered?"

Seriously? She was going to do this right now? "Yes, now if you don't mind…"

"Is he missing something important? Like a hat? What kind of a man doesn't wear a hat?" Rose said.

"What on earth are you talking about?" Bella straightened and turned toward Rose, ready to shoo her right out of the clinic if she was going to talk nonsense. Rose, however, wasn't looking at her. She was gazing out the window.

At the billionaire walking up to the front door.

"Shoot, he is hot," Hannah said, her files forgotten.

As Evan opened the door, Bella reached for the reception counter to steady herself. She hadn't realized how much she'd missed him, but it hit her now. She felt weak in the knees. Suddenly she couldn't breathe.

Evan scanned the small room as he walked in and took in Hannah and Rose's presence. He nodded to them but didn't slow down. Instead he crossed straight to Bella, knelt down in front of her and pulled a small velvet box from his pocket.

"Bella…" He trailed off, his voice rough and unsteady. He tried to speak again and failed.

Somehow she knew what he wanted to say: That they didn't know each other well enough to be married.

That he knew she was her own woman and had her own plans. That she had enough money to fund her own dreams and didn't need his. That he still wanted her—and only her—to be his wife.

"Bella," he said again, taking her hand. "I can't marry anyone else. I love you. But I have to marry someone within the next two weeks. Would you...please...?"

"Yes!" she said. She tossed her clipboard away and dropped down on her knees beside him. "Yes!" She didn't care how crazy it was or how little they knew each other. She didn't want anyone else, either. She loved him with all her heart and that was all she needed to know.

Evan surged to his feet, Bella in his arms, and kissed her until she couldn't breathe anymore. "Are you sure?" he asked when they finally broke free. "Are you absolutely sure? We can write it right into a prenuptial agreement; if you're unhappy when a year's up I'll let you go."

"Is that what you want?" She pulled back from him. "Marriage for a year?"

"No." He tilted her chin up and grazed her mouth with another searing kiss. "I want marriage forever. If I could, I'd put that into our vows. That once you're my wife, you're mine forever and ever."

Bella grinned. "I think that's in there already." She placed a hand on his chest, wanting to know for sure that he was real. She felt his heart beating under her touch, strong and steady.

"Better be," he said. "So what do you think? Will you marry me? Will you be my wife?"

"Yes." Joy overwhelmed her and she trembled as she

gazed at him. Could this be happening to her? Could she really be so lucky? "I know it's crazy. It's all happening so fast." Rose and Hannah still watched them, wide-eyed, and Bella turned their way, feeling like she owed them an explanation. "We got to know each other really well while we shot the show."

"Obviously," Hannah said. She grinned. "Oh, my goodness; it's so romantic. I think it's great! You deserve to be happy, Bella!"

Rose inched closer, craning her neck until Bella realized she was trying to see the ring Evan had placed on her finger. Bella clutched Evan's arm with her right hand, but lifted her left hand into view. She knew the jewelry store salesclerk wasn't evaluating the ring's worth, although from Rose's swift intake of breath she figured it was worth a lot. Instead, the woman was listening to the ring, or feeling its emanations, or however her crazy brand of psychic worked. She waited, heart in her mouth, for Rose's pronouncement on their chances for happiness. She knew too many cases of Rose calling it right to doubt her abilities.

After a long moment, Rose flashed her a grin and a thumbs-up, skirted the counter to grab Hannah and pulled her into the back, closing the door behind them. More relieved than she could say, Bella turned to Evan, just in time to meet his kiss. Desire crashed over her as she pressed herself to him. She wanted him close, wanted him never to leave her again.

"I should have phoned you and let you know I was coming," he said when they finally broke free of each other.

"No. I'm just so glad you came. I don't care how it happened," she said. "I missed you."

"I missed you, too. I didn't know if you wanted me, though. I mean…mmph!"

Bella leapt into his arms and kissed him until she couldn't kiss him anymore, trying to show him just how much she wanted him and always would. "I won't ever let you go," she murmured finally into his neck.

"I will always listen to you. I promise," he said. "I will always be here for you."

"We'll save all the animals and all the people."

"I can't wait."

## Chapter Twenty

WHEN YOU SEND a kitten down the center aisle of a church, trailing after a tempting ribbon dangled by an adorable flower girl, you have to figure your odds of it reaching the altar are mighty slim, Bella thought. Nevertheless, she smiled happily at the sight of the black feline tripping down the aisle, two rings tied to the collar around its neck. Behind it walked Hannah, her maid of honor, and Morgan, who to her surprise had been overjoyed to be her bridesmaid. Although as she put it, it should be bridesmatron. She'd gotten to know Morgan well over the past couple of weeks. Since she wasn't as stressed out about money and losing her clinic anymore, Bella had found that Morgan, Rob, and the rest of the gang were more than willing to include her in their fun.

She lifted her eyes to where Evan stood at the altar in a dark jacket cut to perfection over his muscled frame, his eyes shining back at her with love and happiness, and her heart thrummed with an emotion she couldn't even name. Love, of course, but something more; something like wonder.

She was marrying Evan. Not because he'd won her in a contest, but because she couldn't imagine life without him, and he felt the same way.

Hannah and Morgan had both helped her plan the last-minute wedding. Morgan had endless energy for organizing and getting things done, and Bella no longer wondered why Hannah found her such good company.

The two women also agreed to help her find the best way to spend her new millions—and maybe some of her husband's billions—to the best effect for Chance Creek's homeless animals. She couldn't wait to get started...right after her honeymoon, that was. She and Evan agreed they needed a little more time off from their normal busy lives and had booked a safe, steady cruise down to Mexico for some R and R.

She glanced up at her father, who held her arm as they walked down the aisle. At first he'd hemmed and hawed and rumbled uncomfortably when she brought up the idea of a ranch and rehabilitation center for old and injured horses, but now he'd thrown himself into the plan. He'd come close to tears the day she went home and told him she loved him, and she had a feeling from the way he held her arm so tightly now that the old man might get misty again today. She couldn't believe they'd both harbored so much guilt about the day Caramel died that they'd nearly lost each other forever. Clothed in a bright blue mother-of-the-bride dress, her mother sat in the front row next to Craig, beaming with happiness back at Bella as they progressed toward the front of the church.

A lightbulb flashed, she winced and frowned for a moment as she took in the cameramen and film crew off to the left. She hadn't realized her contract contained language that allowed Madelyn to document any significant changes in her life that happened because of winning the show. At least that clause ran out in a couple of months. She didn't need a film crew hanging around forever. She saw Ellis take Madelyn's hand and she forgave them just a little. She'd seen the ring on Madelyn's finger earlier and the way the two looked at each other when they thought they were unobserved.

She met Evan's gaze again, and smiled when the flower girl—Evan's niece, Katy—and the kitten—arrived at the altar and Evan's brother, Nate—his best man—bent down to untie the rings. Katy picked up the kitten and snuggled it as she made her way to sit by her mother in the first pew. Bella reached the altar herself and took her place beside the man she loved.

EVAN DIDN'T THINK anyone could be happier than he was when the country preacher, Joe Halpern, pronounced them man and wife and he bent to kiss his bride. He hoped no one could read his thoughts, as he considered the night—and the lifetime—ahead of him. He couldn't wait to be alone with Bella, but for now he'd take the time to get to know her friends—his new community.

This small chapel and country style wedding was a far cry from the society wedding the paparazzi always seemed to expect him to have, but it suited him just fine, as did the fresh, delicious food served at their reception and the local band that began to play as soon as dinner was consumed.

Nate caught up with him when he took a break from the dancing. "I guess I can't be too angry that you found yourself a wife. Although I think you're pissing away the family fortune on those pie-in-the-sky environmental ideas you have. I hope you'll invest at least a portion of it in something solid like oil and natural gas. And your niece and nephew's college fund."

"Nephew's?" Evan asked, knowing damn well Nate could afford to send his own kids to school a thousand times over on the salary he earned from Mortimer Innovations.

"Brenda told me yesterday. The sonogram says it's a boy." Nate beamed, and Evan understood the sudden sweetness of his brother's disposition. He knew he'd taken a chance when he chose Nate as his best man, but he figured his brother deserved some sort of recognition. It couldn't be easy watching him control Mortimer Innovations and know he might never get the chance to do so himself. Now it looked like his gesture was paying off. They were talking—joking, even. It could be worse.

A lot worse, he thought, spotting his bride across the reception hall. He could have refused to go on the show and never met his cowgirl bride.

"You ACTUALLY RODE a stallion?" Craig asked, as they waited for the caterers to carry out the four-tiered wedding cake.

In a moment Bella would join Evan for the cake cut-
ting ceremony, but she appreciated the quiet interlude to
connect with her brother.

"Yes. It didn't go too well," Bella said. "Wait until
you see that episode."

"Still, you got in the saddle. That's something."

She waited for him to say something biting, like he
often did. So she was surprised when his tone softened.

"It was all my fault."

"What do you mean?"

"The day Cyclone died. I saw you there. I should
have said something." Craig turned toward her and she
saw anguish in his eyes. "I was too busy showing off to
do the right thing. Afterward—what I said to you—I
hate myself for that."

Bella stepped back, his words echoing the pain that
had lived in her heart for so many years, until her ride on
Thunder had put it all into perspective. "It wasn't
anybody's fault. It was an accident. They happen sometimes. Besides, you've done so much good in the world
since then. Think about your work—all the cattle and
horses…"

"I'm just a vet, just like you," he said.

"But you help people with the animals that provide
their livelihoods." She couldn't believe Craig blamed
himself, too. They'd all sacrificed so much time to the
bitterness of the past.

"But I'm not brave like you are," he countered. "You
save the animals that people love—the ones that are like

family members. There's a reason I don't work with pets."

"Because it doesn't pay as well?" Bella joked, trying to lighten the atmosphere between them.

"Because I'm not worthy of them. I just stood there the day that Caramel died. I didn't even go after her." He shook his head. "It was like I was paralyzed because I cared so much. You're the brave one. You went after her. You held her as she died. Then you went to work for Maggie. And you didn't have to beg money from Mom and Dad like I did when you went to school. You did it all yourself. You became a vet, you've saved so many pets for other people. You kept on loving animals..." He took a deep breath. "I'm afraid to care about anything. I miss you. I miss our family—the way it used to be."

Bella blinked back the tears that threatened to spill over. She didn't want Evan to think she wasn't happy. She was happy, especially now. "I'm right here."

"You don't blame me?" Craig said.

"Of course not," Bella said. "I always thought you blamed me. We've all been torturing ourselves, stuck in our separate hells. It's time to let it go."

Craig drew in a ragged breath. "That sounds good to me."

She pulled him into a quick hug. "It's going to be okay. Everything's going to be different now, you hear?"

He smiled suddenly, though she saw the pain was still fresh for him. "Why, because you're filthy rich?"

She grinned back. "Yep. And because we'll restore

our ranch to its former glory. We'll restore our family back to its former glory, too. You'll see." She squeezed him, then let him go as another guest moved forward to congratulate her. Carl Whitfield, formerly Chance Creek's richest inhabitant. The millionaire had moved to town to play at being a rancher, and had fallen in love with a local girl, Lacey Taylor. No fairy-tale wedding ended that match, however, and she felt a tug of sympathy for the man. Lacey had left town. Rumor had it Carl planned to leave as well.

Craig patted her back and excused himself. She hoped her words had offered him some comfort, and that they really would be able to regain a closer relationship.

"Welcome to the club," Carl said, shaking her hand.

"The club?"

"The Chance Creek millionaires club. Although I guess we'll have to rename it now that a billionaire is moving to town." He didn't look exactly pleased at the thought.

"It's nice that there will be three of us," she said. She wasn't sure how to take Carl. She didn't know him that well.

"Unfortunately, there will only be two pretty soon. I'm leaving. Heading back to California. Chance Creek and I didn't get along that well."

"I'm sorry to hear that," she said, touching his arm. "Really, Carl. I know you thought you would make a life here."

"Well, I've got myself to blame for it, don't I?" he

said. "I'm so used to promoting myself I didn't know when to quit. Folks around here think I'm a braggart and a fool."

"No, they don't," Bella said. "I don't, anyway." Although if he'd showed this more human side of himself right from the beginning, Carl would have found lots of people willing to be his friend. "Maybe a break will be good for you—give you something to do and take your mind off Lacey—but I hope you'll come back and give Chance Creek another try."

"We'll see," he said. "I won't sell my house until next summer, just in case I change my mind. I'm looking for someone to live in it for the meantime, though. I don't suppose you and that husband of yours are looking for a mansion?"

She shook her head. "I need to be close to the shelter. We plan to live in my trailer for now. When we get back from our honeymoon, that is."

"That ratty old thing?" Carl sputtered. "Sorry. I mean, it's a little rough for a guy like Evan, don't you think?"

"He's used to roughing it," she said, her thoughts slipping back to their time in the little tent in Jasper. "Once we're back, however, we'll start hunting for enough land to build our house, plus a new, state-of-the-art clinic and shelter."

"Evan doesn't mind leaving San Jose?"

"No, he says he likes it here." She shrugged. "Plus he wants enough land to run test projects about alternative energy sources and sustainable ranching."

"Sustainable ranching? He better take care he doesn't make himself as unpopular as I am around here," Carl said.

"Actually, Jake Matheson seems pretty interested in that idea." She nodded across the room at Rob Matheson's older brother.

"Let me know if you think of anyone else who'd like to stay at my place."

"What about Cab? Maybe he'd like to spend the winter there."

"The sheriff? Now that's not a bad idea." Carl shook her hand again and made his way through the crowd toward a knot of cowboys. Bella crossed the room to join her husband, her thoughts lingering on Carl's mansion. She was sure he'd filled it with plenty of precious things that needed to be looked after; but it lacked the one thing he wanted most—the woman he loved.

She was so grateful fate had pushed her and Evan together. She didn't care where she lived as long as he was there.

She must be the luckiest woman in the world.

"COME ON, I've got a surprise for you," Evan said.

How many more surprises could her life hold? Bella wondered lazily as she allowed him to pull her up off the chair on the balcony overlooking a nearly deserted beach below. Mexico had quickly become one of her favorite places, after Chance Creek, of course. They'd rented a secluded, but fully-staffed beach cottage, and relished the luxury and peace that surrounded them. "Where are we going?"

"On a little hike."

She cocked her head, taking in the backpack he wore on his back. "I thought you just ducked inside to get your sunglasses."

"I did, but I did a little packing, too. No more questions," he added, putting a finger to her lips. "Just follow me."

She gave the impending sunset behind them a last, longing look. She'd become a connoisseur of spectacular Pacific Ocean sunsets, but she allowed herself to be led downstairs and outside, down to the beach itself. Coming around a curve to a stretch of sand hidden from the building, she stopped when she took in the sight before her.

A tiny tent stood pitched in the sand.

"Is that for us?" she asked, suddenly very aware of her husband.

"Yep."

"No cameras? No interruptions?"

"Nope."

"And you intend to spend the whole night with me this time?"

"Yes, ma'am," he said and drew her into his arms.

As the edge of the sun dipped below the horizon, Bella kicked off her sandals, unwrapped the sarong she wore around her waist and shimmied out of the bottoms of her bikini.

"Hold up, there, beautiful," Evan said, but he

laughed and shucked off his own shorts. "Actually, go as fast as you want." He came and helped her undo the clasp of her halter top.

As it fell away, Bella stood back and let him take her in, familiar by now with the warmth of his regard and the love that shone in his eyes. She tugged him toward the tent and dropped to her knees to unzip the opening, smiling at the hitch in his breathing that told her what he thought of that particular sight.

She couldn't get inside fast enough, and Evan took forever to fold his bulk into the tiny space, but when they'd zipped the netted opening back up for a hint of privacy, she lay back and let the moment draw out.

"Did I do good?" Evan asked her.

"Better than good. I think we need to have one of these pitched in our backyard at all times."

"We can sleep in it every night until we build our house."

"Sleep? What's sleep got to do with it?" She snuggled in close and turned over, spoon-fashion. Might as well finally finish what they started back on that most frustrating night of her life back on the show.

"I was hoping you'd remember this," Evan said, sliding his arms around her, and hugging her close. As he set out to explore her body with his hands, caressing every curve, stroking her breasts, teasing her nipples, the fire within that seemed insatiable whenever he was near began to build anew.

She loved the feel of him nestled against her, the hardness of him pressed along her skin. She loved knowing what was to come, but relishing every moment of the process it took to get there.

She began to rock back against him and heard his murmured grunt of pleasure. As he slid a hand lower, exploring her, stroking her, she parted her legs, allowing him better access.

"You're beautiful, you know that?" he said.

"I love you."

He stroked faster and with a moan of wanting, she eased into position, telling him she wanted more, now—right now.

He pushed inside her, but only just a little, then pulled out before pushing in again. With each stroke he reached a little farther, but his slow pace and teasing motions stoked her fire so high she nearly cried out in frustration. Reaching behind her, she gripped his hip and tried to pull him inside. Evan only chuckled into her hair.

"Patience," he said.

"I've never been patient! You know that!"

"I do know that," he said, and pushed all the way in with a strong stroke. Bella gasped and moaned as he pulled out and pushed in again. This time his pace suited her just fine and she moved with him, every stroke a streak of liquid pleasure between her legs.

"Is this good?" he asked as if he didn't know the answer.

"Yes!" she gasped. "More."

"You got it," he said and redoubled his efforts.

Just when Bella thought she couldn't contain her desire anymore, she went over the edge and came in crashing waves of sensation and pleasure. Evan came with her, his shouts of release echoing in her ears like the crash of the surf on the sand outside their tent. When they collapsed together, spent and blissful, she reached back to give him a kiss.

"Just give me a minute and we'll do it again," he said, kissing her back.

"You promise?"

"As many times as you like. To the victor go the spoils."

She rolled over to consider him. "You sound pretty pleased about that."

"Losing that show was the smartest thing I ever did." He reached up and tugged one her curls. "I love you, Bella."

"I love you, too." And she reached for him again.

The **Cowboys of Chance Creek** series continues with
**The Sheriff Catches a Bride**.

Be the first to know about Cora Seton's new releases!
Sign up for her newsletter here!

Other books in the Cowboys of Chance Creek Series:

**The Cowboy Inherits a Bride (Volume 0)**
**The Cowboy's E-Mail Order Bride (Volume 1)**
**The Cowboy Wins a Bride (Volume 2)**
**The Cowboy Imports a Bride (Volume 3)**
**The Sheriff Catches a Bride (Volume 5)**
**The Cowboy Lassos a Bride (Volume 6)**
**The Cowboy Rescues a Bride (Volume 7)**
**The Cowboy Earns a Bride (Volume 8)**
**The Cowboy's Christmas Bride (Volume 9)**

**Sign up for my newsletter HERE.**
www.coraseton.com/sign-up-for-my-newsletter

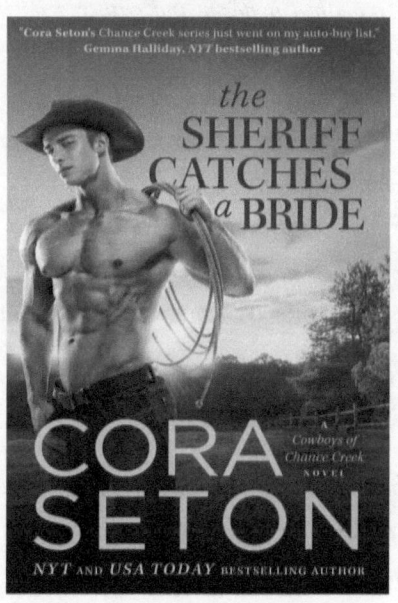

"Cora Seton's Chance Creek series just went on my auto-buy list."
Gemma Halliday, *NYT* bestselling author

*the*
SHERIFF
CATCHES
*a* BRIDE

CORA
SETON

*A Cowboys of Chance Creek* NOVEL

*NYT* AND *USA TODAY* BESTSELLING AUTHOR

Read on for an excerpt of
**The Sheriff Catches a Bride**.

P LAN SLOWLY, RUN FAST.

*As her mother's words repeated in her mind like a well-worn mantra, Fila Sahar struggled to right her clothing in the cramped bathroom of the Emirates-owned airplane she'd been traveling in for hours. She'd waited to escape from Afghanistan for over ten years, keeping her head down, gathering information, cultivating contacts, fitting each puzzle piece together with infinite care. Soon—very soon—it would be time to run.*

*She washed her hands with shaking fingers, turned off the tap, and dried them carefully. In the mirror, her dark, almond-shaped eyes were almost obscured behind the delicate netting of her sky-blue burqa. As she smoothed it down and gathered its folds to cover as much of her clothing as possible, she blessed the covering garment for the first time in her life. The men who'd brought her here weren't relatives and they had never seen her face. That would have brought too much shame to her family.*

*Family. Fila refused to believe any of the radicals who had held her captive for over a decade were related to her in any way.*

Turn the weapons of your enemies so they point at their own hearts.

*Those weren't her mother's words; they were the words of the Taliban men who'd trapped her in their violent snares and swallowed up her life. But the words still fit, and she'd follow them.*

*One last check in the mirror to see that all was well, and Fila opened the bathroom door, retraced her steps to her seat, and submitted herself to the strict care of her guards once again.*

"WHAT THE HELL are we doing here?" Cab Johnson asked from his uncomfortable position in the back seat of Rob Matheson's oversized Chevy. At six foot four and over two hundred pounds, he was always uncomfortable in back seats. Hell, he could barely wear his hat in here. It didn't help that he shared the extended cab with three other cowboys—three men he'd normally call his best friends. Rob Matheson, at the wheel, was a tall, blond, blue-eyed man he'd known since grade school. An all-around trouble-maker, Cab had no doubt he was behind today's shenanigans. Ethan Cruz sat beside Rob in the front passenger seat. A dark-haired, rugged rancher, he'd grown up on the spread next to Rob's and was another of Cab's oldest friends.

Rounding out the group was Jamie Lassiter, a little shorter than the other two, a little slighter, as well, but he possessed a wiry strength and he'd never taken last place when it came to getting the attention of women. No, that distinction fell to Cab, which was one reason he was still single while the rest of them had recently settled down. More reserved than his friends, he'd always hung back when they flirted and talked with the pretty women at bars, at parties, heck, even in grocery stores. He wasn't the flirting kind. As county sheriff it behooved him to keep a more dignified demeanor. Plus, he'd had his eye on a particular woman for quite some time.

A woman engaged to another man.

Cab sighed. It had been a rough few months in many ways. While his friends had gotten married one by one over the sunny summer, he'd helped to track down a killer with the rest of southern Montana's law enforcement officers. A man who had brutally assaulted and beaten to death three young women, and nearly finished off a fourth before he was apprehended. Cab was still haunted by details of the cases and the fact they hadn't caught the man sooner. The fourth victim—a woman named Amanda Strassburg—was still in the hospital and would be for some time. Samuel Grady, the perpetrator, was behind bars awaiting trial. The evidence was solid—they'd caught him in the act—and Cab was sure he'd spend the rest of his life in prison at the very least.

He was also sure there were other Samuel Gradys out there, and that kept him from sleeping well these nights. Today he wasn't working, though, so he had planned to head over to Linda's Diner for lunch in the hopes that he'd forget his dark thoughts in the hustle and bustle of the eatery. Midmorning he'd gotten a call from Ethan, who had asked him to stop by. He did so on his way into town and had met up with the whole gang—Ethan, Jamie and Rob—all getting ready to run an errand. The next thing he knew he'd been coerced into coming with them. Well, coerced was probably too strong a word. He'd been mostly pleased to see his friends all together without their wives for once—not that he minded their wives. It was simply galling to be the odd man out these days. First Jamie became partners with Ethan on the Cruz ranch, then Rob joined in. Now all three of them were married and living on the same spread. Cab was out in the cold. He didn't begrudge his friends the fun they had living and working together. He just hated being on the outskirts of that fun all the time.

He was beginning to have second thoughts about this *errand*, though. Why were they parked in front of Thayer Jewelers?

The call from Ethan seemed innocent enough. He'd asked Cab to come by and pick up an extra pie his wife, Autumn, had baked for him. Never one to turn down pie, Cab made it his business to come right over. As soon as he found the three of them waiting for him, he should have known something was up.

Because something was definitely up.

"Did Autumn ask for an upgrade on that ring you bought her?" he asked Ethan as they all piled out of the truck. He eyed the jewelry store with suspicion. Rose

Bellingham would be in there.

Rose. When he wasn't dreaming about the possibility of a serial killer coming to Chance Creek, he dreamed about Rose these days, even though he had no right to do such a thing. Unfortunately sometimes those two dreams merged and when he woke, thrashing and hollering, he paced the floor of his bedroom for hours, unable to sleep at all. Rose lived alone. Her fiancé, Jason Thayer, was off in North Dakota, making his fortune in the oil fields. Rose rented the carriage house behind Jason's father's old-fashioned house in town. Safe enough, but was a young single woman ever really safe?

Was anyone?

"Nah, we didn't come here for me," Ethan said, giving him a friendly shove toward the door.

"Then why are we here?" He had a feeling he wouldn't like the answer. How was it that everyone else in town respected him except these three idiots? As the county sheriff, he normally called the shots. Not when Rob, Ethan and Jamie were around.

"Come on," Jamie said and pulled the door open. Cab reluctantly went inside. He'd never liked the jewelry store, probably because it made him feel like the proverbial bull in a china shop. Everywhere he looked stood glass cases filled with precious, delicate jewelry.

Definitely not his scene.

"Do whatever you need to do and let's get out of here," he growled. He wasn't in the mood to see Rose, either. He didn't want the reminder that she was engaged to Jason, whose father owned this store. Rose had worked here for a couple of years now. She'd been engaged to Jason for nearly six. What was the man waiting for?

Sometimes Cab wished Jason would get a move on and marry Rose already. That would put the final nail in Cab's coffin and he could get his grieving over and done with. Rose would become Jason's responsibility and maybe he could stop worrying about her. Other times, he hoped Rose and Jason's engagement would stretch out until it finally snapped and she gave him back his ring. It was wrong to wish unhappiness on another man, but Cab did. Often.

"Over here," Ethan called, gesturing for them to join him at one of the cases. Cab figured the sooner they finished this charade the sooner they could leave. He moved carefully to join the others as they bent over a display of engagement rings. Rose, who'd been near the cash register when they came in, crossed to join them, a smile on her pretty face. She was petite with glossy dark brown hair and startling blue eyes that often contained a spark of humor. Cab loved the way she was always smiling, even if sometimes that smile was wry. She was cheerful, sharp, imaginative and lively. Jason was a fool to leave her alone so long.

Cab kept his expression carefully friendly, as always, all too aware of the engagement ring that had been on Rose's finger for as long as he could remember. He knew Jason had slipped the thin silver band on after he took her to their senior prom. Cab hadn't noticed Rose much back then. He was a young buck in those days just establishing himself as a sheriff's deputy. Directly after graduation, Jason moved to North Dakota. Rose stayed in Chance Creek and found herself a job. Cab had noticed her more and more over the years but had kept his distance until Rose became friends with Autumn and started to help out from time to time at the Cruz guest ranch. Thrown together more at social occasions, Cab had gotten to know her better, and as much as he told himself she was off limits—entirely off limits—he couldn't help wishing she wasn't.

"That one," Jamie said, pointing to the most ostentatious ring in the bunch. Cab would hate to know the woman who wanted that monstrosity on her finger.

"Nah, too flashy," Ethan said. "I think that one." He pointed to a wisp of a gold band.

"That's not an engagement ring; that's hardly a ring at all," Rob said. "This one." He jabbed a finger at a circlet of yellowish diamonds that made Cab wince.

It was amazing any of them had wives, he thought, leaning over and examining the case for himself. His eyes immediately lit on a vintage art deco ring with flowing lines and several sparkling diamonds. It reminded him of Rose somehow; artistic, womanly, unique.

"Rose," Jamie said. "Pull out that one, would you?" He pointed to the ring Cab was staring at.

Rose reached in and pulled out the tray. She angled it toward Cab and he picked up the ring, curious to see it without the intervening glass case. Just as he thought, it was a work of art.

"You can't see it that way," Rob said, grabbing it

from his fingers. He snatched up Rose's hand, drew her own ring off her finger and jammed the one Cab picked out in its place.

"Rob!" Rose snatched her hand away and held it up, shock on her face. She stared first at the ring, then at Cab, then back at the ring again. When her free hand grabbed for the counter, and her knees buckled, Cab reached over the case to steady her.

"Rose? You okay?" She looked like she was about to faint.

"Told you," Rob said, grinning at Ethan.

"Son of a gun," Ethan said, "You were right."

"What are you talking about?" Cab was annoyed. "Get her some water, for crying out loud. Rose, do you need to sit down for a minute?" In a horrible flash he wondered if she was pregnant. She'd been Jason's fiancée a long time. Maybe they hadn't always been careful.

Rose stared at him wide-eyed. Growing worried, Cab tightened his grip on her arm and came around to her side of the case. "I think you need to sit," he said again.

She shook her head and seemed to come back to herself. "I'm... fine."

"Really?" Jamie said. "Because you look like you've seen your hus—"

Ethan whacked him on the arm.

Rose blushed furiously, peeled the ring off and thrust it back into the tray. Understanding dawned on Cab and he felt heat creep up his own neck at the trick his friends had played. They'd gotten him to choose a ring. They'd put that ring on Rose's finger.

They'd waited for her reaction.

Everyone knew about Rose's hunches—the ones she got when a couple chose their engagement ring. Somehow she could predict their future—if their marriage would be successful or not. If they were meant to be together. She'd given her approval to Ethan, Jamie and Rob when they'd bought their rings during the past few months, and since all of them remained happily married they believed her hunches were real.

So what did they think they were proving now?

He wanted to let go of Rose's arm. Wanted to apologize for his friends and get the hell out of there, but he couldn't seem to turn away.

"I didn't feel anything," she said angrily, breaking the uncomfortable silence. She yanked her arm away from Cab's grip and set the tray of rings back in the case with shaking hands.

"You looked like you felt something," Rob said with a grin. Rob made a business of teasing women, and he and Rose had been friends for some time. Usually Rose gave back as good as she got, but this time she didn't come up with a stinging reply.

She glanced at Cab again instead, and Cab's stomach tightened when he met her gaze. He saw something there—awareness, interest—fear?—that sent a shiver of recognition up his own spine.

Rob was right; she'd felt something when he put the ring on her finger. The ring Cab had picked out. The ring he wished he could give her.

Were he and Rose meant for each other? Did she

feel the same kind of interest in him he felt in her?

Rose turned away abruptly, grabbed her engagement ring off the counter and shoved the thin circle back onto her finger. Cab's stomach sank.

Of course she didn't feel anything for him. She had made her choice and it wasn't him.

"Let's go," he said gruffly. "See you around, Rose." He knew he should say something else—apologize for Rob's behavior at the very least—but he couldn't form the words. He turned on his heel and headed for the front door, hoping against hope the rest of them would follow his lead for once.

They did and a moment later they spilled out onto the sidewalk. Cab waited until Rob took his keys out and headed for his truck before he grabbed him by the collar of his jacket and slammed him face down on its hood.

"What the hell?" Rob bellowed. "Hey, let go! You can't arrest me for playing a joke." He struggled, but Cab had already pocketed his keys and slapped a handcuff around his right wrist. In a few spare motions he locked the other cuff on his left.

"I'm not arresting you. I'm going to throw you into the creek and watch you drown." He opened the door to the extended cab and gave Rob a shove. "Climb in." Rob did so, cursing, and Jamie got in beside him, chuckling. If Cab had another set of handcuffs he wouldn't be laughing long. Ethan got into the front passenger seat while Cab made his way around to the driver's side.

"You better not throw me in the creek," Rob said as Cab climbed in.

Cab shut the door and turned on all of them. "What the hell was that in there?" he demanded. "What would make you do that to Rose?"

The others exchanged a look. "We got to talking," Ethan said. "That's all. Who you'd likely match up with. Rob said Rose was gone on you. Jamie said no way because she's engaged to Jason. Rob said there was one way to tell for sure. So…" He shrugged his shoulders.

"You've got to be kidding." Cab looked from one to the other. "First of all, I'll marry who I marry, with no help from any of you. Second of all—" He broke off, exasperated. "Even if I wanted to marry Rose, she's taken. It's a done deal. You shouldn't have done that to her."

A long silence greeted this speech, broken at last by Rob. "Engagements can be broken, you know. Jason's been away a long time. Seems to me if he was going to marry her, he'd have done it by now."

"Yeah, well, until his ring is off her finger, I won't go near her," Cab said. He started the truck and pointed it toward the diner. He still planned to have his lunch. Rob could sit back there and starve for all he cared.

WHEN ROSE PULLED into the parking area in front of the Big House on the Cruz ranch, she shut off her truck's engine, but didn't climb out. It was seven in the evening and, being November, nearly dark already. With her engine off, the cold outside air quickly brought the temperature in the cab down. Still, she kept her seat, not ready to go inside and face all of her friends. The incident in the jewelry store this morning had replayed in her mind all day. How could she react so strongly to Cab's ring when she was engaged to Jason?

*Because your heart has moved on even if you haven't.* The voice in her head sounded like Grandma Allison, a plainspoken woman who had died over a decade ago. She would tell Rose it was high time to make up her mind about her engagement.

The truth was her relationship with Jason had been going downhill for months. Years, even. She'd begun to suspect the only reason it had lasted this long was because they weren't living in the same state. If they were, Jason's attempts to organize and control her life would have driven her crazy. Back in high school she'd thought it romantic when he'd boss her around in that slow drawl of his. Sexy, even. Now it just pissed her off, not the least because everyone else in her life seemed to think they could boss her around, too.

Immediately she felt contrite at the uncharitable thoughts she'd aimed at her fiancé. She'd promised herself only last week she'd give this relationship one last real shot before giving up. It didn't make sense to overthrow a six-year engagement on a whim. Even if that whim had lasted for months. Maybe she could change the way they interacted if she tried hard enough. She needed to be more direct about what she wanted. She needed to speak up. Jason would finally listen to her and stop trying to do everything his way. He loved her, after all. He always had.

She pulled out her phone and checked for messages.

None. He hadn't called or texted her in days, and she hadn't reached out to him, either. He'd barely crossed her mind this week until Rob yanked his ring off her finger and replaced it with Cab's. Refusing to think too deeply about what that meant, she called him, waiting as the phone rang and rang.

Finally Jason answered. "Yeah?"

Rose frowned. Hadn't he seen her name on the screen? Why was he being so abrupt? "It's me."

"What is it, Rose?" He sounded impatient. He was somewhere noisy. At a restaurant, maybe?

"I just wanted to say hi," she said brightly. "I wondered what you were doing."

A pause. "Nothing."

He wasn't going to make this easy, was he? This is how their conversations went these days—stilted, with long gaps and awkward questions that betrayed how little they knew about the day-to-day circumstances of each other's lives. Well, she was trying to bridge those gaps, wasn't she? Her last-ditch effort to save their sinking ship of an engagement. She tried again. "Where are you?"

"Jeez, Rose, what are you, my father?"

Stung, Rose snapped. "No, I'm the one who has to deal with your father. You're five hundred miles away, remember?"

"I didn't tell you to move in with my old man. In fact, I told you to keep living with your parents so we could save more money," Jason snapped back.

Rose shut her eyes. There it was, that harping, bossy

tone he always directed at her. Jason knew she hated the idea of living at home. She felt like a child under her parents' roof. When Emory offered her the carriage house three years ago, she jumped at it. The rent was nominal and the place was all her own. At least, that's what she thought in the beginning. Now she knew better. Still, how many times had she and Jason had this particular fight? They could say the lines in their sleep. Jason was right; moving onto his father's property had been a mistake. Emory Thayer was overbearing to say the least. Jason had warned her, but she hadn't truly understood until she moved in.

"Look, I'm not trying to check up on you," she began, ignoring the rest of what he'd said.

"Sure sounds like it. Have you found a new job yet?"

"There are no jobs," Rose said. How many times had they had this conversation, too? "And I don't want another job until I go to school. I've told you that."

"How the hell are we supposed to save up for a house if you're going to spend all our money?" Jason said. "Art school is stupid. You spend thousands of dollars to learn a skill that makes you no money back. It's a bad investment."

"Stupid?" Rose echoed, her voice rising. Jason had always been against her going to art school but he'd never used such strong words before.

"Art is a hobby, Rose. A hobby. Only idiots pay that kind of money for their hobbies."

Was he for real? She remembered the days back in high school when Jason drove in the demolition derby.

How much money had he blown on that particular hobby?

"I'm a good artist. I can make money…"

"No, you can't." Jason's temper flared, too. "It's time to get real. No artist can make that kind of money. It's a one in a million shot, and the chance that it would happen to you is nonexistent. Art school is for little rich kids who don't need to make a living. You need to make a living. What about that nursing course I told you about? A friend of mine here has a wife who's a nurse and she's making a killing! You could go to night school. But first you need to get your ass out of my dad's store and find another job. I gotta go."

He clicked off the phone and left her staring out the windshield of her truck in shock. Was that how he really felt? That she had no chance as an artist? And nursing— that was his idea of an alternative? The thought made her shiver in disgust. Thank God other people liked nursing, but it wasn't for her. She was terrified of illness and death and all the things nurses had to take in stride. She was far too private a person to be comfortable with the intimate tasks nurses faced every day. Whatever she did for a living had to be artistic in some sense of the word. That's why she stuck to the jewelry store even if it meant working with Emory. The rings were beautiful and the variety of jewelry infinite. While Emory didn't let her pick the merchandise, he did let her peruse the catalogs and dream over all the designs. She'd tried jewelry making herself, but unfortunately it wasn't her thing, either. She preferred acrylics. Still, selling rings was better than nothing.

Why should Jason get to pursue his dream but demand that she give hers up? And if he was so set on saving money, why didn't he save more of it himself? He had to be earning a ton of money at his oil patch job, but he claimed living expenses ate up most of his wages. After all these years he still didn't have enough money for them to marry and put a down payment on a house. She was beginning to think he never would.

Which was probably just as well. Because if she was honest, she didn't want to marry him anymore. In the cold, dark stillness of the truck cab, she finally faced the truth. She had promised herself one last try at working things out, but she was out of patience. She didn't want to try anymore. What was the use of it? Jason wasn't going to change. As she stared out at the hulking shapes of the barns against the night sky, she made up her mind. She was done with Jason. Done with Emory. Done with all of it. She would break off the engagement, find a new place to live and get a new job. That wasn't going to be easy, though. The minute she phoned Jason and told him the news, he'd be on the phone to Emory, and Emory would be on the phone with her folks. She couldn't stay in the carriage house or work for Emory anymore once she broke things off with Jason. And she wouldn't want to be anywhere near her parents, either. They were going to flip their lids.

First, she needed a place to call her own and a job. Then she could spill the beans to Jason. Luckily, Jason wouldn't call her back for at least another week, so she had plenty of time to make a plan. She considered going home and getting started on it right away, but decided against that course of action. She'd already had a long day and she needed company to cheer her up. Home alone, she'd have to fully face the mess she'd made of her life so far, and more than likely Emory would drop in and want to stay an hour. At least here she'd be with her friends.

Taking a deep breath, she looked at the band of silver on her ring finger. In one week she'd take it off for good. She expected a stab of pain, or tears to sting her eyes, but instead she felt a lift of anticipation in her heart and then a squeeze of shame. How could she be happy she was breaking off a six-year engagement? What kind of a woman was she?

A realist, she decided as she climbed out of the truck. She and Jason weren't meant to be together. It was time to move on.

Inside the Cruz Big House some minutes later, she perched on the arm of one of the sofas in the living room. Every Thursday her friends gathered at Ethan and Autumn's house for an informal get-together. Usually they played poker, but this week the Cruzes had bought a pool table and they were breaking it in with a tournament. Autumn, nearly six months pregnant, told Rose she was slated to play Autumn's sister-in-law Claire in a while, but right now Ethan and Jamie were up. The rest of the people present stood around, or sat on stools pulled from the kitchen counter to watch. Autumn circulated with appetizers and everyone knew there was beer in the refrigerator.

Rose had always been jealous of Autumn's elfin features and long, lustrous hair. Someone had once described her as ethereal, and the word suited. Originally from New York City, Autumn fit into Chance Creek like she'd been born here. Rose, who had been born here, couldn't remember what the town was like before she came. She'd been the one to transform the Cruz ranch into a guest ranch business. Soon afterward, Jamie and Claire built their home on another part of the spread. Jamie helped with trail rides, but he also was starting a horse breeding business. Claire helped when she could but she was much in demand as an interior decorator. Ethan and Jamie had grown up together, along with Rob Matheson, whose family owned the next ranch over. Rob was here tonight as well. A tall, blond, handsome cowboy, he owned a property that straddled the two ranches. He and his wife, Morgan, had just started a winery on part of that land. Like Autumn and Claire, Morgan was pregnant, although she was only in her first trimester. Rob also intended to work with Ethan on the guest ranch and Jamie with the horse breeding. The three friends had found a way to interweave their lives, and Rose, frankly, was jealous of the way it all seemed to work so well.

A cheer went up when Ethan sank a shot and Rose's attention returned to the room. Everyone else seemed mesmerized by the pool game.

All except Cab Johnson. He was watching her.

Rose frowned. Did the sheriff know what he'd done

to her when he picked out that ring and Rob slid it on her finger? Immediately, a rush of emotion had overcome her: joy, excitement, a sense of rightness she'd never felt before. She'd always had hunches when she sold couples their engagement rings, but nothing like this—never anything half so strong. If it was any other man and woman she'd feel sure their marriage was bound to succeed.

But it wasn't any other couple; it was her and Cab. They weren't even engaged. They'd never gone on a date.

What on earth had possessed Rob to drag Cab in there, make him pick a ring and shove it on her finger? She was friends with Rob, sort of. He teased her mercilessly and she did her best to tease him back. How could he have guessed that lately when she saw Cab she felt... interested?

She crushed that thought with an iron hand. First she needed to extricate herself from her current situation, and then she needed to find a backbone before she considered dating again. She'd let her parents run her life until she was eighteen, and then even though she'd thought she was showing her independence by getting engaged to Jason, it hadn't worked out that way. Instead, she felt as if she'd gone from two parents to four. Her mother, father, Emory and Jason all told her what to do. She hadn't stood a chance at ordering her own life.

This time it was going to be different. This time she wouldn't answer to anyone. Just as soon as she broke up with Jason she'd be free as a bird, and no one, not even the hottest, most eligible sheriff was going to hold her back.

Rose sipped her beer, fighting against the breathless feeling Cab's proximity always conjured in her. What was it about the man that tugged at her in such a primal way? He liked to hang back and let his friends hog the limelight, but to Rose he stood out like a beacon. He was muscular, self-assured, intelligent, and damn him, she wanted to know what he was like between the sheets.

She glanced around to see if anyone else had noticed the direction of Cab's gaze—or guessed the direction her thoughts had taken. Jamie sunk a ball and Claire cheered, her glossy black bob swinging with her enthusiasm.

"Hey—what happened to family loyalty?" Ethan said to her.

"Husbands take preference over brothers," Claire said. She was glowing tonight, Rose thought with more than a bit of jealousy. She and Jamie couldn't be more in love. That was hard to stomach when Rose's own relationship was disintegrating and she was fighting inappropriate feelings for Cab. Still avoiding the sheriff's gaze, she considered another couple who'd joined them tonight; Bella and Evan Mortimer.

The billionaires.

Rose still couldn't believe that sweet Bella Chatham, the local pet veterinarian who couldn't say no to any stray animal, had gone on a national reality television show, beat a billionaire to win the five million dollar prize, then married the guy. With his short, dark hair and athletic build, Evan was as hot as any of the local cowboys, Rose had to admit. While she didn't begrudge Bella her fantastic luck, she also couldn't help feeling jealous. Again. Evan and Bella were camping out in Bella's airstream trailer behind her clinic and shelter until they decided where to build their new house.

Everyone in this room was coupled up and on their way to living their dreams. Even Hannah Ashton, Bella's receptionist, had a boyfriend, although he wasn't here tonight. She and the sheriff were the only ones without partners.

She risked a glance over at him, but quickly looked away when she met his gaze. He was still watching her. Not in an overtly sexual way and not in a weird stalkerish way. Just watching her. As if he was considering something.

Considering her reaction to his ring, maybe.

She glanced down to her left hand where it rested in her lap. The thin silver band Jason Thayer had slipped on her ring finger six years ago still glinted there. After six years of being someone's fiancée, she needed at least six years of being on her own before she considered marriage again. By that time Cab would be long gone.

Jamie sunk another ball and Claire cheered again, startling Rose out of her reverie.

"You won't be cheering when you go up against Jamie," Ethan said to her. "If you beat Rose, you play him afterward."

"He'll go easy on me," Claire said confidently.

"Oh, yeah?" Jamie straightened up from the table.

"You will unless you want to sleep on the couch tonight," she said.

Jamie chuckled. "I tell you what. When it's our turn we'll get rid of the peanut gallery and make it a game of strip pool."

"Strip pool?" Rob said from where he perched on one of the stools. "That's genius." He gave his wife's hand a tug and waggled his eyebrows at her. Morgan rolled her eyes.

*Strip pool?* Rose glanced involuntarily at Cab and met his gaze again. An image sprang into her mind. The two of them alone in the room. Cue sticks in hand.

Half undressed.

She'd seen him without his shirt before when the whole gang went swimming in Chance Creek. Cab was a big guy—really big.

And not an ounce of fat on him. Powerful shoulders, massive thighs, muscles to die for…

The sudden intensity in his gaze told her he was thinking about the same possibility she was. Her breath hitched and heat swept through her. What would it be like to unbutton her shirt, peel off her bra and let Cab take a look? Would he touch her…?

She wrenched her gaze away, the heat in her face telling her she had flushed to the roots of her hair. Quickly she swallowed the rest of her beer and slipped off her stool to make her way to the kitchen. She took her time fetching a second bottle from the refrigerator. Heck, if she could get away with it she'd climb right in the thing to cool herself off.

She couldn't feel this way—not about Cab. Not now.

It would be lunacy to break off one long-term relationship and jump straight into a new one. She needed space and time to figure out who she was. She needed to figure out what she was going to do next. She needed a home. And a job. There was way too much on her plate to allow her the luxury of dating.

But when she returned to the living room her gaze sought out Cab like a moth drawn to a flame.

And he was looking back at her.

A tremor of desire rippled through her and Rose realized she'd waited far too long to break up with Jason. Not because she should be with Cab, but because she shouldn't feel like this for anyone. Not when she was about to embark on an important new chapter in her life—one in which she'd hopefully discover exactly who she was. She'd allowed herself to get so lonely and unhappy that she longed to throw herself at the next man who crossed her path. That meant it was doubly important she create a new life for herself—a life that didn't require her to have a man in order to feel complete. She couldn't keep putting her dreams on hold. Time to put her plans into action.

Before it was too late.

End of Excerpt

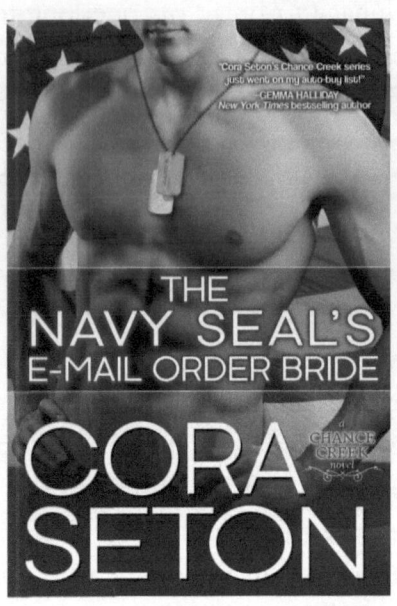

Read on for an excerpt of Volume 1 of
**The Heroes of Chance Creek** series –
*The Navy SEAL's E-Mail Order Bride.*

"BOYS," LIEUTENANT COMMANDER Mason Hall said, "we're going home."

He sat back in his folding chair and waited for a reaction from his brothers. The recreation hall at Bagram Airfield was as busy as always with men hunched over laptops, watching the widescreen television, or lounging in groups of three or four shooting the breeze. His brothers—three tall, broad shouldered men in uniform—stared back at him from his computer screen, the feeds from their four-way video conversation all relaying a similar reaction to his words.

Utter confusion.

"Home?" Austin was the first to speak. A Special Forces officer just a year younger than Mason, he was currently in Kabul.

"Home," Mason confirmed. "I got a letter from Great Aunt Heloise. Uncle Zeke passed away over the weekend without designating an heir. That means the ranch reverts back to her. She thinks we'll do a better job running it than Darren will." Darren, their first cousin, wasn't known for his responsible behavior and he hated ranching. Mason, on the other hand, loved it. He had missed the ranch, the cattle, the Montana sky and his family's home ever since they'd left it twelve years ago.

"She's giving Crescent Hall to us?" That was Zane, Austin's twin, a Marine currently in Kandahar. The excitement in his tone told Mason all he needed to know—Zane stilled loved the old place as much as he did. When Mason had gotten Heloise's letter, he'd had to read it more than once before he believed it. The Hall would belong to them once more—when he'd thought they'd lost it for good. Suddenly he'd felt like he could breathe fully again after so many years of holding in his anger and frustration over his uncle's behavior. The timing was perfect, too. He was due to ship stateside any day now. By April he'd be a civilian again.

Except it wasn't as easy as all that. Mason took a deep breath. "There are a few conditions."

Colt, his youngest brother, snorted. "Of course—we're talking about Heloise, aren't we? What's she up to this time?" He was an Air Force combat controller who had served both in Afghanistan and as part of the relief effort a few years back after the massive earthquake which devastated Haiti. He was currently back on United States soil in Florida, training with his unit.

Mason knew what he meant. Calling Heloise eccentric would be an understatement. In her eighties, she had definite opinions and brooked no opposition to her plans and schemes. She meant well, but as his father had always said, she was capable of leaving a swath of destruction in family affairs that rivaled Sherman's march to Atlanta.

"The first condition is that we have to stock the ranch with one hundred pair of cattle within twelve months of taking possession."

"We should be able to do that," Austin said.

"It's going to take some doing to get that ranch up and running again," Zane countered. "Zeke was already letting the place go years ago."

"You have something better to do than fix the place up when you get out?" Mason asked him. He hoped Zane understood the real question: was he in or out?

"I'm in; I'm just saying," Zane said.

Mason suppressed a smile. Zane always knew what he was thinking.

"Good luck with all that," Colt said.

"Thanks," Mason told him. He'd anticipated that inheriting the Hall wouldn't change Colt's mind about staying in the Air Force. He focused on the other two who were both already in the process of winding down their military careers. "If we're going to do this, it'll take a commitment. We're going to have to pool our funds and put our shoulders to the wheel for as long as it takes. Are you up for that?"

"I'll join you there as soon as I'm able to in June," Austin said. "It'll just be like another year in the service. I can handle that."

"I already said I'm in," Zane said. "I'll have boots on the ground in September."

Here's where it got tricky. "There's just one other thing," Mason said. "Aunt Heloise has one more requirement of each of us."

"What's that?" Austin asked when he didn't go on.

"She's worried about the lack of heirs on our side of the family. Darren has children. We don't."

"Plenty of time for that," Zane said. "We're still young, right?"

"Not according to Heloise." Mason decided to get it over and done with. "She's decided that in order for us to inherit the Hall free and clear, we each have to be married within the year. One of us has to have a child."

Stunned silence met this announcement until Colt started to laugh. "Staying in the Air Force doesn't look so bad now, does it?"

"That means you, too," Mason said.

"What? Hold up, now." Colt was startled into soberness. "I won't even live on the ranch. Why do I have to get hitched?"

"Because Heloise says it's time to stop screwing around. And she controls the land. And you know

Heloise."

"How are we going to get around that?" Austin asked.

"We're not." Mason got right to the point. "We're going to find ourselves some women and we're going to marry them."

"In Afghanistan?" Zane's tone made it clear what he thought about that idea.

Tension tightened Mason's jaw. He'd known this was going to be a messy conversation. "Online. I created an online personal ad for all of us. Each of us has a photo, a description and a reply address. A woman can get in touch with whichever of us she chooses and start a conversation. Just weed through your replies until you find the one you want."

"Are you out of your mind?" Zane peered at him through the video screen.

"I don't see what you're upset about. I'm the one who has to have a child. None of you will be out of the service in time."

"Wait a minute—I thought you just got the letter from Heloise." As usual, Austin zeroed in on the inconsistency.

"The letter came about a week ago. I didn't want to get anyone's hopes up until I checked a few things out." Mason shifted in his seat. "Heloise said the place is in rougher shape than we thought. Sounds like Zeke sold off the last of his cattle last year. We're going to have to start from scratch, and we're going to have to move fast to meet her deadline—on both counts. I did all the leg work on the online ad. All you need to do is read some e-mails, look at some photos and pick one. How hard can that be?"

"I'm beginning to think there's a reason you've been single all these years, Straightshot," Austin said. Mason winced at the use of his nickname. The men in his unit had christened him with it during his early days in the service, but as Colt said when his brothers had first heard about it, it made perfect sense. The name had little to do with his accuracy with a rifle, and everything to do with his tendency to find the shortest route from here to done on any mission he was tasked with. Regardless of what obstacles stood in his way.

Colt snickered. "Told you two it was safer to stay in the military. Mason's Matchmaking Service. It has a ring to it. I guess you've found yourself a new career, Mase."

"Stow it." Mason tapped a finger on the table. "Just because I've put the ad up doesn't mean that any of you have to make contact with the women who write you. If it doesn't work, it doesn't work. But you need to marry within the year. If you don't find a wife for yourself, I'll find one for you."

"He would, too," Austin said to the others. "You know he would."

"When does the ad go live?" Zane asked.

"It went live five days ago. You've each got several hundred responses so far. I'll forward them to you as soon as we break the call."

Austin must have leaned toward his webcam because suddenly he filled the screen. "Several hundred?"

"That's right."

Colt's laughter rang out over the line.

"Don't know what you're finding so funny, Colton," Mason said in his best imitation of their late father's voice. "You've got several hundred responses, too."

"What? I told you I was staying…"

"Read through them and answer all the likely ones. I'll be in touch in a few days to check your progress." Mason cut the call.

REGAN ANDERSON WANTED a baby. Right now. Not five years from now. Not even next year.

Right now.

And since she'd just quit her stuffy loan officer job, moved out of her overpriced one bedroom New York City apartment, and completed all her preliminary appointments, she was going to get one via the modern technology of artificial insemination.

As she raced up the three flights of steps to her tiny new studio, she took the pins out of her severe updo and let her thick, auburn hair swirl around her shoulders. By the time she reached the door, she was breathing hard. Inside, she shut and locked it behind her, tossed her briefcase and blazer on the bed which took up the lion's share of the living space, and kicked off her high heels. Her blouse and pencil skirt came next, and thirty seconds later she was down to her skivvies.

Thank God.

She was done with Town and Country Bank. Done

with originating loans for people who would scrape and slave away for the next thirty years just to cling to a lousy flat near a subway stop. She was done, done, done being a cog in the wheel of a financial system she couldn't stand to be a part of anymore.

She was starting a new business. Starting a new life.

And she was starting a family, too.

Alone.

After years of looking for Mr. Right, she'd decided he simply didn't exist in New York City. So after several medical exams and consultations, she had scheduled her first round of artificial insemination for the end of April. She couldn't wait.

Meanwhile, she'd throw herself into the task of building her consulting business. She would make it her job to help non-profits assist regular people start new stores and services, buy homes that made sense, and manage their money so that they could get ahead. It might not be as lucrative as being a loan officer, but at least she'd be able to sleep at night.

She wasn't going to think about any of that right now, though. She'd survived her last day at work, survived her exit interview, survived her boss, Jack Richey, pretending to care that she was leaving. Now she was giving herself the weekend off. No work, no nothing—just forty-eight hours of rest and relaxation.

Having grabbed takeout from her favorite Thai restaurant on the way home, Regan spooned it out onto a plate and carried it to her bed. Lined with pillows, it doubled as her couch during waking hours. She sat cross-legged on top of the duvet and savored her food and her freedom. She had bought herself a nice bottle of wine to drink this weekend, figuring it might be her last for an awfully long time. She was all too aware her Chardonnay-sipping days were coming to an end. As soon as her weekend break from reality was over, she planned to spend the next ten months starting her business, while scrimping and saving every penny she could. She would have to move to a bigger apartment right before the baby was born, but given the cost of renting in the city, the temporary downgrade was worth it. She pushed all thoughts of business and the future out of her mind. Rest and relax—that was her job for now.

Two hours and two glasses of wine later, however, rest and relaxation was beginning to feel a lot like loneliness and boredom. In truth, she'd been fighting loneliness for months. She'd broken up with her last boyfriend before Christmas. Here it was March and she was still single. Two of her closest friends had gotten married and moved away in the past twelve months, Laurel to New Hampshire and Rita to New Jersey. They rarely saw each other now and when she'd jokingly mentioned the idea of going ahead and having a child without a husband the last time they'd gotten together, both women had scoffed.

"No way could I have gotten through this pregnancy without Ryan." Laurel ran a hand over her large belly. "I've felt awful the whole time."

"No way I'm going back to work." Rita's baby was six weeks old. "Thank God Alan brings in enough cash to see us through."

Regan decided not to tell them about her plans until the pregnancy was a done deal. She knew what she was getting into—she didn't need them to tell her how hard it might be. If there'd been any way for her to have a baby normally—with a man she loved—she'd have chosen that path in a heartbeat. But there didn't seem to be a man for her to love in New York. Unfortunately, keeping her secret meant it was hard to call either Rita or Laurel just to chat, and she needed someone to chat with tonight. As dusk descended on the city, Regan felt fear for the first time since making her decision to go ahead with having a child.

What if she'd made a mistake? What if her consultancy business failed? What if she became a welfare mother? What if she had to move back home?

When the thoughts and worries circling her mind grew overwhelming, she topped up her wine, opened up her laptop and clicked on a YouTube video of a cat stuck headfirst in a cereal box. Thank goodness she'd hooked up wi-fi the minute she secured the studio. Simultaneously scanning her Facebook feed, she read an update from an acquaintance named Susan who was exhibiting her art in one of the local galleries. She'd have to stop by this weekend.

She watched a couple more videos—the latest installment in a travel series she loved, and one about over-the-top weddings that made her sad. Determined to cheer up, she hopped onto Pinterest and added more images to her nursery pinboard. Sipping her wine, she checked the news, posted a question on the single parents' forum she frequented, checked her e-mail again, and then tapped a finger on the keys, wondering what to do next. The evening stretched out before her, vacant even of the work she normally took home to do over the weekend. She hadn't felt at such loose ends in years.

Pacing her tiny apartment didn't help. Nor did an attempt at unpacking more of her things. She had finished moving in just last night and boxes still lined one wall. She opened one to reveal books, took a look at her limited shelf space and packed them up again. A second box revealed her collection of vintage fans. No room for them here, either.

She stuck her iTouch into a docking station and turned up some tunes, then drained her glass, poured herself another, and flopped onto her bed. The wine was beginning to take effect—giving her a nice, soft, fuzzy feeling. It hadn't done away with her loneliness, but when she turned back to Facebook on her laptop, the images and YouTube links seemed funnier this time.

Heartened, she scrolled further down her feed until she spotted another post one of her friends had shared. It was an image of a handsome man standing ramrod straight in combat fatigues. *Hello.* He was cute. In fact, he looked like exactly the kind of man she'd always hoped she'd meet. He wasn't thin and arrogant like the up-and-coming Wall Street crowd, or paunchy and cynical like the upper-management men who hung around the bars near work. Instead he looked healthy, muscle-bound, clear-sighted, and vital. What was the post about? She clicked the link underneath it. Maybe there'd be more fantasy-fodder like this man wherever it took her.

There *was* more fantasy fodder. Regan wriggled happily. She had landed on a page that showcased four men. Brothers, she saw, looking more closely—two of them identical twins. Each one seemed to represent a different branch of the United States military. Were they models? Was this some kind of recruitment ploy?

*Practical Wives Wanted* read the heading at the top. Regan nearly spit out a sip of her wine. Wives Wanted? Practical ones? She considered the men again, then read more.

*Looking for a change?* the text went on. *Ready for a real challenge? Join four hardworking, clean living men and help bring our family's ranch back to life.*

*Skills required—any or all of the following: Riding, roping, construction, animal care, roofing, farming, market gardening, cooking, cleaning, metalworking, small motor repair...*

The list went on and on. Regan bit back at a laugh which quickly dissolved into giggles. Small engine repair? How very romantic. Was this supposed to be satire or was it real? It was certainly one of the most intriguing things she'd seen online in a long, long time.

*Must be willing to commit to a man and the project. No weekends/no holidays/no sick days. Weaklings need not apply.*

Regan snorted. It was beginning to sound like an employment ad. Good luck finding a woman to fill those conditions. She'd tried to find a suitable man for years and came up with Erik—the perennial mooch who'd finally admitted just before Christmas that he liked her old Village apartment more than he liked her. That's why she planned to get pregnant all by herself. There wasn't anyone worth marrying in the whole city. Probably the whole state. And if the men were all worthless, the women probably were, too. She reached for her wine without turning from the screen, missed, and nearly knocked over her glass. She tried again, secured the wine, drained the glass a third time and set it down again.

What she would give to find a real partner. Someone strong, both physically and emotionally. An equal in intelligence and heart. A real man.

But those didn't exist.

*If you're sick of wasting your time in a dead-end job, tired of tearing things down instead of building something up, or just ready to get your hands dirty with clean, honest work, write and tell us why you'd make a worthy wife for a man who has spent the last decade in uniform.*

There wasn't much to laugh at in this paragraph. Regan read it again, then got up and wandered to the kitchen to top up her glass. She'd never seen a singles ad like this one. She could see why it was going viral. If it was real, these men were something special. Who wanted to do clean, honest work these days? What kind of man was selfless enough to serve in the military instead of sponging off their girlfriends? If she'd known there were guys like this in the world, she might not have been so quick to schedule the artificial insemination appointment.

She wouldn't cancel it, though, because these guys couldn't be for real, and she wasn't waiting another minute to start her family. She had dreamed of having children ever since she was a child herself and organized pretend schools in her backyard for the neighborhood little ones. Babies loved her. Toddlers thought she was the next best thing to teddy bears. Her co-workers at the bank had never appreciated her as much as the average five-year-old did.

Further down the page there were photographs of the ranch the brothers meant to bring back to life. The land was beautiful, if overgrown, but its toppled fences and sagging buildings were a testament to its neglect. The photograph of the main house caught her eye and kept her riveted, though. A large gothic structure, it could be beautiful with the proper care. She could see why these men would dedicate themselves to returning it to its former glory. She tried to imagine what it would be like to live on the ranch with one of them, and immediately her body craved an open sunny sky—the kind you were hard pressed to see in the city. She sunk into the daydream, picturing herself sitting on a back porch sipping lemonade while her cowboy worked and the baby napped. Her husband would have his shirt off while he chopped wood, or mended a fence or whatever it was ranchers did. At the end of the day they'd fall into bed and make love until morning.

Regan sighed. It was a wonderful daydream, but it had no bearing on her life. Disgruntled, she switched over to Netflix and set up a foreign film. She fetched the bottle of wine back to bed with her and leaned against her many pillows. She'd managed to hang her small flatscreen on the opposite wall. In an apartment this tiny, every piece of furniture needed to serve double-duty.

As the movie started, Regan found herself composing messages to the military men in the Wife Wanted ad, in which she described herself as trim and petite, or lithe and strong, or horny and good-enough-looking to do the trick.

An hour later, when the film failed to hold her attention, she grabbed her laptop again. She pulled up the Wife Wanted page and reread it, keeping an eye on the foreign couple on the television screen who alternately argued and kissed.

Crazy what some people did. What was wrong with these men that they needed to advertise for wives instead of going out and meeting them like normal people?

She thought of the online dating sites she'd tried in the past. She'd had some awkward experiences, some horrible first dates, and finally one relationship that lasted for a couple of months before the man was transferred to Tucson and it fizzled out. It hadn't worked for her, but she supposed lots of people found love online these days. They might not advertise directly for spouses, but that was their ultimate intention, right? So maybe this ad wasn't all that unusual.

Most men who posted singles ads weren't as hot as these men were, though. Definitely not the ones she'd met. She poured herself another glass. A small twinge of her conscience told her she'd already had far too much wine for a single night.

*To hell with that*, Regan thought. As soon as she got

pregnant she'd have to stay sober and sane for the next eighteen years. She wouldn't have a husband to trade off with—she'd always be the designated driver, the adult in charge, the sober, wise mother who made sure nothing bad ever happened to her child. Just this one last time she was allowed to blow off steam.

But even as she thought it, a twinge of fear wormed through her belly.

What if she wasn't good enough?

She stood up, strode the two steps to the kitchenette and made herself a bowl of popcorn. She drowned it in butter and salt, returned to the bed in time for the ending credits of the movie, and lined up *Pride and Prejudice* with Colin Firth. Time for comfort food and a comfort movie. *Pride and Prejudice* always did the trick when she felt blue. She checked the Wife Wanted page again on her laptop. If she was going to pick one of the men— which she wasn't—who would she choose?

Mason, the oldest, due to leave the Navy in a matter of weeks, drew her eye first. With his dark crew cut, hard jaw and uncompromising blue eyes he looked like the epitome of a military man. He stated his interests as ranching—of course—history, natural sciences and tactical operations, whatever the hell that was. That left her little more informed than before she'd read it, and she wondered what the man was really like. Did he read the newspaper in bed on Sunday mornings? Did he prefer lasagna or spaghetti? Would he listen to country music in his truck or talk radio? She stared at his photo, willing him to answer.

The next two brothers, Austin and Zane, were less fierce, but looked no less intelligent and determined. Still, they didn't draw her eye the way the way Mason did. Colt, the youngest, was blond with a grin she bet drew women like flies. That one was trouble, and she didn't need trouble.

She read Mason's description again and decided he was the leader of this endeavor. If she was going to pick one, it would be him.

But she wasn't going to pick one. She had given up all that. She'd made a promise to her imaginary child that she would not allow any chaos into its life. No dating until her baby wore a graduation gown, at the very least. She felt another twinge. Was she ready to give up men for nearly two decades? That was a long time.

*It's worth it*, she told herself. She had no doubt about her desire to be a mother. She had no doubt she'd be a great mom. She was smart, capable and had a good head on her shoulders. She was funny, silly and patient, too. She loved children.

She was just lousy with men.

But that didn't matter anymore. She pushed the laptop aside and returned her attention to *Pride and Prejudice*, quickly falling into an old drinking game she and Laurel had devised one night that required taking a swig of wine each time one of the actresses lifted her eyebrows in polite surprise. When she finished the bottle, she headed to the tiny kitchenette to track down another one, trilling, "Jane! Elizabeth!" at the top of her voice along with Mrs. Bennett in the film. There was no more wine, so she switched to tequila.

By the time Elizabeth Bennett discovered the miracle of Mr. Darcy's palace-sized mansion, and decided she'd been too hasty in turning down his offer of marriage, Regan had decided she too needed to cast off her prejudices and find herself a man. A hot hunk of a military man. She grabbed the laptop, fumbled with the link that would let her leave Mason Hall a message and drafted a brilliant missive worthy of Jane Austen herself.

*Dear Lt. Cmdr. Hall,*

In her mind she pronounced lieutenant with an "f" like the Brits in the movie onscreen.

*It is a truth universally acknowledged, that a single man in possession of a good ranch, must be in want of a wife. Furthermore, it must be self-evident that the wife in question should possess certain qualities numbering amongst them riding, roping, construction, roofing, farming, market gardening, cooking, cleaning, metalworking, animal care, and—most importantly, by Heaven—small motor repair.*

*Seeing as I am in possession of all these qualities, not to mention many others you can only have left out through unavoidable oversight or sheer obtuseness—such as glassblowing, cheesemaking, towel origami, heraldry, hovercraft piloting, and an uncanny sense of what cats are thinking—I feel almost forced to catapult myself into your purview.*

*You will see from my photograph that I am most eminently and majestically suitable for your wife.*

She inserted a digital photo of her foot.

*In fact, one might wonder why such a paragon of virtue such as I should deign to answer such a peculiar advertisement. The truth is, sir, that I long for adventure. To get my hands dirty with clean, hard work. To build something up instead of tearing it down.*

*In short, you are really hot. I'd like to lick you.*

*Yours,*
*Regan Anderson*

On screen, Elizabeth Bennett lifted an eyebrow. Regan knocked back another shot of Jose Cuervo and passed out.

### End of Excerpt

**The Cowboys of Chance Creek Series:**

**The Cowboy Inherits a Bride (Volume 0)**
**The Cowboy's E-Mail Order Bride (Volume 1)**
**The Cowboy Wins a Bride (Volume 2)**
**The Cowboy Imports a Bride (Volume 3)**
**The Cowgirl Ropes a Billionaire (Volume 4)**
**The Sheriff Catches a Bride (Volume 5)**
**The Cowboy Lassos a Bride (Volume 6)**
**The Cowboy Rescues a Bride (Volume 7)**
**The Cowboy Earns a Bride (Volume 8)**
**The Cowboy's Christmas Bride (Volume 9)**

**The Heroes of Chance Creek Series:**

The Navy SEAL's E-Mail Order Bride (Volume 1)
The Soldier's E-Mail Order Bride (Volume 2)
The Marine's E-Mail Order Bride (Volume 3)
The Navy SEAL's Christmas Bride (Volume 4)
The Airman's E-Mail Order Bride (Volume 5)

The SEALs of Chance Creek Series:

A SEAL's Oath
A SEAL's Vow
A SEAL's Pledge
A SEAL's Consent
A SEAL's Purpose
A SEAL's Resolve
A SEAL's Devotion
A SEAL's Desire
A SEAL's Struggle
A SEAL's Triumph

The Brides of Chance Creek Series:

Issued to the Bride One Navy SEAL
Issued to the Bride One Airman
Issued to the Bride One Sniper
Issued to the Bride One Marine
Issued to the Bride One Soldier

The Turners v. Coopers Series:

The Cowboy's Secret Bride (Volume 1)
The Cowboy's Outlaw Bride (Volume 2)
The Cowboy's Hidden Bride (Volume 3)
The Cowboy's Stolen Bride (Volume 4)
The Cowboy's Forbidden Bride (Volume 5)

# About the Author

With over one-and-a-half million books sold, NYT and USA Today bestselling author Cora Seton has created a world readers love in Chance Creek, Montana. She has thirty-five novels and novellas currently set in her fictional town, with many more in the works. Like her characters, Cora loves cowboys, military heroes, country life, gardening, jogging, binge-watching Jane Austen movies, keeping up with the latest technology and indulging in old-fashioned pursuits. She lives on beautiful Vancouver Island with her husband, children and two cats. Visit **www.coraseton.com** to read about new releases, contests and other cool events!

Blog:

www.coraseton.com

Facebook:

facebook.com/coraseton

Twitter:

twitter.com/coraseton

Newsletter:

www.coraseton.com/sign-up-for-my-newsletter